PROGRESS

OTHER BOOKS BY MICHAEL V. SMITH:

Cumberland

What You Can't Have

Body of Text
(with David Ellingsen)

For more information on Michael V. Smith, see
www.michaelvsmith.com

Book club questions and suggestions
for *Progress* can be found at:

www.michaelvsmith.com/progressbookclub

MICHAEL V. SMITH

PROGRESS

a novel

Cormorant Books

Canada Council for the Arts **Conseil des Arts du Canada**

The publisher gratefully acknowledges the support of the Canada Council
for the Arts and the Ontario Arts Council for its publishing program.
We acknowledge the financial support of the Government of Canada
through the Canada Book Fund (CBF) for our publishing activities,
and the Government of Ontario through the Ontario Media Development
Corporation, an agency of the Ontario Ministry of Culture,
and the Ontario Book Publishing Tax Credit Program.

Library and Archives Canada Cataloguing in Publication

Smith, Michael V.
Progress / Michael V. Smith.

ISBN 978-1-77086-000-1

I. Title.

PS8587.M5636P76 2011   C813'.6   C2010-907032-1

Cover art and design: Angel Guerra/Archetype
Interior text design: Tannice Goddard, Soul Oasis Networking
Printer: Friesens

Printed and bound in Canada.

This book is printed on 100% post-consumer waste recycled paper.

CORMORANT BOOKS INC.
215 SPADINA AVENUE, STUDIO 230, TORONTO, ONTARIO, CANADA M5T 2C7
www.cormorantbooks.com

for Claire Hamilton Payne

'The twentieth-century struggle between capitalism and socialism is, at an ideological level, a fight about the content of progress.'

— John Berger, introduction to *Into Their Labours*.

BEFORE

SATURDAY

EVERY TIME HELEN stepped out of doors these final months, more of the town had disappeared. Today it was the laundromat, which had nothing left inside except a chair with three legs and a can of pop on the seat. Through most of June, trees within ten feet of the highway had been felled, from the old campsite east of town to the overpass of the new stretch of major highway that led to the city. Last week it was the knife-sharpening shack that Tim Ho built from wooden barrels he'd sawed in half. The deli case at the market had been emptied when Helen went looking in the morning for lunchmeat. She'd never noticed how dirty the case was, with nothing to see inside it except the grime along the outer edges where the glass met the plastic moulding.

She'd bought a can of tuna, took herself home, and made a sandwich with cucumbers and lettuce from the garden. She packed it up in a baggie with a handful of yellow pepper slices and a Thermos of tap water. She combed her hair in the bathroom, put on a fresh top, a blue linen skirt her mother used to wear on weekends, and brushed her teeth, surprising herself that she could look more put-together if she wanted. She hadn't been dressing in anything nicer than a T-shirt since her mother passed. It had been practical in the final days and then, afterwards, a lazy habit. Looking after her father a year later had done nothing to encourage her.

She felt good to be wearing something decent. It was hotter than usual, but with rain every other night; people were saying how lucky the farmers were to have this be their last season. An excellent crop for them. In the paper that morning, Helen had read a letter to the editor that claimed the logic wasn't so sharp, because the farmers' last season on the land hardly gave them reason to feel lucky. She chuckled, thinking of it, as she stepped across the wet grass to her car.

She backed out onto the old highway a bit quickly, without her usual checks and re-checks, for there was less and less traffic every week. Piché was kneeling over her pea plants, east of her house. Helen waved to her from the car window as she passed, feeling badly for not visiting this morning. She didn't want to have to explain where she was going. It was her second trip this season to the old Keegan farm, where no Keegan had actually lived in a half dozen years.

The drive was twenty minutes out of town, up to the only hill of any note, which held one of the best apple orchards in the area.

Inside the property, about ten yards before the orchard began, Helen pulled the car into a small gravelled turnoff from the highway and parked. She took her bagged lunch with her and — to give her something to do, a kind of excuse to be there — an old khaki pair of binoculars her father had owned, which she had found in the shed. A small dirt path once trickled along the property line through the thick grass, though in recent years Helen was the only person to use it, and then only once or twice a year, so the hard dirt, for the most part, was overgrown.

It was an easy route, despite the missing trail, because Helen had only to walk parallel to the fenced property line. She could smell the apple trees sweet on the air and, beneath that, the damp earth through the grass and the hot fishiness of the river.

She came to a clearing along the water's edge, with three maples making a canopy over a large grey stone rising four feet from the ground. It was here that the Keegan family had buried their son's ashes, at the base of the large stone, overlooking the river. His name and inscription were carved in neat block letters, a quarter-inch into the face. *GARRETT SAMUEL KEEGAN*. The grass had once been manicured, to a point, but over the past years, since the politician and his wife had retired out of town — to not be reminded so often of what they'd lost, or to escape the pitying looks from their neighbours — Helen was the only one to keep the grass trimmed.

Helen came to this clearing each spring on the anniversary. Sometimes she would bring her hedge trimmers when she was lonely or wanted a good place to think, wishing herself back into a time that was easier, easier than now, with the dam forcing her hand. She would sit at Garrett's grave, take up her place on the right, leaning against the stone, and run her fingers through the grass as though she were still tousling his hair in a park somewhere, wrapped alongside him.

The heat of the sun was so intense, even for the morning,

she was sweaty by the time she reached the small clearing. Some of her toes were covered in foam from the sap of a milkweed. She came round to the side of the stone facing the river, sat leaning against it, pulled a paper napkin from the front pouch of her purse and wiped her toes dry. They were sticky against the vinyl of her sandal. She could feel two of them pressed together. She sat there, the grass scratchy on her bare legs, moving her toes back and forth, feeling them gum together and separate as she pulled from her purse her Thermos of tap water and the bagged sandwich and peppers.

Helen could hear the long, low rumble and whine of heavy machinery from a kilometre or so upriver. She had watched from this spot as they'd rerouted the river to the south with a coffer dam, then cleared the newly dry land of the boulders and detritus the river had buried under it. Hundreds had come down over those first weeks to see what their riverbed had looked like — there was an awesome magic in standing on the river bottom, which felt direct sunlight for the first time. Fences went up in the second week after the temporary dam was completed, with generic signs on the chain-link saying the grounds were private property, which wasn't quite true, for it was crown land. While one article in the paper spoke about the hazards of wandering around the construction site, the next had a photo of the Bhatia twins holding up an old head-stocked anchor and chain they'd found in the rocks.

Two years in, the concrete columns of the power dam were in place, looking like a giant's knuckles. The symmetrical fingers of a great machine. The tops of the farthest three columns were surrounded with a wooden platform and casing. The closest

two were only half-poured, but still a good ten storeys high, rebar
rising a storey or two from the completed base. Helen could
make out a few men walking on the closest platform, black ants
moving back and forth. Then a black spot on the side of the
nearest full column slid straight down from the top, like a spider
dropping with its line. There was another dark blot as well,
hanging lower and to the right of the first. Men strapped into
harnesses, she imagined, dangling from the top, doing heaven
knows what.

It was astounding really, the construction. Thousands of
tonnes of earth moved, concrete poured, rerouting a river so the
land could be cleared and then erecting something so mammoth,
right here. The exposed earth was brown and dingy from the
summer sun. The backhoes were toys at the base of the dam.
From her perspective — better than the costly spots some locals
had set up for the tourists on the other side, downriver — the
landscape looked dwarfed, a kid's toy box, except Helen knew
— and couldn't get over, found it hard to believe — the little
black dots moving around on the construction were the big
hulking men she saw at the lodge. She picked up the binoculars, the plastic casing warm to the touch from the front seat
of the car, and turned the dials to adjust the view. Each little
black dot became a stick-figure man with a large, colourful,
helmeted head.

Their concrete hand was even more impressive, its scale
increased by the appearance of the slivered arms and legs of
the workers. She could make out the thin line of the rope now
for the two men scaling the side of the closest structure. What
a job, she thought, and, with her toes wiggling, she imagined

what it was like to be there, suspended along the wall, so many feet up, air all around, nothing but air beneath her. Her heart raced, and by some strange, unaccountable coincidence, at that moment the inky spot of the man on the outside dropped.

The straight line of rope supporting him flew up and squiggled itself as he fell like a sack, straight down, with one arm waving in circles. He fell past the other workman strapped in his harness, who must have been surprised to see him pass. Mocking the air. It seemed he fell without a sound. A pebble dropped from the sky, a dark twig. He fell, with no one to catch him. His body flashed between the metal rebar, a sparrow between iron weeds, and then disappeared behind the concrete.

He fell quickly, in less time than a breath. Two heartbeats. Helen blinked, her lashes rubbing against the binocular glass. She had a kind of vertigo, a spin, as she sat there. She pressed the lenses to her eyes, straining to see more closely. For a moment three men on the ledge and the other on the wall were looking over the side of the wooden banister at the place where his body must have stopped and, as though a timer went off, two of the men took off their hardhats, another broke into a run and the hanging man looked upwards at his buddies but pointed downward. He gestured repeatedly, and was clearly shouting something, although Helen realized she could hear nothing over the sounds of the site's machines. The harnessed man obviously wanted to be lowered; his arm pointed to the ground — to the injured man — but neither of his co-workers moved. Helen leaned forward, eager for them to pull him up to safety. Why did they just leave him hanging there?

The fellow who ran off — it seemed to Helen it was the same man, though there was no telling from this distance — returned with another four men, one of them in a white hard hat and carrying what Helen thought must be a small safety kit. They engaged the winch, for the guy in the swing began to be lowered into the pit, out of sight as well.

The fellow in the white hard hat — *foreman*, Helen thought — lifted his hand to the side of his head, then shouted into the pit, and pressed his hand against his face once more. He had called someone. Helen imagined the conversation, the clipped messages, the important details. Briefly, she wished she had the perspective of the six men on the ledge — they could see what was happening — then she reconsidered.

Bending on one knee, the foreman cupped his hands beside his mouth and leaned into the pit, shouting. Somebody handed him a megaphone. In a few seconds, Helen thought she heard the faintest electric buzz of his voice. As the minutes passed, her heart slowed; her shoulders collapsed forward when she recognized how tight they were. Her bones felt hollowed out. The binoculars hurt in two round pressure points around her eyes. She felt shaken and exhausted, nauseous from the taste of her own mouth. She opened the water and drank, and was relieved that the coolness of the liquid soothed her. The first swallow made her body relax and the second gulp nearly did her in.

She choked on the water, picked up the binoculars, and couldn't stop herself from watching. They lowered something down the pit on a rope. A small box or square bucket of some kind. Within seconds, it came back up. Then minutes later the man in the harness appeared, rising up out of the concrete. He looked straight ahead to the concrete wall of the dam. When he reached the top, he immediately removed himself from the harness and walked down the platform without a glance backwards.

A large chute — its mouth as wide as a pickup truck — swung into view from behind the next column. Seconds later, a delay caused by the distance, came the squeal of dry metal on metal. Helen wondered what they could be using the machine for, since she didn't see a winch, nor a rescue basket, nor anything that seemed useful to their purpose. Of the six men gathered on the ledge, four of them took their hard hats off, until the foreman gestured to them and each of the men put his hat back on.

Minutes later, grey sludge came running out of the mouth of the chute. Helen tried to figure out what the purpose could be, how that would help them retrieve the body. She pictured him floating atop the sludge until the level had risen to the upper lip and they could pluck him off the grey sea; then, stricken, the length of her spine shaking, she realized her mistake. They were pouring concrete.

Helen's head jerked backwards, throwing her from the scene. A small something flew with a peeping sound onto the tall grass just to the right of where she sat. She looked over at it, to see its dappled head snap to and fro like a mechanical toy. A starling, puzzling her and the bread in her lap. Helen felt her face unbearably hot. She was sweaty around her eyes where the binoculars had been. Within moments, without warning, the bird flew off. By the time Helen turned her attention again to the dam, the concrete had stopped running from the metal mouth. Three men were walking away and two others held their hands to their ears.

Helen burped, tasting the acid of her belly. She might be ill. Her limbs felt loose and rubbery and full of energy. *Home*, she thought.

She packed her Thermos into her bag, roughly tore the sandwich into bits that she tossed into the grass and slipped her feet into her sandals.

The tall grass irritated her knees as she walked to the road. Her fingers felt as though they had disappeared; they were numb, and when she held them, they were cold against her palms. The warm air, sweet with pollen, went milky, thickened, and the field around her turned dreamy, as though she were separated from everything, her senses locked out and peering from beyond a window, but still she stepped cautiously, feeling the ground might rise up beneath her. She walked in waves, the world rising and falling around her, her head unhinged from her body, her body from her legs.

At the highway she walked along its edge with the sound of the gravel under her feet so much louder than the machines behind her. There were no cars on the road until she reached the Chevy. A small green truck pulled onto the highway, heading towards her. She stood at the rear of her car, relieved to see someone else. She rested a hand on the trunk, but realized in a delay that the metal was burning hot. Her hand snapped back. The driver of the truck was a woman in a tidy hat, her arms looking thin and small, her hands holding the steering wheel as she drove by. If she'd have glanced her way, Helen might have flagged her down. Her hand buzzed from the shock of the heated metal.

She regretted throwing her sandwich into the long grass, for she now needed something to settle her churning stomach. She had no idea where the peppers were. She'd dropped them. They'd been in her lap. Now her head was very hot. She wasn't wearing a sun hat. She noticed her feet were pinched; the irritating stickiness of her toes prevented them from resting quite right beside each other.

She looked across the road to see two crows flying into the woods, over the blur of cornflowers and buttercups nestled in the wild grass. The sky was a pale blue. The colours on the ground seemed much richer by comparison. Her car was vibrant red, the trees much more green than she remembered. Her stomach let out a growl. She put a hand to her belly, took in a breath of air, smelling the river behind her, the slightly rotten smell of fish coming from the riverbank. She could smell, too, the chalkiness of the gravel, and the pollen like a woman's powder on the air.

Taking her keys from her purse, she walked to the door of the car and stood there, again, staring at the highway ahead of her.

Only when her hands gripped the wheel of the car did she realize how much they were shaking. She didn't remember unlocking the car door and getting inside.

She felt unsafe, because she still wasn't entirely present. The world was behind glass. She could see the route home laid out in her head and a dozen different turns of events presented themselves to her. She was trapped in a loop of imaginings where the world offered up accidents, a repertoire of tragic coincidences, and despite rationalizing each away, or forcing herself to correct each mistake with a matching turn of luck, another error presented itself. The car stalling on the train tracks through town, the brakes not working, over-correcting from the shoulder of the road, a drunk in the other lane coming towards her. For a few minutes, Helen could see nothing before her but a random menace until she noticed again her hands on the wheel of the car, and the road before her lined with trees. She'd been looking inward, with the familiar fear, and out there, she tried to comfort herself with the old mantra, things weren't tragically laid out.

She saw a man fall from the dam. It was a freak occurrence. He was dead, wasn't he? He must be dead. Yes, of course, pouring the cement meant he was dead. But there was no ceremony. Had anyone said a prayer? *Christ*, Helen thought, she'd not even said a prayer for the man. She spoke a brief prayer in her head and tears came. Tears brought panic with them, black waves of fear.

Behind everything there was darkness, behind every colour, void. The car was a trap. The road. Her clothes, tight against her chest. Everything she could see, in full colour, felt black. On the other side of everything, black, as though the world had a skin, and beneath it lay a void pregnant with nothingness. Tangible nothingness. Weighted nothingness. She was beside herself with terror, as though she'd been on the edge of that cement pit, as though she were dropping out of the world, to a hard death, without a witness. The world again turned itself against her, everything was a sharp edge, and she couldn't move for fear of cutting herself open.

The feeling was familiar, from when she was a child and her father had been at his worst. Helen would wake in the night, screaming to make the walls shake. The first time, the family was terrified. The noise was medieval, animal. She was crazed with fear. For weeks she woke screaming, every other night or so, as though she could warn them their lives would be ruined. Blackness, sewn from the material of her dreams, hung in the room before her.

She couldn't say what the dreams were, though the absolute emptiness of them was something of the same fear she felt now. In the brightness of the afternoon, despite the summer light on the trees and the blue of the sky, the richness of the grass and the random dots of yellow and blue in the fields, she could feel the dark everywhere, she could feel it surround her, laying its arm across her shoulders. A black-gloved hand over her heart. The fear was a profound, massive abandonment, where every sight and smell, every sense led her to one true feeling. She had always been alone, cleaved from the world. Left apart.

She sat for an interminable time, two minutes or twenty, until she could see again. Things in the landscape — pavement, road sign, fields of grass, trees, river — were just that: objects, things, unconnected blobs of things. The steering wheel seemed to become itself, a *steering wheel* in her grip. Her hands were *hands*. She was gripping the wheel; she could *feel*. She felt like a person again.

She had somehow started the car and had already passed the entrance to the construction site and was rounding the first bend in the highway before she was fully aware she was driving. She tried to pay very close attention to the road, but minutes later she was passing the Johnson intersection and again coming out of some daze. Concerned she wasn't alert yet, she turned into the driveway, which was right there, for the cemetery, and nearly laughed aloud for where she'd ended up. Some cruel design, a stab at humour.

A number of vehicles, mostly pickups, were parked along the fence — *there must be a funeral going on*, Helen thought — but once she'd driven through the gates, she noticed in the far corner two more trucks: city vehicles. Backhoes were at work on some of the graves, with a handful of workers in matching coveralls standing nearby.

Helen knew what was being done. Her mother was buried here. She had tried to arrange for her father's ashes to be placed in the plot next to her mother, but he'd died after the construction became too involved, so they'd agreed only to place his gravestone; his ashes waited in a box in the garage. When they'd buried her mother, Helen had presumed her safe. Her mother was left to the earth and its secrets to do what needed doing. Nobody had been told yet the cemetery would be moved. Now, the rules no longer applied. The dead here were being exhumed, their corpses jostled inside their coffins, air leaking in through the panels and their clothes undone. The grisly business of what the men were doing was vivid, immediate.

Helen felt her stomach turn again, with consequence. She opened the car door just in time to vomit into the grass. A small breeze drifted around the door and washed across her face, into her burning nostrils. She was relieved; her back relaxed. Her head cleared considerably. Her hand on the door was slick with sweat. She heaved again, a coarse sugary taste in her throat. As she sat up, she noticed her clothes were sticking to her body. She was thinking she might pull further in, step out of the car, and use the excuse of checking on her parents to get more air, when she noticed the workers standing around the machinery. Each one of them was looking over at the car. Some stared longer than others before returning to their work. Two men in orange hard hats and navy suits discussed something, until the taller of them walked towards her, crossing over the graves as he came. The gentleman in the suit was thirty yards away and Helen could see the deep crinkle in his brow.

He walked slowly. He was reluctant to have this conversation. Helen drew in a long stuttering breath and — she didn't want to hear anything this man had to say — closed the door to the car. He stopped and looked her in the eye, to see what she would do. Helen waved him off, then turned to fiddle in the glove box, pretending she was looking for something, to stall, and realized in that gesture that she hadn't packed the binoculars. They must be on the grass still, by the rock.

She couldn't return, not with the falling man stilled below fresh concrete two minutes up the road. She wouldn't trust herself to pass by there again.

Sitting upright, she could see the man in the suit ambling towards her, eight metres away and wiping a handkerchief across his forehead. Helen started the engine. The man put the handkerchief in his pocket and lumbered to a stop, tiredly, anticipating her, for maybe this time she really was leaving. She put the car in reverse, which made a squeak as it lurched at the ready. She reversed down the drive, cautiously, and steered the Chevy onto the road, with the man watching her until she drove down the highway toward home.

ROBERT RESENTED MUCH of this; he couldn't walk up the driveway without breaking into a terrific sweat; his body wasn't his own, his hands were freezing cold despite the heat of the sun and the slick of perspiration covering his back and arms. He'd eaten breakfast and two dry sandwiches at noon on the bus from the capital, but his stomach felt empty from nerves. He'd burned it up from the capital to the city, and then, in the cab, he'd felt the gas build up inside him and had burped quietly to himself the whole way out. The cabbie had agreed to charge him a flat rate, and hadn't asked a single question the twenty minutes out of the city, for which Robert was grateful, so he'd given him an extra five bucks as thanks.

The house itself was more or less the same, a split-level bungalow, brick and siding, though fifteen years later, it seemed to be smaller. Reduced, which felt odd, and comforting. The window frames were old and weather-worn. But there was a trellis in bloom on the left side of the front landing and the flowerbeds along the front, on either side of the door, had never been so well tended. Robert remembered marigolds, about eight plants on either side, which were never enough to fill the beds his father had dug for them. He had turned the ground, but he wouldn't allow Robert's mother to spend enough to fill them. So she bought seeds for lily-of-the-valley and made do. The front garden was now landscaped, running out in a gentle curve, swelling at the outer edge of the house on the left and, to a slightly lesser extent, on the right. There were bushes, and rocks well-placed, and a small bird feeder tucked beside one shrub with pale green leaves. The front yard was handsome. Things had changed. Of course they had. And for the better. He was encouraged, a strange mix of pleased to see so much life, and concern for what that life might or might not offer him.

He walked up the front steps and noted the wood was grey where the paint had worn through in the centre of each step. The windows were shut. Quickly, he rapped on the door, before he'd even come to a stop. He was ahead of himself. Had he knocked hard enough? He wiped his hand on his pant leg, then imagined his father opening the door. Instinctively, he took a step back.

He waited, and waited longer, willing for a sound beyond the door, for the sound of the lock clicking open. It seemed a great task to decide to knock again. He raised his hand to the door, but set his knuckles against the wood. *Knock*, he told himself. *Just knock. Knock again. Someone will hear you and answer.*

He gave another three raps, hard, so that his knuckles smarted, and still there wasn't a sound. He had to tell himself that they hadn't seen him arrive. There was nobody around the corner, waiting for his footfall to retreat. The house was empty: there was no car in the driveway and the windows were shut in this heat.

He hadn't been on the property since he'd crawled out his bedroom window at sixteen, but he still knew the feel of the place. The black metal mailbox on the side of the house had replaced the large wooden one, the siding was older, the windows more ragged, but he thought he could tell if anyone was home, and they weren't. The quality of stillness told him the house was empty.

It occurred to him that maybe they'd moved already, maybe someone else occupied the house — he'd not bothered to check the directory before coming — but the lace curtains in the window, yes, were the same as when he'd left. They were here. They were just out.

And now what? He'd wait. He couldn't call a cab; he hadn't thought to get a number. He should have asked for a receipt. He didn't want to walk the highway into town, to see if the Inn was open, and risk it not be, and have to pass by the neighbours' yards twice. If he were to leave now, he might not come back. He wanted to stay, and prove to himself that his parents weren't home, or they'd have answered the door. He'd wait then, but not on the front stairs because he couldn't bear the thought of someone seeing him with a suitcase at his feet. Sweat rolled down his back.

Robert picked up his suitcase, trying not to think, but to simply move. Take a deep breath. Descend the stairs. Wipe his free hand dry again.

He walked around the left side of the house, to the gate, and let himself in.

THE SIGHT OF her yard made Helen better in her skin.

The car window down and the radio on had restored her breathing to nearly normal, though her stomach was still tight.

Some song that she didn't know but liked for the doot-doot of its beat was playing as she turned off the ignition. The order of the front yard, her flowerbeds thriving despite the heat, and her clematis abloom up the front steps, calmed her, made her limbs vibrate at a lower register.

As soon as Helen was out of the car, Piché, on one knee in the front garden, called out and waved her over. As Piché clambered to her feet as best she could on two legs that had tried to quit working years ago, Helen had to coach herself to not mention the accident. Her old neighbour was struggling enough with having to prepare for the move; she didn't need extra stress. Piché didn't need to worry after Helen too.

Helen was beside her by the time Piché managed to right herself.

A man come to see you, she said, her accent heavier for speaking quickly.

Another surveyor? Helen asked. Or agents?

Maybe. I see him from the front room come up your steps, but I don't open my sheers. I don't talk at any more men.

Piché threw her trowel onto the grass. Her pale stockings were wrinkled below her knees, looking as though the skin had slid down her legs. This was new for her. Even last fall at the end of her gardening season, Piché had been robust. She'd been tidy.

He waited on the steps. I was going to tell him, 'Go away,' but I went outside and ... gone. She opened her fingers into the air, miming a puff of smoke.

Just as well.

Helen gave a warm smile of thanks to Piché, who looked at her with determination. Her brow was set in its firmness, a signature look she'd give when repeating an argument she'd had with her Éric, when he was alive to argue. There was no changing the mind of a woman, she often said. You'd have to change the world instead.

Are you tying up the peas already? Helen asked, to get her to speak of nicer things.

Yes, Piché said, giving Helen a fast pinch on the elbow. Growing so fast.

If you need more, let me know. I've got a bunch I'm not using.

Piché took her hand. You remember me, she said.

She gave Piché's hand a squeeze. You're not easy to forget, Helen answered.

Head thrown back, Piché laughed, a trio of sounds gurgling through her throat. Yes. I like more twist ties. String is not good on my fingers.

I'll be over soon.

Helen returned to the front step, thirsty, and eager to brush her teeth. Putting her key in the lock, she imagined a man standing on the porch waiting for her. There was no note left behind that she could see. No envelope in the mailbox. Whoever it was would return.

She put her bag down in the hall and stretched her arm out to loosen the muscles. It was stifling hot inside with the windows locked tight. The air was dry with the smell of breakfast from the kitchen. Immediately, she brushed her teeth quickly and felt better. She washed her face, and dried it, noticing the smell of the towel, which she tossed into the hamper. She put on a fresh shirt in her room and felt the urge to crawl into bed, but wanted first to get some air circulating through the house.

In the front room, Helen opened the windows as wide as they'd go. If she was lucky a breeze could cool things off by the evening. She might be sleeping on the couch tonight. The heat in the front of the house would be enough to keep her awake as it is, she wasn't looking forward to the conditions at the back.

She walked into the kitchen to get a cross breeze and remembered Piché. From the cupboard drawer she pulled out a small bag of twist ties, then leaned over the sink to open the window.

With her hand on the lock, she noticed through the glass someone lounging on a patio chair just beneath the back step. A set of legs jutted out. Men's black shoes.

Some man had come to see her about the house and had taken the liberty of making himself at home in her backyard. Her blood ran cold down her back with an uncertain fear of what he'd say — she hadn't signed any of the appropriate papers yet; they still sat in their envelope on top of the fridge — and, at the same time, her hands and face were hot and pulsing. Her heart raced again, compounded by the morning, and boiling with rage.

Mine, she would scream at him. *Get off* my *land*. This was still her property.

She unbolted the latch, threw open the rear door and, feeling her body full of adrenalin, flew onto the small porch at the back.

She made it no further. The man had heard the latch and stood up. He was in front of the patio chair with his arms at his sides like he'd been there a long time, waiting. At first she saw only his suit, a smart black jacket and a rich blue tie. As she drew in air, ready to blast him for his trespass, she stared him in the eye.

At the sight of him, her skin prickled and her joints felt turned to rubber. Helen felt the small hairs on her limbs stand up. Chills zigzagged across her back and arms. She could think of nothing to say.

The sight of him, the simplicity of his body in the yard, not a few feet from her, close enough she could see the colour of his eyes, hurt.

She said his name on the property for the first time in a decade and a half: *Robbie*, a set of consonants and vowels so familiar, and yet distant to her ear, it was like the ground had been turned to reveal an old toy in a box. Robbie, she said again, just to hear the word.

You changed the locks, he said, smiling. It was his voice.

Yes, she answered, quieter than she meant.

No no, I'm kidding. I don't have a key — Robbie's tone was apologetic, thinking her short answer a reproof — but I'm afraid the heat got the better of me. He gestured to the chair, giving a wry, dismissive laugh.

Helen felt the heat of the sun pressing straight into her eyes yet she couldn't bring herself to blink. Robbie was in the yard.

I saw an accident, she wanted to say, but didn't think that a decent hello. She was full of relief. And then she wanted to scream his name, to hear it said over and again, but she was silenced by how awkward this was — she wanted to vomit again — how changed he was, so adult, so foreign.

He was a grown man who shaved, neatly. He wore a suit and very handsome tie with blue stitching. His hands were manicured, Helen assumed, for his nails were perfect. He had the hands of a movie star. She couldn't believe he was here, so transformed, so aged and superior. He'd become a man, which felt in her heart to be at once a glamorous re-creation and the worst betrayal.

He was to return as himself. He was to come back, if ever he did, as the boy who disappeared, for them to resume where they had left off. For them to buy the convertible they'd always dreamed of and drive to the coast to see the ocean. He was to sweep her up in his arms, and to lift her in the air for her to shout his name so loud and so often that the whole neighbourhood would gather round and celebrate that Robbie had returned.

He gave a nervous cough then, and Helen's heart slunk back into her chest. She descended the three stairs to the grass.

We changed the locks when our first caretaker quit. She touched a hand to her skirt to dry it. Dad didn't want her coming back for the furniture, he said, now that she was out of a job.

Helen could taste toothpaste and vomit on her teeth. She wanted to sit down.

So nothing's changed, he said, glancing to the window of the house, though Helen barely noticed for looking at him, soaking in the sight of him, every detail of the body he'd become. Robbie, in the yard in front of her, was terrifying. Her mind raced with an odd, irrational fear. He was a ghost. How many times had she imagined where he was and come to the same conclusion as her father, that he had followed Garrett's example and gone overseas, but had been buried in a dry foreign ground or dumped in some nameless grave? Or had been found in an alley, or a hotel, in a distant city. That he was a living, breathing man in front of her made Helen feel as though her parents, too, were closer. He had his father's features, the same tone and clarity in his voice; his mother's eyes and lashes. Her parents had returned in the body of one man.

She flexed her hands, feeling the dry skin of her palms. She put a hand to her damp forehead and closed her eyes. She needed to slow the moment down, to catch up with how the world had suddenly remade itself.

Are you okay? Robbie asked.

No! she yelled and he winced.

You're alive! she said. She held a hand to her mouth and shook with tears, repeating the words, You're alive, Robbie. You're alive. You're in my yard.

Yes, he said, almost giggling, and the word, the trueness of him standing there to speak it, righted her.

She sobered, straightened herself and sniffed. A bit of a shocker.

She didn't laugh with him, and so he said, rather formally, I'd like to see our parents.

Helen realized by his tone of voice that she was doing a very poor job of welcoming him home. She was no help in putting him at ease. I can take you to them, she said warmly, in a quieter voice.

Where are they?

Just past the Johnson's dairy. Well, it hasn't been a dairy in a decade.

Did you ... did they sell you the house?

Helen's head tipped to the side, slightly, puzzling his question.

I'm not prying, I don't mean to, but I didn't expect to see you here. I thought you'd be ... somewhere else.

Helen realized that Robbie had made a terrible assumption. She knew no way to decorate it nicely. She said gently, They're dead, Robbie.

A moment passed, and he extended his neck, slightly, in a sort of silent, Oh. He hadn't looked her in the eyes since the initial moment of recognition, or perhaps it was that she hadn't looked at him directly. She was busy studying his hands and clothes, his shoulders and trim waist, for something of the young Robbie who left, but he looked her in the eye now with an innocent, disappointed candour that pulled her heart apart in halves. There he was, in the blue of his eyes, clear and brilliant Robbie. Everything they'd left behind was in that look between them. Finally, she felt, someone who will understand what's been lost.

I would have liked to see Mom again, he said, his voice clear and delicate.

He turned then, dropping his jacket onto the deck chair behind him. As he came back round, he lifted his hands wide apart so that Helen didn't know what the gesture was, some sort of clearing of the air, a stretch, until she realized it was the beginning of an embrace.

She stepped forward immediately and pressed herself unbelievably into him.

As he drew his arms around her, Helen's heart sank so hard in her chest she felt as though someone was trying to pull it out of her body. Keenly alert, aware that she was in the adult arms of her brother, after waiting so long, disproving any fears that he too had died, she felt the slight breeze tickling a hair against her cheek, the spring of the grass beneath her feet, the sound of bees in the garden and the river rubbing against the weeds. She smelled the slight musk of his cologne, a damp sweat, and the sweet thick pollen from the gardenias along the eastside fence. Even the sun on her skin felt more intense, as though she could soak up the light.

She clasped her hands behind his back and held him. She had remembered him for so long he'd become a ghost of her imagination. What had he really looked like? How exactly did he hold himself? What was the expression of the grin on his face as he was telling his jokes at the dinner table? With her face pressed against his tie and her arms pulling him even closer, Helen let out a sob of joy that he was solid. Solid never felt so solid. He was real. His body so thoroughly here, in her arms. She saw again the speck of man falling through the air and felt it, his fall, inside her, like a fishing line tied to her heart, pulling downwards, and she grabbed Robbie's shoulders more tightly.

When they let each other go, she wanted to invite him in but couldn't think how to do so without sounding proprietary. *Would you like to come inside?* felt so coloured with ownership.

When he pulled a handkerchief from his pocket and mopped his brow, Helen felt relief. Oh, we're baking out here, Robbie, let's go inside for a drink.

He smiled and said, Good idea, though Helen caught the strain in his right eye as he glanced at the back door.

Taking a step towards the house, Helen's adrenaline began to run cold through her limbs, her heart banging in a chest too small to contain it. Robbie would be in the house. She was winded climbing the three steps of the porch. Holding the screen door open, she stepped back to allow him passage. At the top step, he smiled at her, a nervous, uncertain, friendly smile. Conspiratorial. They both knew the significance of these simple gestures, and they were both nervous with it.

Then he was in the kitchen, ahead of her, taking steps on the tile in his black shoes, so much broader in the back and shoulders than when he'd left, and the incongruence, the change, helped Helen relax. However much the house carried the spectre of her parents' former life, they were dead. Helen was the one who remained and she was thrilled to have him here. It could be that simple. Her brother was home, she'd cook him a meal, they would talk, and the world would continue to turn on its axis.

Draping his jacket over the back of a chair, he sat at the table in the seat where Helen used to see him every morning wolfing down his breakfast before school. She felt her body holding its breath in an attempt to slow the moment, trying to keep it.

I'll get us some iced tea, she said. You still like iced tea?

If you made it, I sure do.

When he smiled, his eyes were sharp and, again, a little pained. He seemed too alert, not the least bit relaxed. She wanted to slap his back and tousle his hair, to put him at ease, though they felt like old tricks, the tricks used on a boy. How did he get to be here, so old; both of them grown and changed? With her brother sitting at the table, it was as if Helen was the one who had been away. She felt like she had stepped into this world out of another, maybe, and she couldn't explain where she'd been. She felt she knew nothing of how she got to be here. So much had passed without him and she could only see the result of it, the product, perhaps because Robbie being so transformed threw everything else into relief. Time had progressed for Robbie, whereas Helen had stepped back into the world to find it changed.

As she closed the door to the freezer, she noticed the twist ties by the back entrance that she'd dropped in a rage. She'd forgotten Piché. Well, she'd have to wait. Helen poured two glasses of cold tea, sliced a couple of lemon wedges and glided them around the rim of the glass before dropping them in the drinks. Robbie was smiling again, infectiously, as she turned to him. Helen giggled, handing him his glass.

She pulled out a chair across the table from him — her mother's place — and sat, feeling light as she landed on the cushion.

He thanked her and took a sip of his iced tea, swallowing with some difficulty.

I ... wasn't sure if I should expect a warm return.

Robbie, she scolded, of course. Then she said more lightly, It was worse the longer you were away.

I suppose there's some truth to that, he replied, with a flatness that made Helen fear she'd been misunderstood.

Mom left your window open for nearly a month, with the door still locked. The morning you left, Dad wanted to take the door off its hinges but she wouldn't let him. It was your room. She was so bent on privacy. He had to slide your bedroom window closed from the outside.

Robbie let out a very small grunt, barely audible, but said nothing.

Mom put a small ladder alongside the house until someone took it. They thought it was Humphries, so we stopped getting our wood from him.

Why would she think I'd come in through the window?

Helen chuckled, and shrugged, raising her palms. Because you left that way?

Robbie said lightly, shaking his head, Glad I wasn't here for that.

Helen set her iced tea on the table, turning the glass, the condensation pooling against the polished wood. I expected you back within the week, she said slowly.

She wanted to communicate how interminable the days felt at that time. Every meal was a reminder that they were no longer together, the routine broken, until over weeks or months, the waiting became the routine, a new pattern in his absence. Her mother set a place for him each meal in the first months. Only once did Helen's father tell her mother not to bother with the extra setting, which prompted her mother to throw supper in the trash and break every dinner plate on the table.

I did, he said. I mean I nearly did. I came back ... I came partway and, well ... changed my mind.

Abruptly, he stood up, stepped towards the hall, which made Helen jump, then he stopped. I'd like to use the washroom, if I may. I see he finally managed to build a new one.

I had it done. Walter McLellan came in with his boys and finished it in an afternoon. He was too sick in the end, and I wasn't going through the winter.

That must have hurt his pride.

I don't know if he realized. He never saw it.

Helen stood as well. Towels are in the cupboard there if you need them. I've got to bring some twist ties to Mrs. Piché.

She's still here?

Oh yes, there's no stopping Piché. Helen touched his sleeve. Make yourself comfortable. Look around. See your old room, which hasn't changed much since you left it. Where are you staying?

I have a bag outside.

Bring it in.

Nice, he said, chipper. I thought I might be staying at the lodge.

Helen felt a flash of anger grip her, that he'd expect so little of them, and then, knowing he would likely have been right had her father still been around, her heart sank for the pity of it. No wonder he'd stayed away so long.

I'm surprised my room is still here, he said, perhaps noting her anger. Not much has changed, has it, other than the bathroom?

Well, they plan to come for the house in a few months, she said warmly. Things need to be packed. They're tearing it down. The structure isn't sound enough to move.

Robbie's head tipped to the side, studying her, and again she noticed the downward pull in his right eye, a tick of stress maybe. In those short seconds she could see him puzzling her meaning, then his face blanched with understanding and his eyes lit with tears.

She put a hand to his head, just over his ear, as their mother used to do. Robbie's face fell in on itself, stifling a sob that burst from him.

Robbie. Oh Robbie, I'm happy you're home, Helen soothed him.

He nodded, squared his shoulders and sniffed hard. It's all a bit much, I'm afraid. He opened his mouth to say more, and nothing came; he was struggling to contain himself. Helen waited, moving her hand from his hair so that she could take his hand in hers.

I'm so sorry Mom is gone, he managed.

She missed you. We all did. The three of us.

His face closed a door then; he withdrew. He gave a short nod. Will you not tell Piché I'm here? he asked.

She'd love to see you, Robbie. She's been a great help to us, Dad and I, especially when Mom was at the end —

I think I've had enough for now, he interjected. We'll see. Tonight. Or tomorrow, when I have the energy, he said. Then he mouthed *washroom*, and turned for the hall.

AS SOON AS he set the lock, Robert leaned his head against the door. The painted wood was cool on his forehead, and solid. He swivelled his head, to press his cheek closer and absorb some of the coolness. He was broiling, overwhelmed. His parents were dead. His father dead. Such a relief to not have to face him ... but he'd also been cheated out of that. So many thousands of times he'd imagined the confrontation; months thinking about returning, three weeks planning it. But his father was dead. When he bought his ticket home, when he checked the schedule seven times to make sure he hadn't misremembered the time, when he lied to the restaurant that he wasn't coming in for a week because he was going on holiday to lake country, when he told Colin, and convinced him not to come, and when his legs buckled three times on the way to the bus depot, his father was already dead.

His mother too. He had imagined she would forgive him, instantly, the moment she saw him, for having stayed away so long. Forgiven. And truer than that, he hoped for the reverse, that he'd forgive her.

Now that they were both gone, he felt unnerved. There was a terror, dormant, in how everything was familiar. Everything he'd imagined, the house, right here before him, the walls and floor and ceiling surrounding him, an embodiment of so much he feared, and longed for. The kitchen just as he'd remembered it, from the dishes on the counter to the wallpaper on the walls, the curtains, the table and chairs, the beige tiled flooring, the placement of spices on the rack above the stove. The cheap paintings and ornamented mirrors.

The front door clicked shut. Helen had left for Piché's, next door. Robert was immobile on the bathroom floor leaning into the door, breathing heavily, trying to slow his breath, to stop perspiring, to turn off his guts, which were boiling. He was inside his body and outside at once. Feeling and not feeling. The bathroom, remodelled, felt like the safest place in the house. The counter was new. The toilet. A striped towel hanging next to him on the back of the door carried the slight smell of river water: seaweed and algae. His sister's swim towel. Behind him, the smell of plastic from the shower curtain. A fruity soap or shampoo. There was a wisp of hair coiled in the corner in front of him.

Robert took a deep breath and pressed his face again into the door. Despite what he'd done, she'd been warm to him. She'd welcomed him. Garrett had been killed, so long ago, that she'd made her peace with what had happened. Robert wondered how much their parents might have also made peace. Had he stayed away too long? He'd spent more than a decade away for no reason but his own useless pride, maybe, and all was right here. All was well between him and Helen. Though she'd received her fiancé's ashes, mailed home in a box, still she had embraced Robert. She had forgiven him. She must have. He was pitying himself. There was nothing in her welcome to make him guilty about what had passed.

Robert shook with relief. He heard the outside door open and click shut again. Helen's shoes muffled by the living room carpet. He stood, quietly, then flushed the toilet, to hide his little episode, and washed his face in the sink.

Stepping out of the bathroom, back into the kitchen, with Helen smiling and glassy-eyed as he came into the room, he thought he should just ask her and have it done with. He should just say he was sorry, and have a good cry with her about it, and move on.

Helen shook her head. You seem impossible, Robbie. How did you get here?

The bus, and then a cab, he answered, and she laughed.

Where did you come from? she asked, performing, holding her palms up and looking around.

Robert chuckled, and stepped to her, then leaned down

between her arms and hugged her slim body to him. She wrapped her arms around his shoulders as best she could, so he leaned a little lower to help her get a better grip.

I'm sorry, he said quietly, speaking into a mouthful of hair. For why I left.

Helen was silent, but gripped him. When they were done, Robert sat down again in his old seat, and smiled, sheepish. Helen smiled back. Then her brow wrinkled, and she cupped her iced tea, and asked, innocently, Why did you leave? and Robert saw in her face that, so many years later, she knew nothing.

HELEN LAY IN bed, her mind too topsy-turvy to sleep. She couldn't convince herself to let go of the day. Similar to the sensation she had when she was learning to float, the more she struggled to relax, the harder it was to accomplish. Sleep felt dangerous, threatening, as though, in order to not drown in the heavy darkness of the room around her, she might have to break something to survive it. Folding back the covers, she slid out of bed and grabbed her summer housecoat from the wardrobe.

The house was so quiet, even walking lightly she could hear the sound of her feet unsticking from the hardwood floor. It had been some time since she'd had to be this quiet, to not rouse someone else in the house.

The click of the lock to the back door seemed unusually loud in the darkness. Out of doors, the night air filled Helen's lungs. Everything outside smelled new. She was better for being out-side. She noticed the terrific tightness of her upper back and tried to relax.

The yard plants were gilded with silver by moonlight. Everything was laced with a soft white, the water's surface a constant blinking of clean light. Helen sat at the end of the dock, as they used to when they were kids, with her feet dangling in the dark water. They would hold themselves with their arms on the edge of the dock, facing the river, and lower their bodies to the water. They were so young their legs couldn't reach the surface. Helen measured her growth from season to season by how far away her feet were from the river's surface, and then how deep she could slip a foot, or leg, in her later years.

Across the river, there were no lights. The land and trees were a dark outline against a sky only slightly less black, a black more luminous for being made of air. She slid a foot into the water and was surprised how chilly it was. There was a ring of cold around her ankle where the water and air met.

Before bed, Helen had stopped in the hallway, outside Robbie's door, with her hand on the doorframe. He was seated on the end of the bed, bent over his suitcase on the floor at his feet. When he looked up, she finally said, Thank you, what she had been wanting to say all evening. He gave her a quizzical look and she said, For coming home. She'd hoped for some reaction, to have him soften, but still there was some reluctance.

She entered her room and closed the door. The minute she crawled into bed, though, she didn't feel right. He was only partially here, partially available to her. Hadn't he been sly all afternoon? Something about him had been busy, distracted, and whatever conversation he'd been having with himself, he wasn't letting on. He'd rejected the suggestion to see Piché, then had taken a nap for most of the afternoon, and when he came out around four, he had suggested they cook supper together so that, it seemed, they had something to keep them busy.

She couldn't deny — as much as she felt a knot of guilt over it — she was worried, and anxious. Fifteen years without Robbie and suddenly he was home. The waiting was over. The questions could be asked, although — here was the sliver in her heel she couldn't pull out herself — all evening Robbie hadn't said a thing, not a word, of why he'd stayed away so long. So he and his father had had a row. Big deal. And why had he returned? Why now? Fifteen years. Her mother's death, then her father's. How she had longed for him at the graveyard, looking over her shoulder to the gates of the cemetery, hoping he'd pass under the ironwork in time. He had failed them. He had failed her.

And now, news of the Power Authority buying up property is published in the papers across the country, and he happens to come home. He'd left a boy. Helen hadn't a clue what influences he'd had during the absent years, where he'd been, or what kind of opportunity he'd had to grow into a man. She didn't know who he was. The boy was there in Robbie's eyes, the quickness, the sparkling warmth, but Helen couldn't deny that he had come home just in time to claim his inheritance. Helen considered it was a prize, possibly, that he hadn't earned. He has every right, she reasoned, and no right whatsoever.

She looked back at the house, the only roof she'd ever lived under, the walls that had seen her conceived, then born, and within which both her parents had died. It looked so solid in the night, so firm, rising out of the ground, and yet Helen imagined she could blow on it and see it disappear like winter steam. Soon there would be nothing left. Robbie was safely inside, asleep in his room; not home, Helen realized, for he'd abandoned home.

Robbie was safe behind those walls, until the demolition crews came in a few months. Helen felt her heart jump at the need to protect him. *He's returned*, she thought. She doesn't have to consider him home, for very soon there won't be a home for either of them, not the same home, surely, built in a new town, but he's returned, and she would have to wait to see the consequences of that, to determine his intentions, however much she wanted to be her mother and to love him regardless, and despite her doubts, and her anger, despite her resentment, like her father, only this time it was not that Robbie had left, but that he'd come back.

SUNDAY

VERY MUCH AWARE of the hard wood beneath her rear, and her arm numb from leaning on it, her face, too, where it lay against her forearm, Helen woke in the outdoors. She'd spent the night on the lounge chair by accident. She must have been comfortable enough, or she'd have woken. It was with a great effort of will mixed with a hardy dose of anxiety that she had learned to sleep lightly when her parents were ill. She forever feared they'd call out and she'd miss an important request, an emergency. In the years since, she hadn't unlearned the habit, for she'd felt important, and going back to a good solid sleep seemed a horrible substitute for what she'd lost.

Sitting up, she felt the corner of the chair's arm pull and leave a dent where she had slept against it. Why she'd have been out so thoroughly as to sleep the whole night in the yard was beyond her, until she looked to the house and Robbie materialized in her mind, beyond the wall, rushing the excitement of yesterday back into her heart, which clenched with nervous energy. Of course she could sleep now, deeply, for there was someone else to rely on. Was it as simple as that? Or was it the exhaustion of so much feeling?

The air was fresh and wet with the smells of river and worm. The trees were brilliant green in the early sunshine, already so bright. From the look of the sky and the sound of birdcalls, Helen guessed it was seven or so. The air was warm and clammy with its relentless humidity. She picked a small johnny-jump-up from across her toe.

Angus Pettigrew was out in his boat again, casting west, downstream, in the same spot roughly that he'd occupied since last week. The fishing must be good, though it was a wonder he had the spot to himself. Too many days in a row in the same area and there'd be more than a few locals who'd get wise and pull up, too far away to curse out without scaring the fish your-self but not so far they couldn't still cast in your general direction. There was no privacy out on the water. Helen saw many a man try for it when they had to take a leak over the side of his boat, and fail. When they were youngsters, her brother and his friends would shout hellos and wave at the men as they peed.

Standing, she noticed her hips were stiff. The grass between her toes was especially sweet. As she stepped into the kitchen, Robbie came from the hall, face full of shaving cream, a razor in hand. He wasn't wearing a shirt, exposing his torso powdered with black hair up his abdomen and spreading into wings across his chest.

Were you out all night? he asked, his brow creased.

Just sleeping on the deck chairs. Helen chuckled, to dismiss her silliness.

That couldn't have been too comfortable.

Helen laughed again. It wasn't.

Am I in your way here? Do you have to get ready for work?

I only do one or two days a week at the lodge. Bookkeeping.

That's nice.

I make as much as when I was turning beds. Minus the odd tip. It works.

She asked, to change the subject, And how did you sleep?

Mm, okay ... Do you have a stalker? There were phone calls in the middle of the night.

Oh damn. I unplug the phone at night, I'm sorry.

Who's calling?

Some prank. They've been calling and hanging up the last week or so, at all hours.

They don't say anything?

Yeah, they just call. So unplugging the phone solves that.

Helen shrugged. Robert thought she had more to say, but she was silent for a moment, which they both recognized as awkward.

I'll finish shaving, he said and, catching her glancing at his chest again, added, And I'll put a shirt on.

You look so *dif*ferent, Robbie. You've grown. Yesterday I thought it was your boots, but it seems like you're taller.

Maybe you shrunk.

Helen leaned in the doorframe, watching him run the razor down his neck. This is familiar, oddly familiar.

Everything is familiar, he said, glancing at her through the glass of the mirror. It's very odd. Everything's the same, only smaller.

Helen knocked on the door jam. So ... Piché? I should tell her. I'm taking her to the meeting at the school tomorrow night. There's a public meeting about the construction. She'll want to know you're here.

I'd like that, he said.

She saw you at the front door yesterday but didn't recognize you. She thought you were with the Power Authority.

They show up often?

I've been delinquent. Haven't signed anything yet.

Helen wasn't sure how much to tell him, and added, as a heads-up, in case he did have designs, I have to bring the papers to my lawyer.

Robbie nodded, going back to his shaving, and said, So how do you want to do this with Piché? I could knock on her door, but I think you should likely go first, no?

Yes ... Helen paused, and Robbie looked at her in the mirror, quizzically.

She forgets things. Sometimes. She might not know who you are, or she might know and then forget again. Though she's better with long term, so maybe you'll be fine. Or not, I guess, because you aren't the same boy she'll remember.

How bad is she? She's living alone. She mustn't be that bad.

Oh, she's okay; it's slow-moving. In hindsight, I think she's been forgetting simple things for a while. Her old dog's name, which wasn't so remarkable. I forget stuff like that too. But I noticed about six months ago she referred to her two boys. Like there hadn't been a third and fourth, like she'd dropped into a time before they'd come along. It's like there are pockets in the landscape. She does well, wanders around like there's nothing wrong, and then occasionally falls into a hole. And she pops out easily, when prompted. She's fine. She's eating well. Her cupboards are stocked. I see her cooking meals and she's always bringing me leftovers and baking.

And what about the boys? Antoine?

Died. Killed himself. It was a real blow to everyone. He was in Montreal and nobody knows what happened. Maybe drugs.

Or a lack of them.

Papa Piché insisted he not be given a funeral. *Not in a Catholic grave*, he said. *Not while I'm alive.* They buried him, oh god, I don't even think I know. The boys were furious. It was very ugly. It took a week after the last one left to repair the walls of the house. And none of them have visited much since. Maybe once a year.

Robert looked at Helen again, in the mirror. She spoiled them, he said.

Which is a good part of the reason why they are so wild. It's funny, she added, that the boys left. Maybe you're the first, and the rest will come back.

She forced a smile, which felt false, and knocked twice again on the doorframe. I'll go tell her you're coming.

Walking down the steps of the house, Helen noticed her hips were definitely tight. She slapped them to try to get the blood moving. Sooner or later they'd warm up. Two sports cars passed on the road, their hatchbacks loaded with blankets, pillows and camping gear.

Stepping into the house, Helen found Piché in the kitchen, with her cotton skirt on backwards, washing her breakfast plate. Good morning, she said, and Piché jumped.

They both laughed. Here, Annick, Helen said, coming behind her, let me fix this. Don't move.

She took hold of the elastic band on the skirt and shimmied it the right way round. You had that on backwards, she said.

I like it like that. Piché was chuckling.

Helen leaned on the counter. Her legs were shaking with excitement, still, as though she might never feel normal again. Annick, she said slowly, unsure, Robbie's home.

Piché looked at her and blinked, then whumped a hand across her chest and said, Where?

In the house. He's shaving in the bathroom.

Helen hadn't even finished her sentence before Piché bolted for the front door, wobbling from one side of her body to the next with effort. She clapped her hands before throwing open the front door and clapped them again when she was outside.

All right then, Helen heard herself say, and followed.

He was wiping his face as they stepped into the hall. Immediately, Piché was on him.

When she hugged him — more like she grabbed him to her chest and hung on — it seemed to Helen as though something from the day before came loose in him, a chair kicked from under a doorknob, and he blubbered like a baby. Helen imagined that seeing Piché somehow made everything feel less otherworldly for him. Piché was older, but still Piché; whereas Helen, being so grown up, some grey in her hair, some laugh lines in the corner of her eyes, heavier in the hips and her legs thicker, was probably something of a stranger, a hybrid of the sister he'd had.

Helen was watching them — Piché clinging to Robbie, his face streaming with tears — when the grandfather clock in the living room began to chime. It was Helen's turn to jump.

As she put a hand on the wall to steady herself, Robbie began to laugh, and Piché released him to turn and see what the noise had been about, keeping a grip on his hand.

I'm sorry, Robert said over the chiming, trying not to laugh harder, tears making the giggles bubble up. I started the clock this morning when I got up.

That's okay, Helen said, I didn't notice. I don't know why I didn't. It just startled me.

The three of them stood waiting for the chimes to stop. The sound of the clock was otherworldly for Helen. When her father had stopped breathing, Helen closed the lids of his eyes, walked into the living room, opened the glass door of the grandfather clock as she and Robbie had done so many times when they were curious children, only this time she did what they had never dared do, she took hold of the weights and stopped the clock. When Dr. Baitz asked the time of death for the official certificate, she wouldn't be stuck for an answer this time, as she had been with their mother.

It was her father who had reset the clock when necessary, so how could Helen restart the workings? It wasn't a job she felt privy to, nor that she wanted. Out of not quite respect, but an honour for the rituals of the house, she had left the gears to rest.

The clock chimed *six*, *seven*, and Helen felt the seconds come to her, rushing at her. He'd wound up her spring with a small key and had set her in motion. She felt, again, as though she'd stepped back into the world, that things were repaired. When the eighth chime sounded, the house was overly quiet, except for the rasp in Piché's throat. The air seemed to whistle through her.

Let's have some breakfast, Helen said, rubbing the goose-bumps on her arms.

.🦐.

PICHÉ HAD ALREADY eaten, so she made plans with Robert to have coffee in the afternoon, at her place, she said, in the backyard, under the gazebo. She grinned ear to ear.

When Helen and he had finished cleaning up the breakfast dishes, Robert told her he wanted to have a look around town. He expected she'd want to join him, and wasn't sure if he could get out of the house alone, but she simply said 'sure' and left it at that.

The walk into town was much shorter than he remembered. His legs were longer and his sense of scale had changed, having lived so long in the capital, and having walked so much further. Much had changed and much more hadn't. MacEachern's had become Go-Mart, the pharmacy was a restaurant, which looked closed. Robert saw kids who could just as well have been from a big city. Did they have kids who looked that urban when he lived here? The streets had more trash on them — paper cups, cigarette packs, newsprint everywhere. Helen had told him the night before that the county decided to halve the pickup dates in the old town, as they now called it, since many families had already moved, but they'd overlooked both the new people in town who were there for the construction and the amount of trash that moving makes. Businesses were piling trash bags onto the street curbs when their dumpsters were full.

There was a knitting store Robert hadn't known and he couldn't remember what had occupied that space before; though the gap in his memory may have been expected, it made him somehow angry. Everything different was something of a relief, a great relief, that things had moved on, that this wasn't the same place that he'd left. The differences held promise, and knowing that he'd missed that evolution, that he'd not been privy to the changes, or an influence on them, that what had changed here did so without him, made him feel cheated, nostalgic for the progress he'd missed.

The payphones in front of the liquor store were gone, but he circled round and found one in the back of the Go-Mart beside the upgraded washroom that had a new inside entrance, though its location was the same. No sign of a MacEachern that Robert could tell, though none of the teenagers working there was much more than a toddler when he'd left. The layout of the store was the same, but the counter was faux granite, a kitchen counter-top, and there was a cash register on it, rather than MacEachern's tin tray below.

Robert picked up the phone with relief, dialled Colin, and realized when he heard *Hello* how desperate he was to hear his voice. He wanted something familiar from his current life to remind him who he was. Colin's voice, his breath on the phone, was instant comfort. Colin, in his chair at the desk. Robert could hear the spring creaking as he sat down.

So how were they? Colin asked.

Dead, Robert replied. Both of them.

Oh god, Rob, I'm sorry.

I don't want to cry on the phone. I'm in the convenience store. Robert glanced around the room and turned his back to the counter.

Okay, sure.

My sister is here. She's living in the house.

Colin paused for only a second. I'm coming. I'll fly in tonight.

Robert's stomach seized. Comfort, he remembered, wasn't Colin's thing. He was good at getting things done, making decisions, seeing clearly, giving frank advice, but not hand-holding.

I don't know.

You've no reason now.

My sister is here.

And ...

I haven't talked to her, really. Really talked.

How's she treating you?

She's thrilled to see me. Genuinely.

So I'm coming. Today.

Robert tried to interrupt him, but Colin continued, I'm looking at my schedule and there's nothing I need to finish until next week. I can take a few days. I'm coming. Where are you staying? What's the hotel called?

From the other side of the wall a toilet flushed. A belt buckle jingled into place. Robert had a brief panic someone had heard him.

I'm staying at home, he said more quietly. My sister is there.

You can't stay there. The lodge is the only place in town. It's downtown, it's still there. You can't miss it.

Downtown? Or the lodge?

Either. Colin ...

The bathroom door opened and a teenager, a pale redheaded girl, stepped out, chewing gum. She walked past as if Robert weren't there.

He lowered his voice again. Colin, I just want to remind you that everyone knows each other here.

I know that.

My sister is working at the lodge. She does bookkeeping. You probably won't see her, but still.

Okay.

And I don't know how much she knows, about anything. He paused, wondering how to say it properly. She seems stuck. I mean, she still has a photo of Garrett in her room.

She doesn't know about me, does she?

I don't think she knows anything. She doesn't know why I left. She asked if I was married. If I had any kids.

Oh fuck, he said, laughing, though Robert could hear the frustrated strain in his voice. He was buoyant, saying, I'll be there tonight. I can tell her.

No. You won't.

Okay ... Okay. But I'm coming tonight. Where do I meet you? How do I get hold of you?

You can't call me.

You're paranoid. You're allowed to have friends.

Just — give me a day. You can meet her tomorrow.

Are you going to send me smoke signals tomorrow? You don't have a phone.

Don't be smart.

Am I to sit in my room for the day waiting for your secret knock?

Can we do this right? I just want to do this right.

I suppose I can't have the number for where you're staying. I don't want to sit around for hours waiting for you to call.

I know, I'm sorry.

You need to get a cell. If I'm coming tomorrow I'll drive. How far is it? Six hours?

That's by bus. Four-and-a-half.

Done. I'm coming, Rob.

Fine ... There's a public meeting tomorrow night in my old school gymnasium. Come in the evening?

When?

I don't know. Get here by eight?

I'll hit the road after yoga then. Easy. What school? What's the name?

There's only one. I'll meet you there. We can talk outside.

There was a pause. Colin was waiting; Robert hadn't offered enough yet.

You can see Helen. She'll be with me. And it'll be crowded; you can watch her if you want, if you're discreet. But you aren't to talk to her until she knows, all right? Do you understand?

Colin didn't answer. Robert continued, to appease him. I'll introduce you but ... Let's be patient. Okay? Let's do this right.

If I can't get into town by eight or whatever, just look for me, he said, softened. I'll be there eventually.

But we'll talk outside.

Outside.

Colin, he said, dropping his tone.

Colin answered, I know, which told Robert that he did.

Thank you.

I've been patient a long time, Colin said carefully. I'm bringing the letter.

I know.

I deserve this.

Tomorrow.

Tomorrow.

I'll see you at eight.

Robert set the phone in its cradle and looked to the redhead, who was at the counter, trying to pull open the buttoned pocket of the kid at the till. He was pushing her hand aside, repeatedly, laughing. They hadn't been paying him any mind.

THE LAST TIME they'd been in a car together, Helen had taken Robert on the back roads to teach him how to drive. Their father had told her not to because he didn't think Helen would be any good at it and didn't want Robbie driving. He didn't trust either of them; Helen was a girl and Robbie, she heard him say to their mother, wasn't much of a man. As it was, Robbie nearly landed them in the Desrosiers' field, so he might have been closer to the mark on both their counts than she'd have cared to admit. Helen, to her credit, had let Robbie keep at it for an hour afterwards. He'd apologized to her up and down, but was greatly improved.

You'll never get it right without making a few mistakes, she'd said, and then, winking, added, But let's try to make them small mistakes, okay, kiddo?

Together again in the car on the old highway out of town,

late afternoon, they drove past the Rideout's barn where the youngest had briefly set up a brewery, and past the corner with the large granite rock which was pissed on and spray-painted each year by the graduating boys. Helen used to wonder if they really did urinate on the thing until one midnight she drove by a handful of them doing so, and wished she hadn't wondered. They drove by the houses their friends grew up in, most of those people moved away, some now dead, with a number of those houses staked with orange ribbons marking them for demolition, and they drove past dozens upon dozens of tree stumps lining the streets, the trees having been felled to make way for the house-moving machine that was to roll into town the coming week. Most of the wood was pulped, but some locals paid to have it made into firewood, and a few cut the trees up themselves. Desrosier, in fact, had been selling furniture from it since the spring.

Helen told Robert what news she knew, most of it gleaned from Ruby across the way, or from Piché, who got it from Ruby. The neighbours, she said, and the papers for that matter, had been talking about the house-mover for weeks. Many locals had driven to this or that site to get a look at it.

Have you seen it? he asked.

I can wait, she answered, crisply, one hand on the wheel. She chewed a hangnail on her finger and looked at him. I'll see too much of it, I'm sure, before it pulls up in front of Piché's door.

On their right, on the Rochon property, an empty hole littered with rubble gaped where the farmhouse once was. The lawn was dotted with the pale beige disks of tree stumps.

What happened here? Fire?

Helen shot him a look. The structure wouldn't support a move, she said. They got a brand new house. Ruby said they chose it out of a catalogue. They match them up based on the value of your property. You'd think they'd have been given a shoebox for the shape their place was in, but they had a waterfront, and the size of the old property was a lot bigger than the one they were moved to, so they got this four-bedroom with a deck out back.

Helen smoothed a finger along her eyebrow, then rubbed, and smoothed it again. She couldn't keep up with the changes. Even places she'd already seen were shocking, like the Rochon's, or Nellie's farm, which sold antiques since before she'd been born. The missing trees, and more homes razed, some leaving their flowerbeds intact, made for a surreal experience, as though they were tearing down Helen's life, set pieces of a movie that were no longer necessary, though the story of her life was still continuing. Houses were being moved around the map like toys. How does one live in a remade world, where everything that once was — this house built here, that store there, the mill, the roads, the trees planted and harvested — was either destroyed, or displaced? Helen was irritable every time she saw it. There could be no authenticity in the new town. It would be Disney. A fake, because it was designed by foreigners with no interest or understanding of who they were, how they got to be where they were. What could be more false than picking up that history and dropping it in some new order, some new arrangement, devoid of the natural process of how things came to be?

It riled her. She couldn't find a way to settle it with herself, to find a compromise. Ruby suggested she ask for more, to negotiate a better offer, and to do so until she was happy, but Helen couldn't find anything that would be a sufficient substitute for what she already had, which was her home. The trick of the thing was simple: she didn't welcome the change, and so she'd been avoiding the negotiation of that change. And perhaps, this late in the game, Robbie beside her, she'd waited too long. Though that wasn't fair to him.

We're just up here, she said as they approached the cemetery. Helen's stomach turned as she got close, because she'd been so wrapped up for the morning imagining what Robbie must be going through, imagining the changes from his eyes, and anticipating this visit to their parents' graves, that she'd forgotten about the falling man until the car was approaching the ironwork gates.

As they parked, Helen coughed, more like a hiccup. She could taste bile. Her hands were sweaty on the steering wheel. Being Sunday, the trucks and backhoes of the day before rested silent at the far side of the yard. The local clergy had insisted they not dig on Sundays. Helen thought about her small puddle of vomit as she drove over the spot where she'd stopped the day before. She wanted to tell Robbie about the accident, but realized he had enough on his plate without her adding her own drama.

When she'd turned the ignition off, she looked at him, then opened her door.

Robert nodded and they both stepped out. As they came round the front of the car, Helen held her hand out and he took hers in his. She walked them the fifty yards to the plots in silence.

The fishy smell of the air gripped Robert, with something of the freshness in the river too, the spring freshness and the sweet blooms of roses, and the wet rich smell that he recognized was worms from their days collecting them in the dewy mornings before the sun had come up.

His parents' stones were simple, grey granite, with their father's five names on it and their mother's maiden name in brackets.

Robert looked at the stones, and blinked, and looked at them again.

The names. Smoothed stone, marking the date.

He gasped. Helen squeezed his hand. Something about the dates on their stones made their deaths more final. His mother's grave seemed somehow impossible, and Robert realized that he'd been hoping, foolishly, that his mother might still materialize. But here it was. Helen squeezed his hand again, acknowledging, yes, their parents were dead. They lived from this day to this one. Their mother was dead not quite a year and a half ago, and their father only five months after her. If Robert had come home last year at this time, when he'd first considered returning, he'd have seen his father, and just missed her. He was glad he'd waited. He didn't think he could have handled seeing him with his mother gone.

Robert squeezed Helen's hand back. It was only a year ago. He asked her, Why did they bury them here if they're only going to dig them up again?

Dad's ashes are waiting at home, in the garage. We put the gravestone here anyhow. They hadn't picked the new site when Mom died. What was I to do? They'd asked me to consider cremation, but Mom was clear she wanted burial. Dad told me point-blank he was going in the ground next to her. 'No burning,' he said, but I couldn't get them to consent. It was Power Authority land by then. They wouldn't approve it.

Helen released his hand and wiped hers on her dress. The wind picked up a piece of her hair and blew it across her nose. She removed it, turning her head, and walked towards the river, giving Robert some time alone. A few hundred yards out in the water were three small islands, staggered one in front of the other, made mostly of rock. There was a single fir on the closest island. Gulls flew round them, circling, and feeding in the river, bobbing white dots on the water.

You don't leave flowers? he said. I wish I'd brought flowers. I wasn't thinking.

Helen turned, but didn't face him. It only reminds me of ... her corpse. She winced a little because she could think of no better word, nothing more apt, as indelicate as it sounded here. This isn't a reminder, she said, gesturing to the ground. I have the house.

Robert nodded. You haven't moved a thing in it, he said. Have you? I don't think you've changed a single piece of furniture. You haven't painted, or gotten rid of that wallpaper in the entrance.

He looked to Helen, and then the plot, which was devoid of sentiment. He hated how spare their graves were. Untouched. If his sister was living in the past, it wasn't out of fondness, or respect for her parents, it wasn't to honour them by keeping things as they were, for it was clear that she didn't come here. Although the lawn was well-maintained by the caretaker, there was nothing familiar, nothing familial about the plots. The lack of flowers, a planter, any sign of Helen having been here made the narrow rectangular space seem even smaller.

I cleared out a great deal of their clothes. Ruby gave me suggestions, families and Goodwill, who could use them. It seemed selfish to keep them when others went without.

Selfish? You wanted to keep them? You would have worn Mom's clothes?

No ..., Helen said. I just haven't wanted to get rid of anything.

Robert gestured to a dozen backhoes parked on the far side of the yard. So they're going to dig them up?

They've started already.

Where are they moving them?

There's a new site past the old one, a mile beyond the railway line. They have to move that too.

It doesn't seem a job fit for a human. You'd think they'd just leave them.

Erosion. Piché says she wishes they would leave them. From the start she's said she wished they'd forget about the cemetery completely, so we could have coffins floating down the new route competing with boaters.

A long silence passed, and Helen turned, intending to walk them back to the car just as Robert threw his coat across the end of both plots. They looked at each other. She paused and Robert sat down, arms resting on his knees. Helen looked around, carefully, should anyone else notice them. No one she could see. Perhaps others were sitting as well. She was surprised to see Robbie settling in, as though here for a real visit, which, she guessed, it was.

This trip was only Helen's fourth. The first time, she came with her father to pick out the plots when her mom was clearly too far-gone to recover. The second trip she'd been in no state to notice much of anything. She'd returned once more, to double-check the inscription on the stone before she had her father's made. To sit in the cemetery, at the foot of your parents' grave. It was a tender, intimate gesture. She believed he was cozying up to the dead in a way that she herself would never have allowed for fear of it being self-indulgent. What would the dead know of my presence? What would they care, now? And then she remembered Garrett, and was embarrassed. But that was different, wasn't it? That wasn't visiting, she lied to herself. That was as much about the place — the view she'd loved, before construction — as it was about Garrett.

She thought perhaps her brother was a greater optimist than she. Moving away had given him access to an entirely different set of possibilities, access to a different life. Helen, again, felt her heart empty, the bowl in her chest tipping everything into her guts, and returning upright, voided. Robbie, away, felt like family still. He was familiar because she was able to invent him, and the real Robbie, here, acted like so little of what she remembered. So little of what he had once been and she still was.

Helen looked to Robbie and saw he was only taking up half the coat. He'd left a spot beside him. Refusing to glance around again, Helen took her seat next to him. Immediately he leaned into her, relaxing against her weight.

His voice resonated through her as he spoke. I came home when I saw the broadcast on television. I didn't realize they'd be moving so many people. I thought, *If I don't get home now, I might never find them again*. I didn't want to have to come back in a boat to see the family home.

He sat up and set his right hand on the ground. It didn't occur to me I'd find them here. Do we get to choose where they go in the new cemetery?

I'm ... I think so. Yes. Helen hesitated, ashamed that she hadn't paid better attention. She'd had no plans to see them once they moved. I haven't picked out the spot yet. We can look at the papers when we return. I have them in the kitchen.

I'd like to pick somewhere with a view like this, far from the road, where I can sit in the sun when I come home and see the river. Mom loved living on the river.

The new gravesite isn't waterfront.

Robbie lifted his head from her shoulder. How's that?

Helen shrugged. They picked new land and it's not waterfront.

But Mom would want to be by the water, wouldn't she?

Helen hesitated from the sound of frustration in his voice. I ... Yes. Sure.

Are there other options?

I don't think so.

There has to be. They can't leave you just one option. We must have some choice.

I'll look at the paperwork again, but I think they just ask what plot you want ...

And what if two people ask for the same plot?

Helen's shoulders went slack, knowing she'd be damned by her answer. It's first come, first served.

Robbie slid a little further right, so he could look at her. You haven't chosen her plot, but they're already digging people up.

It hasn't been easy. Dad was sick ... Dad was a mess. And I've had a lot more on my plate than where Mom should be reburied.

Helen wanted to add, *And she's dead. What does* she *care?* but that felt harsh, given the shock for Robbie.

Her answer made Robert realize that his sister wasn't so relaxed either. They were both sensitive. Staring at the gravestones ahead of him, he thought maybe this was a safe place to prepare her for Colin. They might get there more easily by talking about their father.

Robert waited a long moment, looking at the inscription, rereading the date, giving them time to move on a little, an apology in that timing, so that he might create a new moment, an entry.

I don't know how you lived with Dad after Mom died, he said gently. I don't think I'll ever forgive him —

I don't know what it was like to be him, she said, interrupting, though her voice was lazy, slow. She was tired. I wouldn't want to.

I know what it was like, Robert said. We both felt the brunt of what it was like.

She leaned forward and looked at him, searching his face. He didn't know for what. He thought maybe she was asking him to forgive his father.

He was nothing after Mom died, she continued. He was ... He'd taken very good care of her on the days he was sober, and he was sober more days than not. When she was sick. He was.

A horn sounded from the highway, two short honks, and another mimicked it in reply. Helen shifted her weight, rested on one arm, tapping on the fabric of his coat.

A couple times after she was sick, he would disappear for a few days, which I'd never seen him do, but Mom said he did that before we were born. Both times. It was nerves. *Just nerves*, she'd said. *He'll come back.* And he did. Shame-faced and sullen, as though he was the one who was to be taken care of. I couldn't pity him. I couldn't. I was doing everything those two days — the needles, the meals, the hand-holding — trying to make time pass more quickly, each moment wondering where he was and wishing, as much as I was hating him, that he'd come back, for her sake. I thought he was avoiding her until it was over. Jesus, she loved him.

Helen leaned back on her arms and gave a weak smile, rolling her eyes. After we buried her, he drank non-stop, pretty much, from what I could tell. He had bottles everywhere, maybe he always did, but he was sloppy. He'd eat one or two meals a day, often just supper, never breakfast, and would sit in the back armchair that was hers and stare out at the river. I mean, he did that for months, through some pretty unseasonable weather. It was like he'd taken up a hobby. Horizon-watcher. Well, if he was going to die, I wanted him to do it sooner. And then it was quick. They think it was diabetes that did the worst of it, from drinking.

When it was obvious he was sick, he wouldn't go to the hospital. He wouldn't have lasted much longer anyhow. His liver was collapsing and his heart was in horrible shape. He wouldn't eat; I couldn't get him to eat for nearly two days until I gave him a beer. So I bought him Guinness. Near the end he'd drink it through a straw. I held the can.

See, Robert began to say, but she held out a finger to him.

You can't tell me you know what he was like. You didn't see that side of him. The fear in him. I held the can for him and put the straw to his lips. He couldn't have been more ... I want to say pathetic — she looked to the ground, searching for the right word — vulnerable. He knew what was killing him, he knew he couldn't stop himself, that he was weak in the face of it, and he knew I knew it too. We played the game of small talk and when that didn't work we were silent, trying to downplay wha... trying to downplay it.

Okay, Robert said, dumbly.

I thought it would be better after Dad died. I did, but it's not better. Some things don't get better. You tolerate them better, which doesn't mean it's any less horrible than it was, it only means it's taken something from you, taken enough that you don't care so much, which I don't think is better, Robbie. Not better.

I'm not sure what you mean. Your life, Helen? You thought what would be better?

You don't just get through everything and are a better person for it. Some things don't go away. I'm not a better person for —

She stopped short. Robert suspected it was *Garrett* she meant to say. Not a better person for Garrett's death, or for knowing he'd left her. That moment should have been his opening, but he didn't know how to get them from where they were to where he needed to be. It would have been cruel.

He didn't say anything except, Garrett, and she nodded.

Helen hadn't mentioned him in years. She never spoke of him out of a kind of superstition, an ownership. Her memories of Garrett were hers alone, provided she didn't share them. But hearing his name, she realized how immaterial he had become in her mind, and he jumped back — fresh, substantial, like thick dust wiped off a photograph, the details made sharp.

And then Robert shrugged, a casual, awkward shrug, and said no more.

THOUGH THEY HADN'T set a time, Piché was carrying a tray with two cups and a plate of cookies across her backyard as Robert entered through the adjoining gate. She gripped the tray very high, pressing it against her chest, as a means to steady it.

When he asked if she needed some help, Piché carried on, unanswering. Her lips were sealed tight with effort.

She set the tray on the table in the small green gazebo and then scooped the air with her hand. Yes, you come help, she said.

He was expected to follow her into the house, which felt odd, because in the sixteen years he'd lived next to her, he'd never been inside her home. The tall wooden fence had been erected the second week after the Pichés moved in due to some conflict between the men over a dog that Robert barely remembered. His mother had insisted on a gate because building it was un-neighbourly enough — she wouldn't have them insult the Pichés twice — but it resulted in a coolness between the men that kept the families from mingling. Piché's boys hadn't much interest in the young Helen anyhow, and Robert, being the boy he was, spent more time avoiding the rough neighbours than playing with them. He followed Piché's broad stout back through the door and smelled coffee on the stove.

You take that, she said, gesturing to the coffee pot, and I'll take these. She picked up two plaid cushions from the kitchen chairs and gave a little chuckle.

Once they were settled on the benches under the wood canopy, she poured them each a cup of coffee, added his sugar and cream for him, and handed him the cup. Robert was reluctant to ask after Piché's sons, so they spoke for a long while about small details they remembered from the past: the first time Piché saw Helen, in the driveway coming home from the hospital, and how loud she'd cried; the road trips her family had taken; a story about him and his father at a fishing derby that Robert didn't recall, which made him wonder if she was remembering the right people; and an incident at a birthday party where two of her boys had vomited under the picnic table, first one, then the other in response, which Robert remembered was a party for a Handy kid.

Each time she lifted her cup, Robert noted the loose flesh under her arms. Piché wore a sleeveless floral print shirt, with a small collar. Likely thirty years old, for where would she ever find something like that? She still seemed sturdy, or gave that impression, likely from being ample, but the longer they talked the more Robert could see her struggling to stay focused. She repeated a couple of details, sometimes losing the topic of the previous sentence. Perhaps he was looking too hard for decline, but it seemed to Robert she was worse off than Helen cared to admit, or to acknowledge.

What work you do? she asked, pouring herself a second cup of coffee. She sounded curt, but she'd always been like that. She often spoke in short sentences to avoid making errors.

He told her he worked at a high-end restaurant.

She asked him, You do *what* there?

Waiting.

She took a loud sip of her coffee and set the cup back down.

Waiting is not a career, she said. You do that while you work on getting a career.

The remark surprised him, because she'd never had a job that he could remember. Piché must have caught his expression, or maybe she'd just given this talk before, maybe to her own sons, because she followed up that comment by saying she was lucky that she'd been a mother, so she didn't have to make those sorts of decisions. Maybe if she was a mother today, she might have to, but things were different back then.

I don't know what else I'd do, Robert remarked, excusing the comment.

You're both the same way, she said. Helen doesn't like the work.

I do like to work, Robert said firmly. I work very hard.

Piché was unresponsive. Robert couldn't tell if she doubted him, or disliked being corrected. Her lips pursed a moment, considering.

Your sister is home *toujours*, she said. She visit you. You invite her.

Yes, I should invite her, he said.

She always in the house. Always in the house. That's good for an old woman. She come out, do things in the garden, that's it.

Holding a finger below her nose, thinking, Piché turned her head towards the sheets she had drying on a clothes line suspended along her dock. Then she glanced at the house, to the back window, Robert thought, where Helen could see out if she wanted. She brought her hands into her lap, gripping them as she readjusted herself on the seat by rocking from one hip to the other. Something in the set of her mouth was off; there was a slight motion of clenching and releasing her lips.

You pack? You help her?

She hasn't asked me to. I should check with Helen, but sure, I'll help.

Piché's head tipped to the side and righted itself. You help. She need help. I'm old. I don't want that they move my house. But they pick it up — she made a gesture, pinching the air like she held a sugar cube below her fingers — and move it. Your sister not lucky like me. They take down the house, yes? Take it down. And where she live?

Though he knew she wasn't looking for a response, Robert felt compelled to answer, I don't know.

Piché shrugged. Is no good. What she do? She has not signed papers. Still no papers. Telephone calls and men here and no papers. Me too, I wait. I wait one year to sign papers. No sign, she said, slapping her hands together. I wait for Hélène. Two months, she have no home. Not packed, no home. Me, I stay here, they move me. I have my home. Hélène? No, no home.

Piché was riled. She looked Robert in the eye. So, she said, softening, pointing a finger at him, *you* are here. You help.

I can try to help, sure, Robert said.

Ta soeur is very good with me. *Genereuse*. But she don't want the change. She never wants the change.

Okay, Robert said. Okay. He took a sip of his drink, to move the moment along, but found the coffee had gone cold.

I knew you come back, she said. She leaned across the table and pinched his hand. You not gone forever.

AFTER A SUPPER outside on the picnic table, Robbie told Helen and Piché to stay put as he picked up their plates and carried them into the kitchen. Helen stacked the remaining dishes by the time he'd returned and she and Piché followed him up the steps with what was left on the table. Salt and pepper shakers, glasses, tongs for the barbecue, napkins and salad bowl. Piché ambled home. She was going to iron the bedding from off the line.

Robbie whisked water around in the sink with his hand, to make the dish soap bubble. Those were impressive pork chops, he said. I haven't had a barbecue in ages.

You don't barbecue at home? she asked. She was tidying up, feeling happy to be in the kitchen with him.

I live in a condo. No balcony.

Oh ..., she said, and paused, debating how snoopy she was allowed to be. He was her brother. She was allowed to ask questions. Do you live with someone?

Robert chuckled. No, I don't.

Helen stood beside him at the counter, strategically, to empty salad into a container. I know you said you're not married, but I thought maybe you had someone, she said. She leaned a palm on the lid and it gave a snap into place.

Not recently, he answered, and he turned off the tap.

But you have had a girlfriend?

Robbie gave an odd sort of laugh again, shaking his head no. He leaned a hip against the sink. I don't do girlfriends, he said finally.

O-kaaay, Helen giggled, stuttering out the final syllable. Now we're getting somewhere.

I thought you couldn't tell.

She wrinkled her eyebrows in an exaggerated frown. Have you seen your fingernails?

Robbie lifted his hands from the dishwater and looked at them then said, I was dying to ask — do you have gloves?

Right under there, she said, gesturing to the drawer beneath the sink. They're smalls, though. I don't know if they'll fit.

He pulled out the yellow gloves and began to put them on, but he hadn't dried his hands, so the rubber snapped a few times, slipping through his soapy fingers. He croaked, Ow, each time. They laughed.

I could wash those, you know.

Not necessary, he said. She watched him struggle, until he raised his hands, with the gloves in place, though clearly the webbing between each digit was not matched to his hands. He gave a nod and said flatly, They're a bit tight.

I'll wash, you dry.

Removing the gloves was even more difficult. Helen ended up pulling on a couple of fingertips and, when the glove gave, it snapped so quick that Robbie's hand slapped into the water and splashed both of them. He wiped soap off his nose, looking sheepish.

That's a gong show. Let's not do this one over the sink.

They pulled the second glove off and were both sweaty and giggling by the end of it. Helen wiped an arm across her forehead. I need a shower, she said.

Robbie laughed, putting an arm around her, squeezing her to him. She felt the heat of his armpit on her shoulder as he kissed the top of her head. You're still my favourite, he said.

I'm still your only.

Same thing, he said, grinning. He picked up the dishtowel to dry as Helen slipped the gloves on, with some difficulty herself, because he'd wet the insides and the rubber wasn't as slippery.

So that's why you left? she asked gently, putting dishes into the sink. Is that why you stayed away so long?

Kind of, he said, yes.

She set the salad bowl in the drying rack and picked up a glass. That seems like an awful long time to be away. Mom wouldn't have cared. I don't care, Robbie. You can do whatever you want.

Thanks, he said, and she wasn't sure if he was mocking her or not.

And why did you leave?

He paused. She could tell he was puzzling an answer. She had waited years to ask him. In the weeks after he'd left, she'd found out very little from either of her parents. There had been an argument the night before Helen returned from a week at the Falk's cottage. Her brother had locked himself in his room and some time later he had climbed out his bedroom window and was gone. Her mother had spent the day at Mrs. Piché's.

Her father — with a freshly blackened eye — was out with the car the entire day, driving the highway.

Robbie was still thinking, so Helen added, to convince him, The day after you left, Dad pulled into the driveway alone. I waited at the window, and I could see you weren't in the passenger seat, but I walked to the car anyhow, and looked in. If I'd've had keys, I likely would have opened the trunk.

He nodded, wiping the bowl, his eyes misty. She gave him a minute to sort himself out. She heard the cupboard above the fridge squeak open, and the glass clink into place amongst the other nesting bowls, and then a soft whump. Shit, he said, his voice throaty.

What's that? she asked, craning her neck. He was kneeling on the ground, with the dishrag over his shoulder, picking up the manila envelopes that had been atop the fridge.

The towel dragged them off, he said. She could hear the emotion in his voice. Sorry.

I got them, she said, kneeling as she turned, dripping water on the floor.

Your hands are wet.

That's okay.

I got them. It's fine, he said, and looked at her.

She was awkward — too eager, she could tell, to collect the contracts from him — and couldn't calm herself fast enough.

I'll just put them back up here, he said delicately, waiting for her to answer.

Yes, please ...

These are your contracts?

Her head gave an unconscious, small, nervous sort of nod.

She couldn't speak. She was ashamed by how secretive she was being but didn't want to tell him all the same.

Piché is concerned about what you'll do after here, Robert said.

How do you mean? She turned back to the sink and picked up the same glass she'd been washing moments ago.

Robert stood in front of the dish rack waiting for her to finish. She's worried you haven't signed anything. I think she's waiting for you.

She is, is she? Helen said.

Well isn't she?

I guess so. I haven't asked her to.

Helen was still turning the glass over, wiping the rim, and the insides, then the rim again.

I don't mean to be nosy. You just tell me to quit and I'll stop asking.

Okay, she said, quit.

Robert cautiously reached over and took the glass from her hands, rinsing it in the second sink. Maybe you and Piché should discuss your plans.

We have that meeting tomorrow, right? Well, she can make her decision then. There's nothing stopping her from signing her contracts. She can sign any time.

Maybe you should tell her that.

Helen stood stiff, her arms at her sides and her hands passive in the water. I thought we were dropping this.

We are, sure, he said, and they finished the dishes in silence.

MONDAY

HELEN SURPRISED HERSELF by forgetting that she had to go to work, forgetting it was Monday morning, until Graveley phoned to ask if she was sick. It was a little thrilling to have forgotten, and to have Graveley wonder after her. She had surprises. She had a life going on.

Every Monday Helen did the books at the Graveley Inn so folks were paid out by the Friday. She'd worked there when she was a teenager, making beds and doing cleaning, until one day she was tired of Ruthie Graveley paying her late because the accountant in the city was slow to do the week's work, which meant Graveley hadn't gotten the books to her accountant on time once again, and she told her she could do the job for her, in house, and likely save her some money too. So for half Graveley's cost but twice what Helen earned making beds, she did the books in little more than a day, rather than three, and saved Graveley the trip there and back. End of month, she did two full days of work. When her mother fell ill, Helen gave up being chambermaid altogether and had enough income arranging the books. Now she had the insurance money, which wasn't much after the burial, but enough for a nest-egg, enough to sleep at night.

There was a satisfaction, a tidiness to the way things fell, for it had been Helen's mother who'd wanted her to learn a trade of some kind, a 'workable subject,' so Helen had taken high school accounting, which wasn't something she thought she'd enjoy, but she found some neat satisfaction in watching the numbers stack up and balance out. She was the girl with her dolls arranged by size and her fifty pencil crayons always in the same order they came in when she first opened the box. The bean jars in her kitchen were arranged by colour.

It was still a good set-up for her: living in a home that was paid for, with no other real expenses except the upkeep of the house, taxes, and her food. She didn't travel, rarely took the car beyond the Keegan property. And she now had the remainder of her father's pension, though modest, but less modest than the life she lived.

Helen worked in the office each Monday morning until Norm arrived at noon to work the front desk, leaving Ruthie free to bustle into the office to make her afternoon calls. Helen took lunch when Ruthie arrived, partly because there was only the one desk and partly because Ruthie made at least half an hour of calls every lunch hour. Helen found she liked Ruthie more the less she knew what went on behind the scenes at the Inn. She could leave the books open and Ruthie would be mindful to not touch anything before she got back, at which point Ruthie would take her own lunch, and then head home, or to the pub, depending on her mood and the weather.

Those numbers falling in place for you?

Ruthie set a stack of opened mail on her desk. She was peeling a small orange, its rind browned and splotchy.

Pretty much, Helen said, standing. She gave Ruthie a smile as she pushed in the desk chair.

Ruthie turned her head and looked at Helen sidelong. What's that? she asked.

Helen shrugged. What?

You were late this morning, and you've got something... She shifted her weight, pushing a hip out. You're not quitting on me?

No, Helen said, laughing.

Well, something's up. Did you cut your hair? Am I missing something?

Helen paused, not wanting to tell her about Robbie, for she wasn't ready to share him just yet.

I saw an accident yesterday, she said, hesitating, but relieved.

An accident ...

A man fell at the dam site. I saw him fall. Through binoculars. Straight down.

God. I'm sorry I asked, Ruthie said. She pulled the orange into halves and held one out to Helen. You okay?

Helen raised a hand to decline the orange. The acid was too much for her stomach. Just talking about the fall again made her feel anxious.

I'm fine. I guess I'm fine. It's unsettling.

I bet. No wonder you were late. You want to go home early? Can you finish up early?

Helen shook her head, said she was fine. It took some convincing to reassure Ruthie that Helen didn't need caretaking, but when Helen told her she'd be better with some lunch in her, Ruthie slipped her a twenty and told her lunch was on the house, which seemed to satisfy her.

Helen made a quick escape and walked the block up to Petrie's market, because she'd left the house without a packed lunch, wanting to leave Robbie to himself. She'd written him a note to tell him to go through his things if he wanted.

Walking the strip downtown, she hadn't noticed the other day just how many of the stores on Bailey were closed already. There were no chairs or tables left in the restaurant, though the booths hadn't been touched. The second-hand bookstore that Lynne ran was already gone; Helen had seen that in the paper. The small satellite library and post office were closed. The ice cream and coffee shop was, too. The Go-Mart was open. Barb's knitting store. Helen knew that Petrie's would move soon but she'd seen Mrs. Petrie outside sweeping when she'd rushed in to work. Helen liked how Petrie's husband, Oscar, always called his wife 'my Helen' when Helen was around, as if one might get them confused in whatever story he was telling.

She wanted something cool because it was broiling in the sun already. She couldn't think what would agree with her stomach. She was running on fumes of energy, her mind buzzing on empty, or buzzing to remain empty. She knew she should buy some food for supper, pick up something else, but she couldn't get her mind to focus on any decision. What did she feel like? Sliced ham. Crackers and curds. Ginger ale, maybe, something gentle.

The shelves at Petrie's seemed emptier than Saturday. Today the last row in the market was completely bare. Helen Petrie was trying to dismantle it with a hammer.

There were no crackers where Helen remembered them to be. Maybe they'd sold them from this location. Weren't they with the cereals? She couldn't remember, tried to visualize them on a shelf but came up with a blank. She'd ask Mrs. Petrie where they kept them, if they had any left.

Coming down the front of the store towards Mrs. Petrie in the last aisle, Helen spotted Glinny Ouderkirk, who did local news for the city paper, at the back of the store. *Glinny*, Helen thought. Although the reporters from the city were often said to be around town in the last months, it seemed like a sign to Helen that Glinny should be here in the grocery store too, so soon after speaking about yesterday's accident.

Glinny, she sort of shouted coming down the aisle towards her.

Although Glinny had seen Helen approaching, she jumped, startled by the force in Helen's voice. She held her milk carton to her chest.

I'm sorry, Helen said. I'm just glad to see you.

Glinny giggled, in her babyish way. That laugh, disarming because it was so silly, had served her well as a reporter because it made people hope nothing was that serious, despite whatever mess you might have got into. She wasn't wily, but was clever enough to know that people talked more freely in nearly any situation if they were relaxed, and her particular giggle worked just so.

No, I'm jumpy. Too much coffee this morning. She looked at Helen with a friendly light in her eye, wondering, Helen could tell, what someone like her might want.

Do you have any news on the accident at the dam Saturday? I was — Helen wasn't sure what she would say, but ended — wanting to get the guy's name.

Glinny lowered the milk carton, which left a darkened spot of moisture on her blouse. What accident?

The guy who fell. From the dam.

Saturday? Do you know what time?

Um, noon? Or maybe a little later. It was lunchtime.

We should have heard by now. Why wouldn't they call us? Glinny was thinking aloud, staring intently at the air in front of her. Likely wasn't something they thought we'd be interested in. We only do 'major accidents' — she rolled her eyes a little — if it doesn't postpone the launch, run up their budgets or involve fatalities then we don't cover it.

This man died.

He died? Glinny set the milk carton on a shelf in front of her without taking her eyes off Helen.

Yes, Helen said, feeling some odd relief. Her face relaxed, making her notice that her jaw was sore from tension. She'd been clenching her teeth.

Are you sure he died?

I saw him fall. There was no way he could have lived.

You saw him fall? How?

Mrs. Petrie passed by, with a smile, carrying part of the

shelving unit. Her hair was perfectly set in white curls, like wisps of cotton candy, but her pants, blue polyester, were covered in dust.

I was on the Keegan property, with Dad's binoculars, Helen continued. I left them there.

What?

Helen gave her head a shake. The binoculars, I left them there. I have to go get them.

Right, Glinny said decidedly, giving a little nod of approval, then she whispered, I'll call the morgue.

I don't think he went to the morgue.

Glinny raised an eyebrow.

Helen continued, He didn't go to the morgue. I'm sure he didn't. They ... they poured concrete ... over him.

Glinny opened her purse and pulled out a coiled pad of paper. She had a pen in the coils. That doesn't sound very nice, does it? You said this was Saturday, and just off the east side then, if you were by the Keegan place. Around noon. I'll make some calls, she said brightly.

Helen felt a warm rush of relief and gratitude, punctuated by tears welling in her eyes, but couldn't stop them. Glinny rested a hand on her arm.

Oh honey, it's horrible, isn't it? she said, with a hint of that giggle. You'll be fine. You go home and get a stiff drink in you and watch some TV ... to take your mind off it, you know?

Helen wiped her eyes on her other sleeve. Glinny returned to the pad.

Now can I get your phone number? It'll save me looking it up.

Glinny wrote the number down, took Helen's arm again, and said, I'll keep you posted. You'd like that ...

Helen nodded, and Glinny handed her a business card. You call me if you don't hear from me soon enough, okay? But my best advice to you is: let it go. This is someone else's accident, right? You don't need to worry yourself when you have big things happening to you.

Glinny paused for a second, to see how that sat with Helen, who tried to brave-face it, so Glinny continued. Okay, I'm off to work, she said, bouncing as she turned in the direction of the front counter. She raised her eyebrows. I have a story to follow!

Glinny, Helen called, so that she turned again. Helen wanted to tell her she was right, meaning she had her own problems to deal with, but couldn't bring herself to that much intimacy — someone else might have been on the other side of the aisle — so said, Thank you. I'll call ... if I remember anything else.

Glinny only nodded, then disappeared beyond the aisle.

HAVING WOKEN EARLY, Robert had taken a morning walk before Helen was up, to be alone and settle himself to the thought of Colin coming, and how they might best approach Helen about him. Why was it so hard? He was beating himself up. He had been determined to sit her down when he returned, not an hour later, but there had been a note taped to the unlocked door explaining where she was. There was lunch food in the fridge. She'd be back for supper, which was around six, if he could wait.

She and Piché had that meeting tonight, which, as she'd said, he didn't have to go to, but she couldn't miss.

She left him a house key on the table with another note. *PS: This might be the best time to go through your things.*

It was an immediate relief to think he had the day to himself.

After breakfast, he opened the door to his old room and the shock was nearly the same as the first night he entered it. Each time he came to the entrance he was stopped short. Helen had said it was pretty much as he'd left it, though the reality of that — the posters on the wall, his alarm clock, the bed, the furniture the same, even knick-knacks still piled on his desk where, he assumed, they'd likely been — was like a magic trick for Robert every time he stepped inside. From the look of things, whatever had been on the floor when he'd left had been placed on the desk or dresser, except for the clothes that were always strewn about, which were probably in the closet or folded in the dresser drawers.

This morning, Robert felt pleased with himself because the room was a great reminder how well he'd done in remaking himself into the man he wanted to be. The ball caps, darts, toy tarantula, poker chips and piñata were never his things, in the way that what someone owns says something of who he is. A collection of music, the books on his shelves, the way one organizes his cupboards and what he hides under his socks in the drawer speak to an attitude, to personality. Returning to these objects of his past, the first past, he saw them as evidence of why it had been easy to leave. He was looking at the belongings of a stranger, a hybrid of what felt like someone else's intentions. He had been living another life, buried under the weight of who other people wished him to be, or thought he was, or who they preferred to the person he would eventually become.

He found a few items he wanted to keep — a handful of old coins that he thought might be worth something online, a couple of books, an odd suede hat he'd once worn to a costume party.

Packing up each item — a broken clock in the shape of a car tire, a magic eight ball, a coin bank and binders and old textbooks — he noticed that the room was dusty, but not much, not for how long he'd been gone. His mother must have been cleaning this room too. Waiting him out? Maybe. He wouldn't know. He resisted thinking about the years he missed, for what if he'd made a mistake? He packed faster, tossing nearly everything into boxes. He took joy in packing up because with it came the feeling that he was completing the task of the first departure, tidying that memory up. With it was the reminder that in that other life he'd been drowning. This second time was easier, although running away had had its moments of extreme ease, a sort of airiness, where nothing had been able to touch him. He remembered feeling light in his limbs, walking alone down a city street for the first time, romantically embracing the future open-armed, with nothing to encumber him. Walking away empty-handed, he had then been free to choose what he took into his life so — although limited by money, and opportunity, or chance — he had been able to make of his new life what he wished. He'd walked into his future with nothing; everything he had today, he'd earned. He often looked around him, still, with the thought that everything in his life he had by choice. He'd made himself. There was a great satisfaction in that knowledge, and a great sense of wonder, that he should be the man he was, that he should have managed to escape and to have done so with great success. Not without his demons — he'd walked through fire a few times — but not without some substantial pride too.

As the afternoon progressed, and the piles took on a weight by the bedroom door, the clearing began to change in tone. To touch so much of his past life, tidied and set in order, then to see it ready to be discarded, he wondered if he was betraying the young self who walked out, because he had so little tenderness for what he'd left behind. But no, he didn't lack tenderness for that kid. It was mostly self-love that got him through those first years. It was love that drove him out in the first place. He hoped his sister would understand that and not judge him unfairly, though he'd done plenty of that in her stead. How much of those years being away was a rejection of who presented himself here in his room and, seeing how insignificant those items were, he also wondered if he'd not been running from something else. Self-loathing, maybe. Guilt. Could he have spent fifteen years away just to avoid the great discomfort of facing his sister?

It took him the better part of the afternoon to box everything up and pile it in a corner of the bedroom. That done, he donned a ball cap and sunglasses and walked the twenty minutes into town. Each time a car passed, he wondered if he knew the driver. Who would he recognize? How many of the people here were the same as those he knew when he'd left? He bought supper food at the market from Mrs. Petrie without removing his sunglasses. She greeted him, they remarked briefly on how the store was emptying out, he handed her cash for the groceries, and she wished him a good day as she gave him his change. She hadn't recognized him, which sent a little thrill up Robert's back, that he should be unknown here, so transformed, an adult, from the big city.

The highway home, he was tempted to remove his glasses, stop to look around, stand in front of the yards of his neighbours to see if he might run in to someone. But when a truck passed him carrying two shirtless men with their arms out the windows, one of whom tossed a pack of cigarettes out the window into the ditch just twenty feet ahead of Robert, he picked up his pace for the house.

Once back, he made Helen a supper that he thought she'd enjoy, partly to spoil her, and partly, he had to admit, to show her how adult he had become. He was cooking so she would welcome him, the new him, the better him, into that home. He wasn't the mistakes he'd made in the past.

Their mother had cooked with three spices: salt, pepper and sometimes garlic powder. He didn't see fresh garlic in a kitchen until he was eighteen, when a man handed him a garlic press and he hadn't a clue what to do with it. He made Helen a curry with peppers and chicken, without the best part, he explained when she arrived. The market didn't have kaffir lime leaves, just lime, so he used a bit of rind.

Helen stood in the doorway, beaming. I love it, she said.

Robert turned back to the counter and slapped his hands dry on his jeans. *It's all going to be fine*, he told himself, repeating what Colin had said a hundred times since they'd met.

On her way to wash her hands for dinner, Helen stopped dead at Robbie's bedroom. She was stricken to see the entire room dismantled. With little more than two months from when she was supposed to move, she'd not packed a single box. Just the garage was going to take a week to sort through.

Wow, she said.

I figured you had enough to do, he said, coming up behind her in the hall. I worked fast to get this out of your way.

How are you getting this back? You going to rent a car? I could drive you ...

No no, I have a box of things in the living room I'm taking.

Helen wasn't sure what he meant. You're coming back for this stuff.

I ... Robert began, but paused. I don't need any of this stuff, he said, apologetically.

Right, of course not. Helen lifted the flaps on one of the closest boxes and looked inside.

I made two very general piles. Stuff I was pretty sure you didn't need, he said, gesturing to the bigger bulk of things along the wall as he first entered the room. It's clothes and old toys and stuff. And this pile over here has sheets and some things you might want. The lamp. Clock radio. Tapes if you want them. I didn't label any of the boxes so nobody will know what's what. I didn't do such a great job, I guess. But it's done.

Over the years, the times Helen had gone into her brother's room, she felt like each of the things inside had been patient to begin again. The sneakers, waiting for her brother to step back into them, the books to be thumbed open once more, clothes to be donned, and the pens ready to spread their ink. With her brother's clothes covered in dust and he ready to toss out the remnants of his past life, Helen remembered her mother, determined to keep Robbie's things safely stored in the face of her father's angry bout of 'cleaning house' once Robert was gone. *I am the mother of this house, Peter, and I clean house. You want to tidy, go to the garage.* Helen wanted to tell him of their mother's fight, how precious he was to her, but she couldn't find the means to relay the story without pointing to their father's actions. He didn't know what these objects meant to her, to their mother. They were a testament to his mother's affection, of their shared hope, mother and daughter, that one day he would return for them.

All Helen could find to say was, Goodwill is always looking for stuff. They'll be happy to have it.

Okay then, Robbie said, slapping his hands together, lightening the tone for both of them. Supper.

Robert prepared their plates, with yoghurt, laying the food out just so. Helen said again, Wow.

Your new favourite word, he answered, handing her a plate.

She giggled. To be honest, I'm worried. It smells great, but I don't know what it is.

Just curry.

Yeah, I've never eaten it, she said, staring at her plate.

Really?

She shrugged, screwing up her face. Where would I?

You don't eat in the city? he said, sitting down at the table.

She sat across from him, gingerly. I wouldn't know where to go.

Well, now you do, he said, you can get it here.

Helen smiled.

Picking up his fork, Robert stole a look at his watch. He had an hour till the meeting. Hey, who do you think will be there tonight that I might remember? Who's still around?

Helen opened her mouth and closed it again. For two days she hadn't thought it through that Robbie would be at the meeting with the whole town there. She hadn't connected the two thoughts: Robbie is coming to the town meeting, the town will be at the town meeting. Her stomach turned to stone.

Robert caught Helen's look. She held her fork over her plate, pale-faced, and he said her name, Helen, and she looked up at him and pretended to shake it off.

I'm not sure, she said. Everyone.

Robert laughed. Okay, everyone. I wonder who I'll remember.

I can hardly think. I don't know. Not that many people we went to school with. The Jacobs. Both Witherspoon sisters. I see Dave Handy from time to time. Les Oakley got married but Barbara left him years ago so I don't even know if he's around. I don't know, she said, shaking her head. I don't keep in touch. I haven't been to many of the meetings.

Helen took a bite of food and scrunched her nose, which made it hard for him to tell if she was sincere when she said, This is amazing, Robbie, thanks.

It's great to cook for someone other than yourself. I hate eating alone.

Helen only nodded.

So have there been many meetings?

No ... I don't know.

Robert gave her a quizzical look, but didn't ask, to avoid the tension of the night before.

I don't know. I have been very bad. It's been too much, so I've just been avoiding the whole thing. Our road is to be moved, everyone, by the end of August, for sure.

Right, Robert said cautiously.

I just don't want to sign the papers.

It was everything she could do to not look to the top of the fridge. She'd been tempted to take them down last night and put them away, but surely he'd have noticed, and that would have been even worse.

What's that mean for you? Robbie asked. You have, like, nine weeks or less. We don't have to talk about this if you don't want to.

Helen felt her shoulders slacken. She was gripping her fork very tightly. It's fine, she said.

Do you know where you're moving? Do you know where you want to move?

No.

But if they aren't moving the house, what'll you do?

Helen held her hands out, raising her shoulders, to say again that she had no idea.

What happens if you don't sign the papers?

Helen laughed. Her nerves were riding her. I don't know, she repeated, and sighed, leaning back in her chair. I guess I'll find out.

That makes me worry about you, Helen.

They can't just move me if I don't have anywhere to go. If I haven't signed anything. What'll they do?

Well, it's a wonder there's been no court order. Can't they do that? Something like that? They expropriate land, so they can just force you out.

I don't know.

I'm sure I read that. Right? There are groups here, fighting this sort of thing. The Algonquian.

Yeah, they settled that, I think. They're getting way more land than they have now. And a skating rink.

Good for them.

There are protestors of some kind or another at every meeting. Vince Markou's been doing a lot of work.

Markou?

From the cemetery. The caretaker, his son runs it now. He doesn't like the new site for the cemetery either.

Because it's not waterfront?

Because he doesn't think you should dig up the dead. *One-way job*, he said in the paper.

See, you could get removed, right? They have legal rights to move people. Isn't that what part of all the fuss was about?

Helen didn't answer. She chewed a bite of her meal, slowly.

Do you have a lawyer?

Again, she was silent.

You might be shooting yourself in the foot if you don't sign anything. Nine weeks, Robbie said, running a hand through his hair. It might be too late even.

That's why I'm going to this meeting, Helen interrupted. They're talking about the relocations. I'll know more tonight.

Helen raised one shoulder, and gave Robbie a look like she knew what she was doing. That she had everything under control. Pretending to be calm meant she was calm. It was the same sort of avoidance tactic she'd always practised. Problems will go away if you don't see them, which worked the years living with her father. It was a mode she hadn't outgrown because she'd had no reason to outgrow it.

You let me know if I can help. I don't want to see you stranded. I can read your contracts. Or I can help you find a lawyer, Robbie said.

I have a lawyer, she said.

Okay, he replied, and continued eating. There was that same coldness from the night before.

When supper was cleared and the dishes were done, Robbie walked into the bathroom to freshen up. Helen waited until she heard water running, then took the envelopes from atop the fridge and tucked them into her purse.

AS THEY PULLED onto the school grounds, a couple of neighbours outside waved to Helen and Piché, though most were preoccupied with the event and barely glanced their way. Helen was relieved not to have to face anyone in the parking lot. There must have been some people, though, who wondered who the man was helping her and Piché.

Before Helen entered the room she could smell the familiar sourness of the place, decades of sweat absorbed into the pine floor and brick walls. She felt the familiarity on her skin, and was aware of the hallway walls and the florescent lighting. Growing up, she'd spent more hours in this building than anywhere else. Most of her growing had happened under this roof.

The pine cleaner smell, the intimacy her body felt with the place, would be gone in a matter of months. This wasn't a building to be moved. In the hallway, Helen breathed in deeply to wrap the smell into her memory as best she could.

In the decade after graduation, she'd only stepped foot inside the school a couple times to vote in civic elections. Others her age were at the school regularly, of course, for pageants, bake sales and dances that needed chaperones. They had married and had had children that brought them back. Maggie Sullivan, the dog-breeder's daughter, who'd been nasty to teachers all those years, now sat on the board.

As they were about to step through the entrance, Helen grabbed Robbie's arm, giving it a gentle squeeze. Surely he must be feeling this as well, the gesture said. He'd not been in that room since he was sixteen. Helen wondered if he'd finished high school elsewhere?

He put his hand on hers, leaned in and kissed her on the cheek, then held the door for them. Their shoes clicked along the halls — the sound of teachers' shoes. They weren't kids in sneakers anymore.

Lined with nearly two dozen rows of chairs that fit thirty across, an aisle down the centre, the auditorium was full. There were people crowded around the side of the gym, shoulder-to-shoulder, talking to each other, and many people already seated. As they passed in front of the first row, Helen wished Robbie invisible. She didn't want him seen and she didn't want to draw any attention to herself. Her gait felt stiff. It didn't help that the room was overly hot, before things even got started. Did the school not use the air conditioning in the summer?

They were late enough that it seemed they wouldn't be sitting together, if they were sitting at all. Helen gave Piché a shrug. Well, we won't be getting seats together, Annick, but we'll find you something.

Robbie craned his neck and found two seats on the far side. Here, he said, and strode across the front of the room. As he walked ahead of her, Helen tried to see recognition in the faces of people in the front row. Would they know it was Robbie? And then what would happen?

None seemed to pay him much mind. Perhaps they thought he was one of the dozens of strangers here from the government, or from the construction team — the architects, planners and muckymucks of the hydro company — who always had the best suits in the room. All eyes were on them, the men with answers and chequebooks. Dan Cruikshank, at the table set up front and centre, was the star of the show, in his well-tailored suit with the broad pinstripes. He was the local face of the Power Authority. A handsome man at fifty, with an odd lick of grey hair on the very top of his head.

In the front row sat Glinny, with her notepad at the ready. The way she perched with her slim legs crossed made the pad of paper look enormous in her lap. It occurred to Helen that Glinny might know something already of what happened on the dam site. Were she not so self-conscious crossing the room, she would stop to ask her what she'd found out.

As the three of them approached the row, Piché shuffling in the lead, someone in the middle moved down a seat, and each person did so in turn, so that they were together, with Robert on Helen's left and Piché on the right.

The gymnasium was much smaller than Robert remembered. The walls seemed to have shrunk closer together. The stage was shortened, the doors smaller. Even the coloured lines on the floor seemed not as thick. But the wood-and-ammonia smell was the same.

They'd barely sat, Piché was pulling a tissue out of her purse, when the sound system was turned on and a plump man in a baggy suit leaned into his microphone, introduced himself as Reeve Sandy Peterson and called the meeting to order.

Sandy? Robert mouthed to Helen. Sandy had dated their regular babysitter, Joylene, when Robert was barely more than a toddler. One night, the story goes — Robert still remembered flashes of it — Joylene and Sandy had locked both kids out of the house so they could have it to themselves for an hour. Their father had had some few words with both teenagers the next day. Joylene never acknowledged them again.

Helen rolled her eyes and held her palms up, shrugging.

Robert had to admit, though, Sandy held his own given it was a challenging meeting. From the get-go the crowd who embraced the move resented the questions and complaints of those who didn't. Sandy rubbed a hand across his bald head in frustration each time someone asked a question that challenged the schedule as laid out, or expressed some inconvenience to the delay, or when, many times, people presented themselves at the microphones without questions, but simply to vent disappointment.

The public meetings had been like this. The national papers were full of stories of rivals in the community who had found allegiance with each other and friends who were divided on issues: the camps were split into those who invited in the change and those who wished the project ill. This was simplifying it, Robert knew. There were neighbours like the Adamsons, who asked three questions that were procedural, and others like Svenson, who was happy to be getting a basement thanks to the new foundation, but wasn't happy with her location in the town — she didn't want the back of her house to be south-facing, even though she'd chosen it.

There were a few, like the Sudeykos, who were still on well water, with a high unpleasant-smelling sulphur count, thrilled at the new town, which would bring them water and sewage — drinkable water and non-septic tank sewage — or the two Kilger boys, who were Helen's generation, happy to have an excuse to give up the farm without insulting their aging parents who hadn't been able to manage the land and livestock alone. For many, this was the best quick fix — new land, new plumbing, new streets. They were eager to get their chance at everything the developers promised.

But there were also those who were well settled, like the Andersons, who'd lived on the land for five generations, with a productive apple orchard for three of them that would take a generation to replace. There were people being asked to make great sacrifices with little reward. What did financial remuneration mean to the decades families spent working the land, or the memories they lived in, or the value of the land parents were born on and buried in? A big man in army pants at the back of the room held up a large cardboard sign with cap letters reading: WITH WHOSE POWER? ON WHOSE AUTHORITY?

Helen whispered in Robert's ear, That's Markou. He's not allowed to speak at these anymore.

Robert only nodded. He was surprised how many people he recognized, and who were now caught up in this drama. A couple of times when Sandy Peterson was at his most exasperated, Dan Cruikshank stepped in to clarify a point or give technical background on a decision. Cruikshank was steady, each time, reminding them that this wasn't the forum for voicing concerns. Those consultations were held in camera, between each party with a complaint and a representative of the Power Authority. He could appreciate the need to get personal details resolved, but the purpose of the meeting was to explain the revised schedule for relocation, due to the delays in laying down plumbing. The construction crews had slowed considerably in the east end of the new town site when they hit a hard clay they hadn't planned on, which made their original plans moot. This meeting was an information session and a chance to ask questions about the changes. Red streets weren't being moved first; blue were bumped up. The majority of blue were in better shape than either yellow or green, which meant their move was scheduled for three weeks Monday.

Tabernac, Piché said flatly.

Helen turned to Robbie and said, That's us.

So we would like to get the last blue relocations resolved as soon as possible, Sandy said. We still have some of those agreements outstanding. I would ask that if you haven't yet finalized details, we set up a meeting to do so before the end of tonight. If anyone has their agreement tucked in a pocket, we can sign them here, he said, chuckling, trying to sound jovial, though the lightness in that approach was a tone only a colleague might appreciate.

Helen leaned over to pull her agreement from her purse — maybe she and Robbie would sign it, finally, and have it done with. They had only three weeks now. Maybe she'd be smart to cut her losses, and give him the papers, before someone here recognized him. He was looking at his watch.

He leaned in to Helen and whispered that he needed some air and would be right back.

As he crossed the room, Helen swivelled in her seat to see where he was headed, to gauge the odds on how many people he might run across. She tapped the envelope absent-mindedly in her palm.

As Robbie exited the auditorium, a man passed by him in the doorway, opening the door wide as he came into the room. The door swung slowly shut, so that Helen caught sight of Robbie speaking with a man leaning against the wall in the hallway. Robbie held him at the elbow. Helen saw him take the man's arm as he stepped away, bringing him with him.

For a second, her stomach sank, thinking it was someone from town. There was no stopping the inevitable now. But then she recognized him as a man she'd seen checking in at the lodge as she was leaving. He'd been dressed in clothes from the city — a navy suit and soft green dress shirt — so she'd noticed him, assuming he was one of the many new faces in town who were here for the construction. She'd thought maybe he was part of tonight's meeting. Consultants, lawyers, investors, architects and engineers — there was a long line of business types coming through town. Nobody from town wore suits, except to funerals and weddings. Seeing Robbie with this man, Helen didn't question her assumption that he was with the power dam, only she wondered what he was doing talking to him privately, and how they knew each other. When someone else left the auditorium and the door was opened again, they were gone.

Helen flicked her nail against the edge of the contract, wondering after him.

STEPPING OUTSIDE, ROBERT was glad for the air. He walked towards the open field, to draw them away from the door, so they could talk more freely. Colin had been uppity in the hall, so Robert walked them a good forty paces onto the grass until they were in the middle of the school grounds, darkened beneath the night sky. There was some risk, too, just walking them through the grass. Colin was in his dress shoes, which he hated to get dirty, but the sight of him — his suit and tie, his hair freshly combed — made Robert nervous. Colin was here, and determined.

As soon as they stopped walking, he accused Robert of showing up only minutes before the meeting started.

There'll be lots of time after.

And you didn't look for me.

Because I knew there would be lots of time after.

You promised, Rob. I came a long way.

I know. We didn't mean to show up this late. It just happened — supper, and Piché is slow. We brought our neighbour with us. I forgot she'd be slow.

Robert tried to rationalize with himself that Colin, wearing his new light green Armani shirt with his suit, made him too dressed up to meet Helen. It was the wrong strategy. He looked far too professional to set her at ease.

So am I coming back to the house with you?

When, tonight?

Colin gave a frustrated nod. Ya, he said.

Robert didn't know how to answer.

Colin put his hands in his pockets. You haven't thought about this for a second.

Shrugging, Robert began to speak and stopped, again unsure.

Colin softened. You have to think about how you want to do this, if you want it to go well. Do you want me to do it?

No.

I'll be nice. Extra nice. He made puppy-dog eyes.

Robert tilted his head slightly, to show he wasn't impressed, and Colin continued. I can introduce myself. I'm not scared.

Colin.

That's not a judgment. I'm just saying, I have a lot less invested. I don't have the history you do.

That's why it's up to me. I need to do this, right?

A pickup pulled into the parking lot and the two expanding lines of its headlights swept across the pavement and then over the two men. Robert squinted for a second as the lights travelled over Colin's shoulder. For a moment, Robert could see the pinstripes in the suit. He realized Colin had worn it for confidence.

I'm here, Robert said, softening. I'll do this. After.

Okay, Colin said. Okay ... Where? Here?

Robert answered, I don't know, giving his hands a shake, trying to throw out the frustration.

Look. This is what you do. The meeting ends and you say, 'I have someone I'd like you to meet. He's over here.' And I can do the rest.

The pickup driver jumped out of his cab, slammed shut his door, and sprinted to the school entrance.

Colin thumped Robert over the heart with the back of his hand. I can do the rest, he repeated.

Robert nodded.

It can be easy like that, Rob. This doesn't have to be a big deal. I can do the talking. You're here. You've done the hard part. That's the hard part and you've done it. Okay? Now you trust me. It's going to be all right.

Robert sighed, to hear that phrase again.

Okay?

He nodded. Okay. *I have someone I'd like you to meet. He's a son of a bitch, but give him a chance.*

Exactly, Colin said, and gave Robert a clap on the side of his arm. I'll be in the back. I'm one of the ones standing. By tonight this will be over. Worry, done. Waiting over. The waiting is the hard part. You're at the easy part.

Robert chuckled. Yeah, he said, sarcastically. It sure feels that way.

Colin squeezed his arm, then pulled him closer and hugged him, patting him on the back. They turned towards the entrance, but Colin leaned over to tie his shoe.

I'll say this for you, he said, looking up from his squat, you made the right decision leaving. It's dog-eat-dog in there.

Robert only shrugged. I should get in there, he said, and before Colin could reply, he began a trot for the door.

I'll see you after, he called, and his voice in the night was oddly cheery. Robert felt none of his lightness. The sound of Colin's voice irked him, as though he'd no sense of what this meant for Robert. He'd no idea, really, and not enough consideration for what Robert faced.

AS ROBBIE SAT down, Helen whispered to ask how he was holding up. He said he was fine, a little beside himself maybe. It was weird being back with so many familiar faces looking right through him. He wasn't sure if he should say hello to people he passed, or leave it be.

Have there been sightings? Speak to anyone yet? she asked.

Robert answered, No, thank god.

Helen saw him swallow. She waited, to see if he'd say more, but he didn't.

Calmly, she slipped the brown envelope into her purse and pulled out some wrapped toffee, offering one to Piché and then to him.

He'd seemed so relaxed lying. He couldn't have been more of a stranger. Everything — the power dam, the meeting with the whole freaking town crowded around, Robbie's return, and even her father's death — suddenly felt part of a fabulous trick to rid her of every security she knew.

Cruikshank was at the microphone again. Now as Sandy mentioned, we have arranged for all our representatives to be on hand tonight if you would like a consultation with regards to your contracts, he announced. Please, if you haven't made arrangements, if you have outstanding details, visit one of our people tonight. Make an appointment, say hello.

Sandy interrupted, sounding panicky this late in the meeting. We've got to get that business done.

Bile crawled up from Helen's belly. She could feel it accumulating as it rose, hot and burning in her throat. She'd been a fool, delaying the inevitable, with some slim hope the inevitable, simply, wasn't. The most recent offer from last October had sat on top of the fridge alongside papers from the lawyer to settle the house as per her father's will. She couldn't sign off on the agreement until she'd finished with the will. She had used her father's decline last summer and into fall to delay deciding what to do.

Which meant, by showing up before those documents had been signed, Robbie's half of the house was still up for grabs. Robbie couldn't have known that, but for Helen, the house was all she had, and his lie, at that moment, with so much up in the air, the decisions she had to make so threatening for her, couldn't have come at a worse time.

Sandy called the meeting to a close before Helen realized what had happened. The crowd seemed to shift at once. Nearly half the group was standing.

If no one had eyes for anyone before the proceedings, the opposite was true afterwards. Everyone looked around at their neighbours for comfort, or an ear to bend, or a comrade in arms, or someone to celebrate with, depending on where they stood in the face of unexpected delays and the surprise dates.

The first to recognize Robert was Joe Fortin, the son of the pig farmer who used to win nearly every blue ribbon in the counties worth driving to. For a moment Robert thought he was Joe Senior — the son had been a slight man of Robert's age the last time he'd seen him, but he'd gained thirty pounds, aged two decades, and was the spitting image, and shape, that his father had been when he and Robert were boys. As soon as the talks were over, Joe stood and looked behind him to see who might be around. He glanced at Robert and then, having caught sight of something familiar, looked back again. A second later he recognized him.

Well, son of a gun, he said, incredulous. Robbie. He grabbed the arm of the person next to him, not taking his eyes off of him, and said, Mom, it's Robbie. It's Robbie Massey.

Mme. Fortin didn't hear him, she was busy in her own conversation with another woman on her left, so Joe shook her arm a little, as though he were still a kid, and said again, much louder, It's *Robert Massey*, Mother. Robbie Massey.

She turned to him then, with a snap of her neck, a fierce look on her face. Others nearby stopped and stared. Helen was already five paces away, walking Piché to the door. He heard his name travel around the auditorium. He spied Oscar Petrie looking over, from a distance, so Robert looked to his feet, should his wife be beside him. He was embarrassed that he'd not said hello.

Then, like an enchantment, a hush fell over him, because everyone within ten feet of him stopped talking the moment they laid eyes on him. They were taken aback that he should be standing in the room with them. Mme. Fortin still stared at him, scowling. Her mouth a hard thin line of dark lipstick. For ten minutes there were people all over him, shaking his hand, touching his sleeve. What the hell, he heard over his shoulder.

Someone slapped him on the back as the family's old papergirl — Annabel? Angela? — took his hand. He overheated, crowded by so many people, his back and neck slick with sweat, for he wanted to burst into tears, again, of gratitude, and spite and resentment at the people so eager to get a look at him, some of them to put their hands on him with genuine affection. A small part of him was grateful that anyone would care, and another was doubly furious — that he'd been denied this tenderness when he was growing up, that people who looked askance at him as an outcast teen had any right to appreciate his return and that he had missed out on every familiarity they shared in his absence. He couldn't wait to get out of there.

He glimpsed Colin following Helen and Piché out the gymnasium door. Robert tried to seem casual about moving away, taking a step backwards, shifting his weight, then another step, until he spotted someone else who wanted to say hi and he could walk two paces to them. He wasn't sure he recognized half the people. Holy shit, some big guy said, and squeezed his hand. His eyebrows were scrunched. Holy shit, Robbie.

He didn't stop for a second, working the crowd, until he was at the doorway to the hall, with Colin suddenly at his side — waiting for him, not with Helen, thank god — and Robert made apologies to the people standing with him that he had to get Piché home.

There was the same hush as he walked away. An auditorium full of people who were just given frustrating news about their old and new properties and there was a noticeable hush among them, as though they were thinking something, each dying to say the same thing.

As he and Colin walked towards the exit down the hall, he was stopped by a man who used to work with his father. Suggars shook his hand. Well, by god, it is Robbie Massey. You aren't dead? They took you for dead, Robbie. How are you, son?

Mr. Suggars, Robbie said.

Tim.

Tim. Suggars. Yes, I'm alive, thanks, he said, faking a chuckle. I can't talk now. I can't talk; I'm sorry.

Robert released his hand and Suggars said, Right right. He stayed still, though, and Robert had the sense the man was watching them walk away. Robert followed Colin briskly to the door. Before they stepped outside, he grabbed Colin by the hand, with his back to the hallway, which he hoped was a bold enough gesture, tender enough, to undo what he was about to say.

Not tonight. We can't tonight. Trust me.

Colin began to protest, and Robert interrupted him. I can't tonight. I can't.

Colin heaved a sigh and looked Robert in the eye, testing him. Robert said again, Not tonight. Did you see that? I ... I just can't.

Colin shook his head, slowly. There was a trail of sweat on his temple an inch long. It's not just about you, Rob, he said, staring ahead, at nothing. He continued, teeth clenched, looking over Robert's shoulder, I will not let you make this just about you.

Joe Fortin passed him, slapping him on the back. Hey, good to see you. Glad you're okay, he said, as his mother stepped out the door ahead of him.

When then? Colin asked Robert.

Tomorrow.

That's familiar.

Robert squeezed his hand to reassure him, but Colin shook himself free. I want the phone number for the house —

Colin —

— because if you don't call me tomorrow morning to make plans I'm going to visit. It's not hard to find; I'm sure everyone knows where she lives. And I'm going to have the conversation.

He looked at Robert.

Is that not reasonable?

Colin, don't.

Is that reasonable?

Yes, Robert said, looking in his pocket for a pen.

Okay, Colin answered, relaxing visibly. Okay.

Robert wrote his sister's home number on his bus receipt.

I haven't used this number. Just so you know. I can't imagine they changed the number, but I haven't actually used it.

Well, I shouldn't have to, right? Because you're going to call me tomorrow morning. I'm going to wake up to good news.

Yes, promise, Robert said, and tried to smile, though moments later as he was jogging towards the car, he recognized he was in too much of a rush to get away. He slowed, but not enough. He couldn't make himself relax, despite what it might look like.

Robert found Piché and Helen in the car, with Piché settled in the passenger's seat and Helen in the back behind the driver's seat.

Sorry, he said, as he climbed in behind the wheel. He blew out a *phew* of relief to try to pretend his mood was light. I'm driving, am I?

I thought for a change, Helen said. She spied Piché squeezing the fingers of her right hand with those of her left. Helen spoke to her. We can have your place packed up pretty quick, Annick. You're set, really.

I don't know, she answered in little more than a hush.

As he turned the engine over, Robert tried to shake off the puzzled expressions on his old neighbours' faces. His hands and feet went through the motions of starting the engine, applying the brake, putting the car in gear, turning on the lights and reversing out of the parking spot but he could only think of how everyone in that auditorium had been dumbstruck to see him. They'd been more awed than happy.

Helen leaned forward between the bucket seats and touched Piché's arm.

They only need you to pack breakables out of the cupboard, that sort of thing. You can leave most of your dishes as is.

Piché nodded, but wrung her hands a little harder.

Is that true? Robert asked Helen in the rear-view mirror.

The house-mover is so enormous it's very steady. There was a big write-up in the paper about how it works.

They give me a booklet with this... Piché gestured a little whirlwind in the air and made a dismissive sound.

A pamphlet. I got one too. I didn't read it. The paper came out first.

They give me English. *Stupide!* Piché spat, her top lip curled.

Robert tried not to smile at the emphasis she could get into a word. The force of her voice recalled Joe Fortin's mother. Amidst the questions from Joe, and the many who came forward to shake his hand or to embrace him — most of them mothers of the boys he'd gone to school with — there was a kind of awe on their faces. And like Mme. Fortin, that bewilderment was mixed with some kind of anxiety, or fear.

Why would they be threatened by him? Not just because he was a homo; they couldn't care so much.

Suggars words and their tone, the surprise in it, didn't sit right, rolled back on him. *They took you for dead ...*

They.

Not 'we,' as one might expect, but 'they.' Robert asked himself who was 'they' and a cold slow hand slid down his spine. Suggars hadn't been speaking for the family.

Robert looked in the rear-view mirror, to catch his sister's eye again, but she was busy trying to soothe Piché.

Each face, he was beginning to realize — he could see them accumulating — had said the same thing, hadn't it? That he had cheated them. Deceived them. *What the hell?* someone had said. The town, some of them people who'd known him since the day he was born, had believed — *yes, they were frightened by him, their tone was clear* — that he was never coming back, as in never, as in dead. *They took you for dead. They* being the town, being his family.

Though in Helen's case, no, in Helen's case when she first laid eyes on him saying *You're alive, Robbie*, she was surprised that he was alive in front of her, but not not-dead. She wasn't entirely surprised. He was sure of that.

As he turned from the main street onto the highway, he

glanced at Piché. Had she thought he was dead? What had she said to him yesterday, *I knew you were not gone forever*.

His sister was talking to her about packing. Piché was struggling. She was agitated, repeating herself.

They give me English.

Robert was sure Helen must have known him to be alive. She wasn't just thrilled to see him because it's what she hoped, or suspected, but what she knew. Someone had told those neighbours he had died and the whole town had believed it. His family had conspired to make them believe it. They must have.

For a curious moment he thought the car was malfunctioning; his hands vibrated against the steering wheel. And then he realized the shaking was only in his arms — it was coming from him.

He opened the window an inch, to allow the fresh air to soothe him, for surely he was overreacting. They couldn't have thought he was dead. They knew better. His father knew.

What kind of lie would that be? Had he been so disowned? *You're dead to me*. He remembered those words, in the kitchen. But how would he have followed through? Would he have dared lie to the whole town, for they wouldn't have believed him without a funeral, right? Unless his mother had lied too, and Helen. Had Helen really told them this? How could she not have been complicit?

He had expected a certain homecoming. Some neighbours would have heard the rumours of how and why he'd left and would choose to ignore him, others would have preferred to be in the dark, or wouldn't have cared for the stories, wouldn't judge, regardless. Old classmates would be happy to see him and a few lesser-known folk in the community might have even forgotten who he was. He'd be spit on and celebrated both. He looked forward to being the wayward black sheep; a man who returned, made new, beyond their critical eye. He'd anticipated reactions, imagining who might not speak to him and who he could count on, but nothing had prepared him to be the walking dead.

Helen rubbed Piché's arm, and the gesture told him this was deliberate, that she was making busy to mask her shame. That auditorium of people hadn't forgotten about him. How could they? They'd left him behind, in their collective past, which meant someone had told them he was gone. She must be waiting for him to calm down, or for them to be alone. Had she walked out of the gym without noticing the looks on their faces, without hearing what they'd said to him?

He pulled into their driveway and parked. His hands still shaking on the wheel. He was relieved to turn off the engine; he'd barely noticed the drive home.

Piché grabbed his hand on the wheel and gave it a squeeze without looking at him. Her hand was soft, fingers spongy and cool. He wondered if she noticed his tremor.

We have coffee tomorrow, she said.

Robert nodded.

Helen opened the passenger door to help Piché out.

I'm home all day, she added, then hoisted herself off the seat. Her throat made a gravelly hum from the effort. Robert could still smell the rose perfume of her lotion after the door was closed.

Helen walked Piché to her house to get her settled as Robert stepped out of the car and locked the doors. He quickly entered the house, to get into bed before Helen returned.

Inside, he stepped out of his shoes and took two strides to the coffee table to drop the car keys, but, his hand over the tabletop, he hesitated. His hand remained closed around the keys, reluctant to let them go. He wanted to pocket them, for later, to crawl into bed and wait for Helen to fall asleep. His legs quivered with a cold familiar chill, which shook its way up his back and into his arms. He released the keys and they fell to the table with a clink.

He could feel where their teeth had pressed into his fingers. In the bathroom, peeing before bed, brushing his teeth, opening the door, in the hall, closing his bedroom door, undressing, he remembered the weight of the metal in his hand. He saw the keys on the table, waiting for him. He imagined driving the car to the park, or the gas station, somewhere. Driving into the city. He crawled under the covers of his old bed, thinking, Where in the city? Where would he find someone? His body shivered even harder. He was chilled through with a frightened excitement. If he got up now he could retrieve the keys before Helen came in and drive to the city and get a fix within an hour.

In the dark of the room, light from the moon angled past the blind. Robert wrapped his fingers into the edges of his bed and gripped firmly. An old trick to keep him at home. He hadn't felt such a dark rush in a decade. He was a giant in the bed. He counted the lines of white light slant across the wall of the room. Twenty-one. He counted again. Twenty. Twenty on the third count. Twenty-two on the fourth. He took a breath and noticed the shivering had stopped. He was here; he was present. He was not out in the car. He was naked in bed in his old room.

There was the shuffle of footsteps on the front entrance, which meant he'd missed his chance to collect the keys. He was relieved. He released the edges of the bed and felt his limbs grow heavier with relaxation. The door opened, and clicked shut. A pause. Helen was listening for him, and likely could tell he was in bed. His lights were out. There wasn't a sound. Robert heard his own breathing, felt it against the sheets, which were moist. His entire back was damp with sweat. He wiped a hand across his face, then rested the crook of his arm over his eyes. He fell backwards into sleep.

TUESDAY

ROBERT WOKE IN the morning to the monotonous buzz of a chainsaw, nearby, at a neighbour's. He'd slept surprisingly well, he thought, which was maybe a result of being on the downside of the stress of the night before. Or maybe it was simpler. Maybe it was just the old familiarity of how his feet hung over the end of the bed, as they used to. When he'd left home as a teenager, he'd found he couldn't fall asleep for the first many months unless his feet were dangling.

He stared at the wall, at the brown smudges of dirt on the blue paint that must have been nearly as old as he was. He heard not a thing from the house. Helen must have been up, for the sound outside was too obnoxious to sleep through. His first thought of her warmed him. She was here, in the house. He was here in the house. He'd lasted the night, and hadn't taken off to cruise whatever dark corner he could find. He wanted the comfort of talking to Colin, and knew, today, that wouldn't come easily. Colin would be furious, wouldn't he? How late was it? He reasoned that Colin could show up at any moment. The longer he waited, the greater the chances he'd just walk up to the door and knock.

With a day's distance, Robert wasn't so sure of himself as he had been the night before. Who could say what Helen knew? Or what the town had thought. Maybe he'd invented everything. Nobody had said anything outright, really, nothing solid, nothing damnable. Maybe he was imagining it, maybe he was reading into their tone. He heard again Suggars voice and was still convinced. But if it was true, how complicit had Helen been? His father was a tyrant. The thing to do was ask.

Robert climbed out of bed and put last night's clothes on. The house was empty. The floorboards just a little cool to his feet. The keys were still on the table from the night before. He was surprised how harmless they seemed today, how quickly they had turned threatening, after so many good years.

Helen wasn't in the house. The front door was open and the screen on the outside door was raised.

Outside, further up the block, there was a large flatbed on a yard piled with tree branches. The Thomsons', though he didn't know if they still lived there. He found Helen in the yard, in flip-flops, cut-off jean shorts, and an old T-shirt that must have been their father's, kneeling with a trowel in hand, and empty green plastic pots piled up on the grass.

She might have looked over as he'd stepped out of the house, and he'd missed it, because she didn't look now. She was digging with some effort, enwrapped. Again, he thought it was false focus, to appear occupied.

Are you planting?

I'm digging them up, she said, dropping a handful of wild pansies into a pot.

Digging them up? Robert asked.

Well, I'm not leaving them behind. If I don't move them now, who knows what will come of them.

The chainsaw started up somewhere again, but further in the distance, its dull whine lazy and insistent at the same time. Robert looked up the block but couldn't see anyone. Helen pointed the trowel in the direction of the sound. They're taking down the trees to make way for the house-mover. I thought I should get a head start on these, before they make some other decision and I find them ruined.

If we get some breakfast, I can help you afterwards.

Helen paused, her hands over another plant. Robert wondered if she'd heard him.

That's fine. I enjoy it.

I was hoping it would give us some time together. I wondered if we could have a talk.

Sure, she said, dropping the trowel. She lifted another clump out of the ground.

I wanted to ask you about last night.

Again she didn't answer, though he suspected he saw the slightest pause in her digging.

And ... I have someone I need to introduce to you. And I'm not sure how to do it.

Helen stopped digging, her heart in her throat, waiting for him to say more.

He was there last night, she said, looking up. She noticed Robbie was in yesterday's clothes. That man in the hallway.

He raised his eyebrows and she nodded.

I saw you.

He held up a hand. I'd like to clear up any confusion about last night, so we're just ... clear. So we're good.

Okay, she said flatly, making Robert doubt again if she understood what had happened for him in that place.

Everyone ... everyone I saw last night thought I was dead, didn't they? He tried to not sound accusatory, though the words themselves sounded overdramatic. He felt a flash of ridiculousness, like he was surely nuts, because it sounded so unreal. He was being stupid.

Helen took her gloves off as she stood, then dropped them on the grass. She looked at them for a few moments, long enough to indicate that he wasn't being ridiculous. She wasn't sure how to say it, to say it in such a way that it wouldn't hurt him more. She knew she'd likely made a mistake, to simply walk her brother into that auditorium to undo her father's doing. But how to tell the whole community that her father had lied and Robbie was home? She couldn't call up every living soul in town. Other than Ruby, and Norm and Ruthie at the Inn, and Piché, Helen didn't share more than passing words with anyone. And she couldn't bring herself to tell Ruby, who'd ask countless questions, and then let it spread like bad gossip. Though maybe that's what gossip was. Their dirty secret. Robbie was alive. Her father had deceived everyone, except her, except her mother. It had been easier to let it be what it was. Robbie, alive, in the room. If they recognized him, fine. She'd tried not to think, really, beyond that. Come what may. She was guilty of not thinking what it might mean to them, let alone to him.

Dad told them you'd gone overseas. To work or ... help.

She grimaced at the word 'help.'

And then you never came back, and folks asked, and he said you'd gone missing. And then years passed. It was easier for him, I think ... for people to not ask about you. They stopped asking.

As she spoke, Robert wanted to grab his sides and laugh. Although she was confirming what he'd thought, he hadn't wanted to be right. He coughed, anxiety bubbling out of him.

You were gone for so long, without a word, and it was easier ... it was easier and easier to believe. You don't know how we missed you.

No, I don't, he blurted out.

She was calm, which made him resent her more. She was in no position to be patient.

None of us knew where you went, she said.

Bullshit.

Bullshit? she asked, like he had made some sort of mistake, like he hadn't used the correct word.

They never looked for me.

Dad went out every day for a week, looking.

Who fed you that line?

I saw him leave. Every day, Robbie.

He ran a hand over his face, frustrated.

Either she was lying, he thought, and incredibly stupid to think it would work — which he knew wasn't the case — or she was wildly naïve. And that, too, made her culpable.

Let's say he looked for a week. Why didn't they do something later, any time in the fifteen years? Like, when Mom was sick?

When she died? An ad in a paper? Check hospitals? Google me, for fuck's sake.

We don't have a computer.

At work?

Then he counted more options out on his fingers, holding them up in front of her, to rub her nose in her own short-sightedness.

Make a couple of phone calls? Check the phone books? Did they wonder aloud where I was? Or say they wished they could find me? Anything? Did they say anything about wanting to find me? When Mom was dying did she not say she wanted to find me?

Helen was red-faced and speechless. She knew he was trying to humiliate her.

Nobody wanted to know what happened, he said, baiting her.

He wanted her to tell him their mother did care, that she asked, and when Helen didn't say it, he was even more enraged. He let out a heated growl and clutched the back of his head.

You never asked, did you? I've been home three days and you haven't even asked me. Did you even ask our parents? What happened to me? Where I went? Did you try to find me. Like, maybe, when Dad died even? Was it not safe then either? Are you afraid of his ghost?

You have no idea, she snipped back, a tight defensive tone slipped into her voice. She wanted to be calm, to calm him. No more rages.

No, you have no idea, Helen. He wasn't looking for me. He never went looking for me. He knew where I was.

Why would he pretend to us?

Us, Helen? You think Mom didn't know?

Her brow furrowed, and her mouth was open, wondering it over. How did they know? I don't understand.

The look on her face, puzzling how she'd been deceived, calmed him for a moment. He snapped his head upwards, to the sky, and noticed a breeze on his neck.

Let's just do this later, Helen, he said wearily. We'll meet my friend Colin and we can talk —

You're saying they lied to me?

For god's sake, he said, glaring.

That she was so blind. That she could have known, if she cared. She could have worried enough about him to come looking. The maw of the future that had been taken from him, the hole that had been left, a desperate void he'd struggled to ignore, then worked even harder to stare down, or he would never have been able to come back, so he could be here in this place with one of the people who never came looking for him, a decade and a half later, the anger riding on the back of that desperate loneliness, rose inside him, raging, like he'd never been, as though all he'd known these years was its overspill and here the lid had been pulled off to reveal itself, rancid with neglect.

He pushed the yellow handle of the spade with his foot, setting it at right angles to the flowerbed.

They knew where I was. Garrett told them, he answered coldly, staring her in the eye.

How did Garrett know?

Dad didn't go looking for me everyday. He was talking sense into Garrett. Your father drove him to that job.

How did he drive Garrett to the job? she asked.

In his car. It was Dad's idea. He drove Garrett to the interview and talked to the recruiter, who he knew. They fished derbies together.

Helen stumbled. She hadn't been walking but tripped just the same, reaching an arm out to the wall to catch herself.

They didn't tell you anything, Robert said.

Helen's eyes darted back and forth, as though scanning inside herself, trying to collect her thoughts, to sort through the memories to see if she'd forgotten something, a hint of the truth, a sign she'd missed where she could have figured it out.

They did. You ran away. You were gone for a week — I counted the days, every day I waited for you — and Dad would leave the house to look for you and he'd come home and I would wait at my window until he drove in again, praying you'd be in the car. And then, then Garrett signed up for work. He wrote me a letter. He ... he wrote me a letter saying he'd signed up to work.

She looked at the flowerbeds, and the shrubs along the yard, looked at the ground at her feet, then stepped aside and pounded past him to the front of the house.

Where are you going?

I'm making tea, she snapped over her shoulder, and he heard her stomp up the steps and into the house. She called from the other side of the door, calmer, I'm making us tea.

Robert followed her into the kitchen and after she'd put the kettle on, they sat at the table in their usual places.

A lazy fly hit the window over the table with a surprisingly loud thud of its body against the glass.

Okay, she said, I'm asking.

Helen watched her brother stare at the fly for a long moment. He was having the same argument with himself as he had been since he'd arrived. She was determined not to make this her responsibility. She had spent years with their father in this pattern of guilt. She had given up friends because, with her parents sick, because they died despite her tending to them, she grew tired of feeling responsible. She grew tired of failing, which, it later became clear, was a failing on their part, and, almost selfishly, had nothing to do with her.

Helen, once she'd resolved to not engage the guilt, looked at Robert again with infinite patience.

What about Garrett? she asked.

Garrett, he said, incredulous. That she'd asked after him, and not her own brother, couldn't have made him angrier. Such innocence, it seemed to him, from such ease, from such ignorance.

The man yesterday, last night, his name is Colin. Does that name mean anything to you? he asked.

Helen shrugged, confused. Should it?

Colin and I have been friends a long time. We met — and he paused here, checking his anger, struggling to go slower — through a friend.

And Colin's been your friend this whole time? Is he from here?

He looked at her pityingly.

What? she asked, dismayed. She noticed she had a teabag in her hand. How am I to trust you if you lie to me? Or tell half-truths? You left me, Robbie, she said gently. You abandoned us. I don't know what Dad said or did but I'm not him. I love you, Robbie.

He caught her eye, and began to speak, feeling the terror, again, of that time, a sharp chill in his limbs. You don't know who you loved.

Was it because you fell in love with this man? I can handle that. That's just fine. Mom would have understood. Even Dad, eventually. You didn't need to disappear.

He began to talk, losing any sense of himself, any sense of the immediate moment, and though it was a story that he'd told dozens of times, first to intimates, then over the years more randomly, sometimes as a great gag for parties, full of shocking bits, salacious details, full of ironies, only with Helen did he finally feel he was telling the truth. It was a watershed, that he had someone to tell who knew what it meant, who would understand the terms. Not revenge — not just revenge. He'd come back so someone would understand him ... where someone would understand. He'd come back so he wouldn't suffer it alone.

I had a boyfriend in high school, or something of a boy-friend. A lover. Outside of the times when we had sex we existed only as friends. I could only touch his body in the fields of grass on the other side of town where we used to go to drink, but then over a few weeks of doing that alone, drink led to sex, and sex with drinks became routine. He would drop friends off at home, making circuitous trips around the neighbourhoods, so that we'd be the last two in his car. Nearly every night he had a six-pack in a cooler in the trunk —

The phone rang, giving them both a jolt. Helen went to answer it, and Robert, knowing it would be Colin, asked her not to.

She dropped the extra teabag on the counter, then placed the teapot and two cups on the table. When she sat across from him, her hands around her empty cup, her eyes were wet.

When the fourth ring sounded and stopped, likely because the answering system had picked it up, Helen wiped her eyes.

I could never have loved you less for this, Robbie. How could you think I'd love you less?

Robert coughed, his throat constricted. He picked up the teapot. He poured the tea, sloppily, filling both cups. He smelled lemon as he took a sip.

He knew it wasn't fair to Helen, but he didn't think he could tell the worst of it on his own. He couldn't tell it without Colin and he didn't want Colin here. He didn't want a mediator. He didn't want anyone who might soften him. He skipped to the end.

When this guy and I had a falling out, I asked Mom for advice, but she had none. She didn't know what to say. She wanted time to think about it, she said, and get back to me, but she told Dad the second they were alone. And when Dad heard, he waited for me. He stood up from the table when I came in that day and I knew Mom must have told him, Robert said, gritting his teeth.

I went up to him, to get it over with, and he lunged at me. He took me by the throat, and slapped me across the face with enough force that his red handprint was still there an hour later. So I hit him back.

The black eye, Helen said. It was nasty.

Robert was relieved to hear it. He had wanted to prove himself. He could recall, vividly, staring his father down until they both recognized that the moment had passed, so that when he drew his fist back and punched him, his father would know very clearly that it was a deliberate gesture. It was not in the heat of the moment. It was from a much more longstanding rage.

It's odd to be telling the story here, he said, where it happened. Dad only let out a small grunt, then turned and walked out the back door. He was gone two, three minutes. When he came in, he had that old set of luggage that granny gave him when he left home. Dad brought in only the two largest bags. At first, I thought Dad was leaving. Then he pitched the bags at me and they fell at my feet.

He looked like he would kill me. *Take these, and get out of my sight.* He was dangerous, he looked ... dangerously out of control, or on the verge of it.

I'll give you thirty minutes to pack and then I'm driving you. He didn't say where. I locked myself in my room and was gone in less than ten, out the side window. I figured I had twenty minutes or more on him. Hitching. Garrett's was only five minutes away.

Helen interrupted him. You went to Garrett's?

His heart sank, for he hadn't meant to say it. He hadn't planned on it.

Yes, he said.

Why?

He couldn't look her in the eye. He touched a finger to the lip of his teacup and rested it there. The steam was warm on his finger. *This is why you're here*, he told himself.

He answered, To ask if he'd come with me.

Where?

Away, anywhere. He wouldn't leave, but he gave me a couple hundred dollars he had hidden in his desk.

I don't understand, she said, and placed a hand down on the table. Why would you ask Garrett to go with you?

And in the end, he didn't know how to say the words. He'd come expecting she already knew and didn't have it in him to speak. For shame, he guessed, quite simply. Some of the same old shame from that time, which he hadn't been able to lose. He returned with hopes she'd have had time to forgive him, to understand a little what position he'd been in, to let their past be just that.

But she didn't know. Despite fifteen years of running, he had still ended up here, her blue eyes on him, asking.

And he didn't answer. They sat at the table for long minutes, with their pasts running through their heads, Helen asking him, once, and twice, Why would he go with you? Why would Garrett go with you?

Until the answer was obvious. He could see it in Helen's face, the truth creeping in, and so looked away, rather than witness the slow pain of that awakening.

She pushed back from the table, stood for a moment, looking down at him, he assumed, but he didn't look up to meet her eyes, not till there was something more than rage. She turned after a short time and walked out the back door. She was going back to her gardening, he figured. He picked up their teacups and put them in the sink. Rinsed the pot out, then the cups. As he placed the last one in the rack, less than two minutes from when she walked out, Helen stepped back through the door with something in her left hand, behind her torso as she came through the door. She held the small third piece of matching luggage, the red and brown colours of the plaid still sharp. She placed it on the counter beside the dish rack, saying, not coldly, for that implies some intention, but as though she was speaking from a great distance, without feeling, uncannily, Now you have the full set.

As she walked into the living room, he said, quickly, Colin knew him overseas. He came to meet you. You should meet.

He heard her pause then, and thought, maybe, he could get her to come back to the kitchen. After the accident it was Colin who made the arrangements overseas. They were lovers, Helen. Boyfriends. I think you should meet him.

And then he heard the jingle of her keys lifting from the coffee table and the front door open and close, gently.

Within a half hour, he was out the front door, which locked behind him. He walked to Graveley's, to meet Colin, so he could drive Robert home.

AFTER

TUESDAY

AS HELEN DROVE back to the house hours later, sure that Robbie must be gone, she was slowed by some kind of accident on the highway. Yellow lights flashing, the road blocked with machinery. She wondered if the big machine was the Jaws of Life. She'd wondered what they looked like, but they wouldn't be this big, would they? As she approached, she realized the machine was the house-mover.

Travelling up the highway at a snail's pace, still a hundred yards ahead, was a mammoth flatbed house-mover. It was two and a quarter tonnes and had to be shipped up on a freighter from Florida, where it was last used to move a sinking subdivision. There was a truck in front and one behind with flashing lights and a *wide load* sign. There were at least two dozen cars lined up behind it, which had been unable to pass. Helen wasn't sure where on the highway they were going next. Though she knew pretty much the fate of every house on the street, she hadn't a clue who was scheduled when.

The truck was nearly at her house, so that Helen wondered briefly if Ruby was first on their list, since she'd likely signed sooner than anyone else. She and her sister had asked for lots next to each other. They'd both signed the day they got their offers, though Ruby's sister had them handwrite in an addendum — a last minute request she hadn't thought to ask for beforehand — that they'd pay to transfer the water fountain from her backyard, which had underground plumbing. Ruby had bragged at the audacity of her sister, her cleverness at getting a little extra, especially that it had to be handwritten. Imagine, she'd said to Helen, watching them print that up in front of you! I would've liked to have seen that, I tell you.

Looking across the way, Helen saw Ruby was on her front lawn now too, looking up the street, in slippers and a robe. She clearly wasn't greeting them undressed. As Helen rolled up the street slowly, Ruby looked over at the drivers and spotted Helen amongst them, and waved, all smiles. Helen put up a hand out of the car window in return.

Trying to guess who it would be wasn't easy, as the house-mover was touted as being able to lift the home, carry it out of town to the new site and lower it on your new lot without so much as disturbing the dishes in the cabinet. Pack what was most precious, to be careful, but pretty much everything could stay in place. The report on the television had given a scenario where a woman slept in, and her home was moved without her knowing, though when Helen had seen it, she'd missed the beginning so couldn't tell if it was meant to be a re-enactment or an example of what was possible. Either way, it was an impressive claim. People had been anticipating the house-mover for months. The news had tracked its progress from day to day, with now and then a new detail or two, or an anecdote, and always the same dumb map with a small animated machine crawling across it, closer and closer to Helen's stretch of the highway.

And now here it was crawling past Helen's house, ready to slide itself under the propped up home of some neighbour. Helen wanted to watch to see where it would stop, but she was eager to get inside and make sure Robbie was gone. Trying not to seem too eager, on the off-chance he was still home, she walked to the box at the corner of her lawn and removed the newspaper, then waved once more to Ruby. As she turned, she noticed the johnny-jump-ups in their pots were wilting. They hadn't been watered that morning. She hadn't watered anything since the day before yesterday, she realized.

She went inside to the kitchen, taking the elastic off the paper and dropping it in a jar above the sink. The house was quiet. Robbie's shoes were gone from the entrance, and his door was open. Helen tucked her head in his room, still pretending to be casual, and saw the bedsheets were folded and his luggage was gone.

She stepped into the room, less superstitious than usual, and picked up the sheets. She tossed them in the laundry basket in the bathroom, which filled it, and went back to the kitchen. The small hand luggage was still on the edge of the counter.

At the table, she opened the paper and scanned the front page headlines for news stories. A hurricane in Florida, a possible new dietary link to cancer, some child mauled by a bear in the west who had been saved by her great aunt. A crisis in Burma.

A celebrity wedding. Nothing local on the front page, nothing about the dam, for what seemed like the first day in months. Nothing from Glinny about an accident, or death, at the dam site. Helen read the headlines through the entirety of the paper, twice, then triple-checked the obvious places, then scanned the news highlights from the front page column, and even confirmed each of the sections was accounted for in case one was missing. Nothing, not a word. She wished she'd have been checking the news over the weekend. Or the radio, maybe, might have something, though she didn't know anymore what time they ran the news.

She turned on the stereo and put the radio on low. She collected the sheets from the bathroom, started the laundry, and then scrambled two eggs for breakfast. The smell of the melting butter alone turned her stomach. She'd barely touched the eggs before she got up, leaving her plate behind, and went to the side yard to fetch the pots and her trowel, dragging the garden hose to the front yard to do something about the flowers.

They'd grown like weeds, quickly spreading, and though all this digging was a waste of dirt, too many pounds of dirt to move, she couldn't leave them. Leaving them to be flooded when they were thriving was a betrayal, however inconsequential, that she didn't care to regret. She would think of them, submerged and rotting, when settled in the new home because she was thinking of them that way already. She found herself imagining a new home, and for the first time, there wasn't blind panic. The move was beginning to be inevitable, rather than menacingly possible, which likely came from seeing the dam site. Or maybe Robbie's return, and, as soiled as it was, the news he brought with him. How could they have been lovers? Garrett and he, lovers. Her stomach clenched, collapsing like a paper bag.

Even as she was watering with the hose, she recognized that the flowers were a distraction. She was busying herself. Already, something was moving in her — she'd woken up to a different future, from a different past — and she didn't welcome the change.

She had a sense, an impulse, to take as much with her from this place as she could. If it was possible to take the lawn, she would, for what else did she have? Without the house, what was left? Everything within the house was hers simply by default, not for having asked for it. Then there was the yard. Well, the yard was hers. She'd made it what it was. It was the only change on the property, changed by her hands and with intent, rather than by wear and tear of weather or by use. What she cared for most was out here. She recognized the house as a museum of her parents' life, and without the walls, floors and ceilings, what they held would be worthless, misplaced.

A horn sounded up the highway. Helen looked to see a stream of vehicles rounding past the house-mover by driving across a yard, which didn't matter, since it wouldn't be a yard for long. The machine had stopped at the Garloughs', who were far less eager to move than Ruby.

A blue half-ton broke from the line of cars and pulled into Helen's yard. Bill Marchant's truck. He stepped out of the cab with his signature hop, though a little less spry than he once was. He'd come over the same way the morning after they'd buried her mother, when Bill brought a forty-ouncer of rum to drink with her father in the lounge chairs out back. It was to help him get on with things, though every other toast was to his wife, and by noon her dad was pissing in the middle of the backyard.

As soon as his foot touched the grass to the yard, Helen knew he was here for a favour. It was an awkwardness she saw on him when he came to borrow money from her father, or ask a favour he knew her dad wasn't likely to say yes to. He greeted her, and they exchanged some talk about the weather, and Helen, in no place to be able to help him out, didn't invite him in, nor offer him a drink. She began digging around a patch of johnny-jump-ups at the front of the house. She'd become accustomed to this now, so she could cut a perfect square of dirt and roots to fit inside her green cartons.

Bill hadn't shaved, so his whiskers were white, though they made him look younger because they filled out his face. His skin nowadays was always paper-white. She knew he'd been working nights as security on the construction site, so, by the paleness of him, it meant he clearly hadn't been fishing this season, which made Helen sad for him. He must have missed her father. Three thin blue lines Helen hadn't noticed before snaked around his temple.

Well, howdy, Midget, he said, as though he was surprised to have run into her somewhere, rather than having just pulled into her yard. He meandered through various questions, asking after Helen, and the lodge, and then talked about his ex-wife's leg, which had swelled to three times its size from an allergy, she said, though he doubted that was possible.

Maybe he's just lonely, Helen thought.

And then Bill said, Say, Helen, you know what you're doing yet? I mean, where you're moving?

No idea, she said.

He nodded his chin out and looked away. Oh yeah.

Helen had the absurd idea that maybe Bill was going to suggest they move in together. He needed some taking care of.

You thinking you might take the money and move into the city? Can't say I'd blame you. I'd do that. Well, if I was twenty years younger. Nobody wants an old man in the city, he said, chuckling, but it only made Helen uncomfortable.

I thought you're never too old, Bill.

Yeah, maybe, he said, scratching the whiskers on the side of his face. Well, what's keeping you back? From deciding, I mean.

Helen shot him a look, so he continued, speaking slowly. I had told your father from the start that people were signing papers all over the place, and he wouldn't want them to run out of money, you know, and him not get what is squarely his. Get them while they still feel generous, right? Before they find out how much is left in the bank. I think he figured that out, but never got around to it, you know, before he was too far gone.

He ran a hand across the back of his neck, which showed the scar on his arm from a stray hook her father cast that ripped open a flap of skin on Bill's forearm. When she was young, Helen loved to catch sight of the scar, and, when she was emboldened, she'd run a finger along the two-inch bump of whitened flesh, marvelling at the skin.

Your father was a smart man.

When Helen didn't answer, he rubbed his neck again. You digging those up?

It's better than buying new ones.

That's just what I wanted to come see you for, Helen.

To offer advice on wild pansies?

Bill grimaced. Have you thought what you're going to do when the lodge closes? This could be your ticket, kid. I mean, you don't have to stay here. If you don't want to move into the new town, don't. You can go anywhere, a pretty woman like you, with some money in the bank. Get some schooling, maybe. Or travel around a bit.

His tone dropped, with genuine concern, Helen could tell. She'd only heard him like this at her mother's funeral, giving the eulogy, when he'd broken down mid-sentence and then, sort of too lightly, said he was poor at this and apologized. It was an unselfconscious, unguarded voice. And for all that, because he was unguarded, Helen tried hard to be patient and not seem dismissive.

Well... He paused, finding a new strategy. What's your brother think of this? Bill looked to the front door. I hear he's back? Scared the shit out of a few people, let me tell you.

He's gone. Left this morning.

I'm sorry I missed him. You'll tell him, will you?

I don't think I'll be speaking to him, Bill, she said flatly, to put an end to that.

Okay. Yeah, he gave a few folks quite the shock, I guess. Quite the shock for *you*. Bill rubbed his beard and waited for Helen to say something more, but she didn't. I guess that'd be your father's doing. No, he was a good man, but we both know he didn't make the best decisions, Midget, and I don't want to see you repeat them.

I'll make whatever decisions I please, Bill.

Okay, okay, he said, raising his hands. He took a small step back. It's your contract. I just don't want to see you throw this away, he said. They can give you a lump sum, you know. It's law. If you refuse to negotiate. They can give you a lump sum and you have no recourse.

Helen put the trowel down and stood, slapping the dirt from her gloves. She answered, steadily, trying to sound relaxed about it, That's my choice too, then, isn't it, Bill?

He hesitated, not sure what she meant. They don't give you a choice, Helen. They just tell you what you get. And if it's less than what you expect — less than you could have negotiated, right — that's your tough luck. It's law, Helen. It's right there in the law.

If I don't negotiate, Bill, that's my choice.

She watched him for a moment, looking him in the eye, until his head nodded backwards again, bobbing his chin forward, an Oh, like he'd figured it out.

Well, I'm sure you know what you're doing.

I'm going to get back to my gardening, Bill. I have lots of work to do out back too. They're trying to move me two months sooner.

I know, he said, turning to go. He sounded let down. I know you do. You'll let me know if you need anything.

And when she didn't answer, he turned back, again, twisting at the waist, a bit stiff in his joints. Okay? You'll let me know?

She softened a moment, her shoulders dropping, though her voice didn't come out that way. It was dry and strained, with a hint of patronizing, which Helen immediately hoped he didn't catch. Of course I will.

All right then, he said, and his voice caught. He took a few steps and Helen heard him clear his throat. She recognized that coming by to give advice couldn't have been easy for him. Bill was smart enough to know what people thought of him, or, at least, knew Helen well enough to know that she was unimpressed, but she couldn't bring herself to be warm to him.

When he opened the door to his truck, he raised his arm straight up in a wave.

Helen waved back, her heart double-timing. Bill's arm in the air, and hers matching it, brought the falling man to mind again. Her senses irked by it. She felt her arms and legs go loose. She vaguely heard the truck start up and the engine recede. Her vision was full of the black lines of his limbs speeding downwards. She saw him, his arm flapping as though he were doing a backstroke, travelling feet-first.

She squatted again and went back to potting, but her mind counted one, two, and he was gone. She imagined his face, imagined the wind whipping his hair across his forehead, imagined her hand could stretch the distance and catch him before he fell, catch him like a black bug in her palm. She saw him, falling further than he'd fallen in actual life, falling down and down without end, the camera eye of her mind following him, matching his speed as he fell. The speed. The squiggle of him racing to the base of the dam with its reedy rebar. She saw it slowly, his arm moving in warm circles, like a stretch, his body calmed, his breathing steadier. She imagined something soft beneath him, a canopy, from the movies, or a secondary rope she hadn't seen drawing him up tight with a bounce.

Her hands, immobile in her lap, held a clod of dirt. She hadn't got around to telling Robbie what had happened. She'd made him leave without saying goodbye, and he'd not left a note. After so much time, he'd come home, a stranger, really, and they hadn't survived more than a weekend.

She had no idea if she could trust him, then she wondered why not? He'd come home to tell her the truth. No, he'd returned to find out she'd no idea of their past, but her parents had — Bill was right about her father — and Robbie had only taken two days to tell her. Her parents had kept the circumstances of his departure a secret for fifteen years, had died with it, and she couldn't spite Robbie that. It was their doing, their betrayal. But his betrayal too, so many years ago, his deception. Can you hold that against someone so many years later? How do you forgive them?

She saw again the small suitcase in front of him, which had to have been cruel. There was much going on for him too. More for him. He'd found out in a day that his parents were dead, the father that had kicked him out of the house and the mother that he'd once adored. Still adored, by the look on his face when she'd told him. Though they'd abandoned him, had lied to her, and had gone to their graves satisfied enough that they'd done the right thing, for they'd kept their silence, hadn't they? And they were both dead before he could reconcile with them. He'd never see their faces again. He had returned home to find only his sister, tired and cold and untrusting, accusatory. Betraying him. *I betrayed him*, Helen thought — the penny dropping, the falling man. She'd followed her father's example. She'd known better and had done the easy thing. She'd followed her father's lies, unquestioning. She had been a fool. And her brother couldn't be blamed for hating her, for distrusting her, for questioning her motives. He was entitled to half the house, surely, by will and by birthright and so who was she to question his meeting people? Who was she to question his secrets, or motives? He'd lost his parents, a second time, in a day, and she'd met him, in the end, with suspicion. Judgment. The same as what drove him away the first time.

And like that, her heart panicked. And in its panic, flew open to him. She wished she could do it over; he had only just left.

Noticing the clump of dirt still in her hand, a hot dry breeze on her face, she set the dirt back and dropped the cotton gloves which bounced on the grass. The image of the falling man slammed a third time in her chest. She jumped. Two sets of emotions raced through her veins: her love for her brother — the safety she wished on him, the peace, the security, the maternal kick in the gut to protect him from whatever hurt he was facing — and the concern for the man in the concrete — her desire to catch him, hold him. The emotions mixed in an alchemy of despair Helen had been trying to avoid without recognizing there was despair. She had lived fifteen years of her life mourning Garrett, wearing his promise on her heart like an iron glove. A false promise. He had been living a lie with her, through her, and she'd carried on the ruse these years beyond him. Damn him for that ... maybe ... or not; she could figure that out later. But for now, in the heat of the yard, Robbie and the falling man were here. There were fresh mistakes that needed attending. She would do right by them. She would protect them, save them, bring them home.

COLIN DIDN'T EVEN look at Robert when he met him in the small lobby of the inn. He was sitting with his legs crossed slowly turning the pages of a magazine as Robert walked in. Colin flopped the magazine on the table, breezed past him out of the inn, and unlocked the doors to the car. Robert heard the squeak-squeak of the Volkswagen's alarm as Norm at the front desk called his name, but Robert kept walking, as though he hadn't caught Norm's voice.

In the driver's seat, Colin buckled up and turned the engine over while Robert loaded his things in the back. He wasn't in his seat a moment before the gear was in reverse, so that he had to rush to close his door.

On the drive out of town, inevitably, they passed the house, but Robert knew Helen wasn't there, so he didn't dare tell him. He was in a bad place to hear it.

The wind was loud whipping in the windows, rattling his hair against his face. The trees were thick on either side of the new stretch of highway. The route had been cut straight through pine forest, then opened into a cornfield, with a blue tractor parked at the far end of the lot. Corn on both sides of the asphalt. More forest, the trees rushing past. As a kid, Robert had loved looking straight across, to see into the bush. He was moose-watching, thinking if he looked straight in he'd have the best angle, though he never managed to spot one. His father had told him there were few moose this far south, but one season, when Robert was eleven or twelve, a truck came into town just around noon with a giant antler rack from a bull in the back of the truck, so he knew the hunters had to have caught it close by.

The highway took Robert and Colin a bit north of the city, then it was nearly four hours straight through to the capital. Once they were beyond city limits, the flat valley floor began to buckle, the horizon rolling and falling. Stretches of road had been blasted through rock, such that the lines of sediment were visible. Kids had spray-painted on the rock walls *Tommy + Geni*, *Roadgun*, and *Save me*. Next to that, *Eat Shit*. Robert wondered if it was a response to *Save Me*, though the latter could just as easily have preceded it.

Then, with the dark asphalt ending in a coarse line, the new road met with the original highway. Robert thought he recognized half the billboards they passed in the fields inviting him to praise, buy a pickup, take the next right for antiques, tour a historic fort, pick his own strawberries.

For more than an hour Colin drove twenty kilometres over the limit, which was faster by ten than he ever drove. Twice Robert thought he might speak — say any of the practised apologies in his head — but he couldn't think how to begin. He was afraid to open his mouth. Sometime after that first hour he felt worn down enough to give up waiting, and let out a long slow sigh, quietly, releasing something of the anxiety, resigned to Colin's anger.

He turned the button to adjust his seat back slightly, so he wasn't sitting so far forward, when Colin swallowed, licked his lips, and spoke.

I'm speeding ..., he said.

I know.

I'm speeding because if I don't — he glanced to the left, out the side window — I'm going to find out where she lives. I'm going to knock on her door and I'm going to have it out. My way.

He turned to Robert.

Do you understand me? I am driving this fast for her, Rob. I'm not mad. I'm disappointed. I've waited how long for this, that's all, and I came a long fucking way, and now I'm expected to wait longer. That's not your fault. Or maybe it is. I don't fucking know. But I do know that I'm really really really fucking disappointed, he said, gritting his teeth and gripping the wheel. His knuckles were white. I'm impatient. Why does she get more time?

He paused.

I want to see his grave, Rob! I want to bring a cheesy fucking bunch of flowers and lay them —

He swallowed, and stopped speaking. Arms extended, he was pushing himself back from the steering wheel and into the seat. His forearms were taught.

When he relaxed, he released his foot off the gas, and clicked on the turn signal.

Where are you going?

You haven't had breakfast, have you? We need to eat.

He merged right into an off-ramp for a rest stop. The building was seventies-brown, its roof shaped like a shallow large-mouthed cone turned upside down, with a little handle at the top. A lid to a wok. There were a number of them across the country, but this was the only one of its kind on the highway west of the city.

Trippy, Robert said as they pulled into a parking spot.

What's that?

This is the first place I got dropped when I left.

You didn't get very far, he said, looking for parking close to the door.

I kept expecting Dad to pull into the parking lot at any time. I was terrified, he said, trying to massage Colin's mood. Then I got a ride with this sketchy guy. He had radar, and anti-radar radar, so he went one-sixty the whole way. That made me happy.

Although Colin didn't respond, maybe it worked because he seemed to lighten as they stepped out of the car. He was slowing down.

Inside the cone-roofed building, there was a short lineup at the fast food counters. They'd arrived just in time to catch the tail end of breakfast before the lunch menu started. The girl at the counter took Robert's order first, and as he was pulling out his wallet, Colin added his own order to the bill, and said he was paying.

I'm apologizing.

You don't have to do that, Robert said. I should be paying.

You should, but shut up and put your wallet away.

I wish *I* had one of those at home, the girl said. She smiled at them.

Robert was tempted to tell her that wouldn't be too hard, from the look of her busty uniform, but suspected that was too friendly. He smiled back, and said, mock-whiney and sibilant, But he doesn't do windows.

Hey, Colin said, and slapped him on the arm.

Better than nothing, she added.

Colin washed his hands in the bathroom as Robert picked up napkins and straws. He found them a table by a window. The seats swivelled, but Robert's had a terrific squeak. When they were seated, Robert asked candidly, So what do we do now? What do you want to do now?

Colin unwrapped his egg sandwich. The hair on the left side of his head stuck straight out in all directions. Usually he would have fixed that on a trip to the can.

I don't know, he said. Do we go home and wait till she calls you?

I gave you her number.

You want me to call her.

I want you to do what you want to do. I just ... I fucked up.

He shrugged and took a bite of sandwich.

It's like ... I walked right back into that other person, he said, looking at his napkin. Right back into that fear.

Colin set his muffin on the wrapper on the tray. He went to speak, then took a moment to wipe his mouth, reconsidering, and asked, So is that triggering for you?

Robert shrugged again, strategically. Sure. What isn't? he said. Although he'd answered honestly, he felt like he was play-ing Colin.

You'll call me if you're tempted? I can stay over.

I'm fine, he said, as though saying so would confirm it.

What are you doing tonight?

Movie. I don't know. Time alone.

Though he knew he might be lying, he also rationalized that he was fine. For years he had been, and although there were nights where he was tempted, some worse than others, he was well into a new pattern where he didn't follow through on a hookup. He'd managed himself fine. So he would be fine again. Part of it was having faith in himself, acknowledging his strength to resist, and knowing he could be well.

Let me know. I'm happy to come by.

Colin rose from his seat. More napkins, he said, his hands slick with oil from his muffin.

Watching Colin navigate the crowd, approach the counter, light on his feet and so sure of himself, so steady, his fit shoulders and small little waist, reminded Robert of the first time they'd met, when he'd attempted to get Colin into bed. They'd had the same lover, whom they'd both loved, and he'd died. What was between them wasn't sexual, Colin had told him. Robert remembered his hand on Colin's leg as he'd said it. How embarrassed Robert had felt, both cheated and flattered, that someone was interested in more than his body.

Now and again, his lust came back and told him he wasn't good enough. They were friends, invaluable friends, with a shared history. Colin had done very well by Robert all these years, a genuine support, yet, Robert always felt, Colin wanted someone better. He was waiting for someone.

Maybe it's Garrett, Robert thought.

But then he snatched his napkins from the counter and turned, so that Robert could see his face. There was that calmness in him, a steadiness, a kind of surety; Colin knew who he was and so wasn't deceived by himself, couldn't be longing for the dead in place of the here and now.

Colin sat down, drying his hands.

Robert smiled at Colin, and said, I'm sorry too, but it felt, somehow, false. It was the right thing to say, but he wasn't sorry. If Colin wasn't deceiving himself, if he was simply waiting for something better, what exactly did that say about Robert?

So tonight, Robert said, I think I am going to hole up. Alone.

Okay, Colin replied, satisfied.

It was that easy. Robert felt his heart race, his stomach run a little, and the blood speed down his arms, tingling through his hands.

NOT LONG AFTER Bill left, Helen went inside to find Glinny's card from the other day. When she phoned the paper, Janet told her Glinny was over at the Debellefeuille's new lot but she could take a message. Or here, she said. Here's her cell.

Rather than call, Helen showered quickly, careful not to get her hair wet, and slipped on some fresh clothes. She stopped in to see Piché and told her, too quickly — she was still standing in the back doorway — that Robbie wasn't coming this afternoon for coffee.

Okay, when he come? She was slicing peaches from a jar she'd canned the summer before, preparing to make a pie. The air was sweet with the smell of them.

Well, I'm not sure. On his next trip.

Piché held the peach and knife over the table and shot her a fierce look.

He's gone, Helen explained.

Gone? she asked, clutching the knife to her chest. Where?

I'm sorry, she said, regretting that she hadn't softened the news. He's just gone home.

Piché scowled. Pfft, she said, and batted the air with a hand, dismissively.

He'll be back, Helen said gently.

You think he comes back here? *Non*, Piché said with an abrupt shake of her head. She put the hand with the knife on her hip, then asked again, incredulous. You think he comes back here?

I'm sorry, Helen repeated, unsure what else to say.

When her neighbour went back to slicing peaches, silent, as if she weren't there, Helen waited a few moments and then took a step backwards, closing the screen door with a click. She'd check on her later, after the news had settled, and likely tell her what had happened, if she hadn't figured it out already. If she hadn't heard it.

She jumped in the car and, in less than a half hour, Helen was pulling off the highway and driving across the fresh black asphalt of the new community.

The roads in the town site were curved, wiggling this way and that. The north-south ones ended in cul-de-sacs, to avoid the monotony of a grid, and, as the planners said, to mirror the course of a river. The sewers were laid, which had been a huge selling point to the project, that locals could trade in their sulphur water and septics for clean new drinking water. Ads in the paper showed housewives throwing their water filters in the trash. Sewer grates featuring a long narrow fish stretching around the edge and eating its own tail — what Helen had read in the paper was supposed to be an environmental message —

were designed by a high school student in the city as part of a contest. There were no trees anywhere, which seemed a shame, that they'd dug them up to build a new site. The town looked very flat, scrubbed raw, despite the curved lines to the streets.

She felt relieved that there were only a handful of old houses here yet, one or two per street — part of her hoped maybe she wasn't as alone in delaying as Bill had said, though she knew better, she knew the stats from the papers as well as Bill — and few of the newly built houses were quite complete. Many were either skeletons of a home, or the walls were up but the insulation exposed. Some without the windows in yet. These houses belonged to those owners whose homes wouldn't make the move, or, in a few cases, those who preferred to be bought out, trading a larger older house for a new bungalow. Helen had delayed so long she'd have to rent somewhere for a year or more before they'd be able to finish a home for her. Would she do that in the city? Or maybe she'd just live with Piché for a year.

Though one of these plots was meant to be her new place — would be, as soon as she selected one — it was Helen's first time here. She drove to the end of the first road and pulled over in front of two neat matching bungalows, both new of course, set on either side of the Ronkkonen's two-storey brick home. She pulled over once she was here to just see what this place felt like, then, in short order, wondered which sites were still available. From her purse, she pulled the stack of envelopes and removed a map that came with her proposed agreement. Much of the map was shaded grey, indicating which sites were taken. The available sites were multicoloured, for various price points. Each property had been assessed for its value and new home sites were marked within ten thousand dollar increments. If someone wanted more land than the value they'd been assessed, they could pay the difference. One could also ask for less land and be paid out the difference, in cash, which a couple of farmers had decided to do, trading farmland for a large chunk of money that would help them figure out how they would earn their livelihoods.

Because the town planners anticipated growth, there was more land available by half than what was needed, meaning some residents wouldn't have neighbours on one or both sides of their property for the near future.

Searching the map, Helen found the street she was parked on. The properties with these two new homes were greyed out, but the Ronkonnen property showed it was still available. She needed a fresh map to find out what was still free. There must have been updated ones given out at the town meeting; she remembered seeing people with maps in hand.

There were no names to any of the taken plots, so Helen wondered how people could know in advance who their neighbours would be. She had heard folks say they were beside so-and-so, and realized, now, that they had simply arranged it to be so, or had talked about it enough that they were all keeping each other in the loop. A grapevine, of which Helen wasn't part. So be it. Having folded the map, she slipped it inside the envelope and turned the engine over.

There were curbs on each street but no lines yet painted on the roads, just small markers the paint truck would follow.

Helen realized the first street was empty of development because it would be the busiest, of course. There were far more foundations laid on the interior streets. With fourteen roads in total, four snaking east-west and ten north-south, Helen didn't have to drive far to find Glinny's car with its magnetic *News* sign on the side. She was parked in front of a new bungalow, half blue clapboard siding and half awful yellow brick. A dusty white landscaping truck was outside, its bed full of pink rose bushes tied up with twine. The tight branches reigned in, abloom, looked like a float in a parade, ready to be released.

Glinny was in the side yard taking photos of two men planting a rose bush. There were a handful of holes spaced evenly along the side of the house where the bushes were meant to go. As Helen stepped onto the springy sod, Glinny put the cap lens on the camera and said something to the men working, who both laughed when she did so. She turned then, seemingly unsurprised to see Helen, and stepped forward to meet her as she slipped the camera into her shoulder bag.

Glinny greeted her and walked them both to the sidewalk, telling her about this story she was doing for the 'House and Home' section in the weekend paper. Forty rose bushes were to be moved, including the trellised set that were to go at the side of the house where she'd been. When they were standing next to Helen's car, Glinny pushed her sunglasses atop her head and squinted at Helen.

Are you here to see the new site? Something tells me this isn't coincidence, she said, smiling.

Helen gave a grimace, trying to smile, but feeling too miserable to fake it.

Well, I didn't find out much, Glinny said. Nothing really.

Nothing? Helen asked, surprised.

Glinny shrugged. I don't think there was an accident.

But I saw a man fall.

No no, sorry, not an accident, she said quickly. I don't think there was a death. I'm sure you saw an accident, but the man didn't die, Helen. They have no deaths on record.

What? she said, confused.

I checked the morgue, Glinny said, sounding a touch defensive, as though Helen had questioned whether she'd done her job and she was letting her know she'd been thorough. As she did so, a dump truck rattled towards them, slowly, with a second hold attached on the back. Helen and Glinny turned to look at it round the corner. For a moment it seemed it wouldn't make the turn, but it did, narrowly missing the curb.

Helen turned back to Glinny. But they didn't take him to the morgue, she said.

I know that, but they still have to process a death. I also checked with Patty in Hospital Admitting in town. Nothing. No reports.

When Helen didn't answer again, Glinny dropped her chin, sympathetically, like Helen was slow to catch on.

Helen had long warm bands, like vines, slipping around her chest, then tightening. She could feel her heart thump in one and a half time, irregular. She was sweaty, and short of breath, light-headed.

Are you okay? Glinny asked. Come sit down, she said, stepping to Helen's passenger door and opening it. Oh, Helen, sit.

She pulled on Helen's arm and Helen must have sat, though

she didn't remember the sensation of it. Her vision cleared, she hadn't even noticed that she'd lost it, until dots of colour emerged out of blackness, and then she noticed she was leaning to her right against the seat. Glinny was standing with her hand on the door, looking down at her. Are you better? Maybe you need some water?

She wanted to say, Anxiety, but Glinny reached in her purse and pulled out an unopened bottle of water and handed it to her. Helen unscrewed the cap and drank a sip. The bottle was heavy. She took a large gulp.

Better?

He didn't walk out of there alive, Glinny. Helen's voice was thin, but firm, which Helen knew, despite feeling like shit, would be effective. Say what you will, he didn't walk out of there alive.

Helen took another sip, which was soothing on her throat. She wiped a hand against her forehead and dried it on her slacks, then repeated the gesture.

I'm not saying you're lying, Helen. But ... but I have no story. Nobody is talking, so there is no story.

The foreman? Someone at the site, there must be some emergency services? Though Helen knew that they weren't used; there had been no emergency service on the scene. There was barely a scene. And what scene there was got buried under cement.

A chill ran through her. What if it was murder, rather than an accident? There were four or five men there in total? And the concrete was poured as if on schedule, within ... how long was Helen actually there? Half an hour? How could someone die on site and there be no report? How could they get the go-ahead to pour concrete so quickly? Who would allow that? Who would make that decision ...?

Helen ran the idea by Glinny, who barely blinked. She wasn't listening, only waiting Helen out. Helen regretted seeming so frail. If only it wasn't so hot. Or she'd eaten a better breakfast. She'd been eating so little.

I'm not sure how to put this to you, Helen. Nobody's talking. Okay, that doesn't mean there was no accident. No death. You saw what you saw, but there's no story. I phoned a couple of people and ... I probably shouldn't say this but my boss phoned me to kill the story.

Maybe if I talked to your boss —

Helen, I hadn't called him yet. He didn't hear about the story from me.

Who didn't?

My boss, Helen. Glinny looked at her, patiently, waiting for it to sink in. Helen could tell she did seem frail to Glinny, and maybe stupid.

Helen, Glinny said, her voice lower, and suddenly seeming more present, as though this were her real voice in place of the professional one. Did you see the man in the pit? Could you see him from where you were, Helen?

No.

So you couldn't actually see him in the pit. You couldn't see the concrete on top of him.

I saw the concrete.

But not the man. You didn't see the man buried, did you?

He didn't come out of there. I know he didn't.

Helen saw something close in Glinny's face again, the expression gently shut. She blinked slowly. I'm sorry. I really can't do any more. They've killed the story, so there isn't a story, really. No offence, Helen, but they won't admit to having a death on record. Nothing official. Nothing they're releasing.

But it happened. I'm a witness, right? Helen looked for the right words, saying, An eyewitness? and heard in her voice that she sounded desperate. She wouldn't win Glinny over like this. So awkward with people, she couldn't figure out what tactic would work. She wanted magic words.

Glinny slid her bag further onto her shoulder and noticed some dirt on her arm.

Please, Glinny, Helen pleaded.

Glinny paused, wiping her arm, then flicked her eyes to Helen's for a flash of a moment, smiling weakly, in such a way that Helen couldn't tell if it was genuine or performed. You call me if you think of anything else, she said, a little furrow in her brow.

She stepped back from the car, and then, seizing on the intimacy of that moment, faced Helen. You know, she said, it is terrific news that Robbie is back... I'd love it if we could do a story there. People would be keen to hear what adventures he's been up to — it's been so long since anyone's set eyes on him.

Glinny smiled brightly, showing her signature look, with lots of teeth, one of her canines recessed. Helen thought perhaps there was some mischief in there, some malice, was there? About her father's lie? No, Glinny was beaming sweetly. Helen was being suspicious, and guilty, and shouldn't be projecting that onto Glinny, who was trying to change the subject to something positive. However misguided, she was trying to help.

I-I don't know, Helen stumbled. She made herself as calm as anything. No, I don't think it's worth it.

Not the right time. That's fine. Maybe later. You have my number. Robbie can use it too. You'll share that with him, yes?

I will, Helen answered.

She gave the door of the car two quick knocks and stepped back. Can you get yourself home? I can always take you, though I don't know what we'd do with your car.

Helen said no, she was fine, and Glinny told her to keep the water. You should sit for a while, finish that, and relax a minute before you head out.

When Helen lifted her legs and slid herself to the driver's seat, she saw one of the men in the side yard coming to the front and give a wave to Glinny as she got in her car. As Glinny waved back, a truck horn from one street over boomed, and Glinny jumped again, as she had in the market. She climbed in the car, and started it, then gave Helen her own wave as she pulled out.

The nervousness in that jump reminded Helen that Glinny was a simple woman. She didn't do hard news like this — they never covered the site as hard news, except in the business section — she was always local interest. Glinny wrote about the community: births, festivals, new neighbours or odd-shaped produce, and local elections, neighbourhood opinion pieces, school events. Roses being replanted.

Well, Helen wasn't going to forget what she saw. She couldn't trade in her peace of mind. She'd seen a horrible accident, handled gruesomely, and someone other than she had to care.

But why did it matter so much that someone care, someone beside herself? Why follow through? Wasn't it enough that she did? Who is to say what those people on the crew felt at the time, which led them to their decisions, or what they felt now, for that matter, given what they did decide?

And that was the thing, there was no knowing. Helen wanted a news report, to lay out a few neat quotes on their regret, to claim responsibility for a safer workplace in the future, assure people that it would not happen again, name the horrible loss, speak it into the world so that it exists, the man existed.

Without a news report, it was like the man simply vanished. He had a family somewhere, or friends, he was probably loved by someone who mourned him right now. Surely they let his family know, so why not the rest of the world? His hands touched that structure. His work was evident in there, his hours on the job, and whether she knew his name or not, he existed, and Helen wouldn't let his death be hushed up. There was news for a reason. We had names for a reason. What kind of future were we building if we didn't name our mistakes, or our dead?

Helen inserted her key in the ignition and started the car, put it in gear. One landscaper was pulling another tree from the back of the truck and still managed to raise a gloved hand goodbye as she passed. His wide face was tanned, smiling, making his teeth, which were small for his head, seem very white. A long thin strip of white in a brown face.

Friends. He must have had friends in the construction crew.

ROBERT HAD TAKEN a week off work, optimistic that the trip home might be worth a week. Hoping it would be. It had been easy; Tanner had hired a pair of students for the summer who fought to pick up extra shifts. When he arrived back in his apartment he was saddened by the furniture where he'd left it, a cereal bowl soaking in water in the sink, the windows shut and the air dull because it hadn't moved in days, the sun on the wall cutting across framed photos of friends, his bed made and the sink with whiskers from where he'd shaved before he left. He felt singular. Without work or plans for the remaining days of his free week, he knew it was a bad idea to sit around the house, but he deliberately dropped his bags in the entrance, stepped out of his shoes, toured every room in some insensible impulse to ensure nothing had changed, and, with signs of the day before he left just as they were, he lay on the couch, doing nothing more than staring at the wall ahead of him. He might have checked in to see if there was a shift or two he could pick up, but he was feeling self-indulgent. Pitiful. That should have been his first sign, but it wasn't.

His mishaps, as his counsellor had called them, had always begun with online porn. Within ten to twenty minutes of browsing, he'd be logging in to some internet chat room; inevitably he'd carry on four or five conversations with various men, turning each one down, thinking better of it, recognizing he was in the pattern. The earlier in the night, the better quality the men were, and the more he chatted. If someone were sketchy, or blunt, if they didn't have a name or facepic, he wouldn't continue the conversation. He had his list of undesirables: if they were married, lived too far away, barebacked, didn't know their HIV status, wanted group action, sent their stats by way of hello, only had a dick photo in their profile, didn't like body hair, didn't kiss, smoked, did drugs.

The later it got, the shorter the chat, and inevitably someone he would never have agreed to talk with early in the night would say hello and within a few short sentences they'd be making plans to meet in the next half hour. He'd pull on warm clothes to correct how his body would begin to shake with an excited, almost anxious, chill. He shook so much his teeth would chatter. If it had been a long day, he'd perform a quick scrub in the bathroom sink, taking a washcloth only to below the waist, because rarely was anyone interested in the rest of him. Brush his teeth, throw on a ball cap with a long brim for how it shadowed his face. It was important to be out the door as quickly as possible. The faster and farther he was from home, the greater the chance he'd follow through. Once he'd arrived at the man's house, regardless what the guy looked like, he'd come in for a drink. Sometimes he'd have a running conversation in his head that he should leave, that he was clearly acting out, that this man wasn't hot, that he could easily just get up and walk out, that no harm would be done, that he could avoid the next morning when he had to get up early for the breakfast shift, that this guy was suspicious, or not very clean, or clearly on drugs, or more compulsive than he, or into something that wasn't a good match, that the apartment was dreadful and he'd never be friends with a guy like this, would never willingly speak with him in a bar, that he could call Colin and tell him what was happening. But if, while the many reasons to get out were running through Robert's head, the man touched him, if he moved in close and let their knees graze, or put a hand on his leg, or took him by the neck and pulled them together, the chatter in Robert's head would stop. He'd follow. He'd be done in.

Early in the days of being on his own, when the casual hook-ups became boring, since they were too often soulless, he'd ramped up the thrill with poppers, or pot, or both, sometimes alcohol, and then, when that too stopped making his stomach tight with excitement, when the fear died down to a cliché, he moved to crystal. The first time, he'd been drunk enough that he hadn't realized what the guy had called *crystal* was crystal meth. *Crystal* sounded pretty. Sounded harmless. He snorted a line — which friends later told him should have been a sign, though that was obvious only in hindsight — and looked at the clock radio just before they resumed fooling around. A short while later he spied the time again and forty minutes had passed, in what had felt like ten. Then, again, he thought to look at the time, and nearly another hour had gone by, but Robert had barely noticed it. What had they been doing? Was he getting the digital clock numbers mixed up, or had he lost track of himself, lost consciousness, passed out? Had his eyes been closed? He was pretty sure he'd not dozed off, they'd been active, but large gaps of time seemed missing between the actions he could recall.

He wasn't concerned about the shrinking time. He was intensely in the moment. Everything surrounding him felt far away, and what was beneath his nose, inches in front of him, on his tongue, was gigantic. The world felt expanded, so that he could see deeper into things. He could taste more acutely, smell more acutely, see the finer details of things. The world expanded, and his senses crawled slowly through the cracks between things, to catch the finer points of their scent, taste, touch. A sigh had many layers to its register. He played the guy's body, drawing him out. That first night on meth he chafed his skin from trying so hard to cum a third time that he bled. He couldn't tell his doctor if the broken skin had come into contact with any of the man's bodily fluids because he couldn't remember.

Lucky for him, the months where he spiralled, spending more money than he had, skipping meals, losing one then two then three days at a time, were early, when he was young enough that he had little to spend and less to lose. Nothing to take to the pawnshop. Hitting bottom came quickly. He had no idea how he'd avoided sero-converting, but he had. He was negative. Now he had been clean more than a decade. Though he still found himself switching in and out of his compulsive modes. Too much shopping one week, sex with a handful of strangers in half as many days, craving sugar, climbing out of bed at two in the morning to get a chocolate bar at the 7-Eleven. Sometimes, while he was out on the street, the chocolate bar led to sex. Sometimes shopping led to chocolate. Sex never led to anything but more sex.

It made sense, in therapy, when he began to talk about the years after running away. Sometimes he'd groan at the cliché, for the problems, and their sources, were so ordinary. Following a man home had been an easy way to find affection. Food was huge comfort after he'd given up meth, since he'd gone without it so many days, so many times, that eating was a reminder he was healthy. If he was eating, he was sober. Chocolate was a neat, safe thrill. An indulgence without harsh consequences. His therapist had congratulated him for choosing such a smart substitute. Robert had felt embarrassed at the obviousness of it. Open book. But that's why therapy works, Gary had told him, because someone else could see what he couldn't.

A breeze coming through the apartment window felt cool on Robert's neck. It had rained in the city, cooling off the concrete. He wasn't home on the couch more than a few minutes before he sat up, realizing he could check email. He got a glass of water from the kitchen to convince himself he was taking his time. As the computer started up, a small familiar rush — like the lightest of breaths — slipped up his arms and down his legs, and back again. As email was downloading, he logged into his chat site to check for messages there too, just in case. He wasn't wanting to hook up, because he knew it was a bad sign, he knew it was bad timing. Though he'd agreed he was to call Colin if he was feeling triggered, he wasn't logging in to cruise. He was checking messages. He could check messages without being triggered — though, at the same time he was rationalizing, he noticed that as he clicked the tabs to get to email, his left hand had dropped into his lap to cup his groin.

He knew he should get offline, but couldn't be bothered to do it. How bad could it be? Asking the question was a means to ignore the answer, since he wasn't asking himself for the answer. He was speedy; his leg shook rapidly, bouncing at the heel; his hand gripped his jeans, squeezing in an unconscious rhythm. Within fifteen minutes he had an address only eight blocks away for a guy who said he was twenty-three, but listed nineteen in his profile.

⁂

RATHER THAN DRIVE home, Helen took a left down the highway and turned off onto a connector road heading north. She had been up this way rarely in more than a decade, so was surprised how little had changed, save for the colour of a few houses; it was a comfort for Helen to see how the Demarais' place was still swampy green and the Spies had the same red doors to their barn. Slowing down past the small hobby farm with the mailbox reading *Handy*, she pulled up in front of the son's place, one driveway over from his parents. The Handys had given three acres to Dave when he turned twenty. Over the years, he'd built two additions onto his trailer home himself, back then front, so that the trailer part wasn't recognizable anymore. Helen hadn't seen the front of the place, though she'd heard about the second addition.

She stopped the car in the driveway, behind Dave's truck with the Chevy letters painted over, so they were just embossed on the back of the gate. The sun was still hot, but behind a thin cloud. Helen smelled oil, thick and dirty, heavy in her nostrils, as she passed a baking pan sitting next to the wheel of Dave's truck. About to knock on the front door, she heard a voice from the back shout, Here!

She found Dave in the backyard on a green lawn chair with a broken strap dangling down. He was in flip-flops, with a beer in one hand, and was bent over to pick at a blackened nail on his big toe.

Dave, she said.

Hey! he answered, standing up, clearly surprised to see her. What brings you here? You want a beer? he asked, which was a tease, because a decade earlier at a barbeque Dave once spilled a drink that had belonged to Helen's friend and Helen had made him stand in the lineup in the hot sun to get her another.

Helen laughed and said, Sure.

Well all right then, Dave replied, enthusiastic, playing it up.

Helen rarely drank beer. Wine, occasionally, when her parents were alive, or a gin with Piché. Beer, on a hot day, when she was feeling rebellious against her own sense of self, when she was her father's daughter. Or when she wasn't at odds being so.

Dave hop-limped inside the back door with his foot pointed up in the air. Helen heard the fridge door clink open, then another door do the same, and in a few seconds he returned with a beer and frosted glass in one hand.

He handed her the beer and glass, sat back down on the lawn chair with a tired sigh, and pointed to another, saying, Well sit down, Helen, sit. Take a load off.

A small mist swirled out of the mug as the amber beer filled it. Helen sat and took a large gulp. Dave smiled at her, bemused, and curious too. Looks like you needed that.

To answer, Helen dropped her jaw and let out a little belch. Dave roared with laughter. Rough weekend?

Something like that. You heard about Robbie —

I did, yes. He just show up on your doorstep?

He was in the backyard Saturday when I came home.

Wow, Dave said from the corner of his mouth as he pulled a swig from his bottle.

And he left this morning, suddenly. I'm reeling a little.

It went that good, he said dryly.

I kinda threw him out.

Dave nodded, slowly. That was a lot for you two to take in. I'd say three days is pretty good after fifteen years.

Helen slipped off her sandal and pulled at some long grass with her toes. Spread out on the lawn behind Dave were the guts to a ride-on mower, each part, including the yellow casing, laid out in neat rows on broken-down cardboard boxes.

You been fixing that a long time, she asked.

Just since yesterday.

You're a little late, here, Dave, she said, swinging her foot across the grass.

Yeah, I'm not much for yard work. Rose used to come over to help — well, we worked out a little deal: I'd loan her the mower to do her lawn if she did mine — but she stopped recently.

Why's that?

The mower broke, he said, then grinned.

That would explain the look of Rose's lawn.

Nah, she just stopped cutting it. Why bother now? I thought I'd give this a clean before we hauled it over. No point messing up the new sod, eh?

Dave had been interested in Helen, years ago, when he was barely twenty and they worked at the lodge together. He'd bring his lunch by, when she was still cleaning rooms and making beds, and would chat with her. He'd invited her to a half dozen things, to which she always said 'maybe,' but then never followed through. He was the closest thing to another future she'd been offered. She liked him; Dave was irrepressible, but he wasn't Garrett.

When her father died, Dave had attended the entirety of the wake and the funeral. He'd bought fish from her father over the years, when he was too busy to get out on the water himself and, when her dad needed a hand for some business around the house, he phoned Dave, because he knew his way around wood and electricity both, and he nearly always said yes.

I want to ask you a favour, Dave.

Before he could respond, Helen told him what she'd seen at the dam site and then about her encounters with Glinny. He asked a couple questions that she thought smart: Had Helen considered asking one of the larger papers? Could she call the construction companies to ask after the death, not to ask if it happened, but to just assume it as a given? Might that work?

Just the thought of it made Helen anxious. She knew Dave was telling her the options, in case she rose to them, but that he'd not expect more. When she told him she didn't have it in her, he was nodding before she'd finished the sentence. He rose from the chair, wincing.

You think you can get me another beer, he asked? I gotta rip this damn thing out today. I'm drinking anaesthesia.

Helen said sure and headed for the back door.

The ones on the door are cold. On the shelf are still warm.

Perfect, she said.

The kitchen was surprisingly tidy. Like the lawnmower, the items in the fridge were orderly. His countertop, too, was reasonably well-arranged. In the sink, though, was a pile of dishes. Two small plates, a large one, and a plastic cup were stacked inside the pots and pans.

I'm sorry for the mess, he said when she'd returned outside. I hit this toe one too many times at the counter and said *fuck it* last night. I can't do much until the nail is gone.

It doesn't look too nice.

It feels worse, he said.

Why don't you get someone to look at it?

Ahh, I'll pull it out. I've had this happen before. It'll be fine when the nail is gone. It just hurts like a bitch when it moves. It's so loose.

Helen stuck her tongue out in a sour face.

I'm sorry, Dave said, chuckling. He opened his beer and took a long swig, swallowing three times.

Helen noticed a pair of pliers in the grass next to him. She wasn't interested in sticking around for when he decided to use them.

You know a lot of the crew, right? she asked. You meet a lot of them.

Enough, he said, suppressing a burp.

Nodding, she took another sip of her beer. I want to find a friend of his, she said, someone who knew him, anyone.

Okay. Dave didn't sound exactly convinced.

You'll do it?

I'm not saying that, he said, then he raised a hand for her to hold on. I'm not saying no either. He looked at his big toe again, and wiggled it, then scratched the back of his head, slowly. Helen could see he was balding, in a round little spot at his crown.

I don't know how to say this any other way, but I'm not sure why, Helen.

What do you mean?

Why do you care about this guy, this accident? What are you going to get out of it —

Do I need to get something out of it, Dave?

He took a second to let the edge off, for he likely knew the answer to his question, but she wasn't getting the entirety of what he meant.

He said cautiously, No one is going to like me asking questions. If it's true the paper can't find anything out, why would I? So I guess I'm wondering why I'm going to do this?

Helen wasn't sure she had an answer, but she answered spontaneously, quick and confident, saying, Justice.

It wasn't the best sort of answer, because who was Helen to say what was the right thing to do? As Dave tipped his head, ready to say no, Helen felt her face drain of colour. He regarded her for a moment and Helen felt she was letting him see right through her. He knew enough about the years living with her father, caring for him to the end of his days, the humiliating bathings and the meals brought back up, blackened with blood. He knew what losing Garrett had meant, and he must understand something of what Robbie's return, and leaving a second time, must be doing to her. She felt it empty from her face.

Dave likely felt sorry for her, and because of his own guilt at recognizing that, it passed between them, in the candour of her look, the unguardedness. In the way a person can know another for so long he needn't listen to the words to know the other's thoughts, Helen knew Dave understood her in that moment, and what he understood was that she had nothing left to care for. Knowingly or not, she was giving him an insight into her that no one, likely not even Piché, had seen. Not since Garrett. Dave might have been a rough man, and wild, but that was as much from trying to reconcile being a man with a big heart as from any kind of recklessness.

He finished his beer in a long swig, tossed the bottle in the grass, and asked, What do you want me to do when I find someone?

HE WAS A young guy, for sure, but just how young was hard to say. He'd answered the door in sweatpants and a T-shirt, barefoot. His toes were knobby. His shoulders slim but broad. From the look of his beard, he might have been a teenager, but Robert suspected he was in his early twenties, like he'd said. The guy probably hadn't shaved for a few days, but the hairs were so fine and sparse that it was clear he'd never grow a decent beard. He had the type of skin that would make him look baby-faced for years. He didn't shake hands, or say hello, but closed the door behind Robert and sort of nodded. Robert, in turn, was silent.

He stepped out of his shoes and the guy turned and sauntered down the hall. He led them into his bedroom, which was a mess of clothes on the floor. There was little furniture in the room: a box spring and mattress without a frame, a TV in the corner, and a computer and keyboard placed directly on the carpet next to the bed. The white walls were bare as well, except for a small hole over the bed, and some nails where paintings had once been hung. Were it not for the clothes everywhere, Robert might have thought he'd just moved in. Student, he thought. Slobby student.

He removed his T-shirt; he had a hairless, white chest. Nipples dark, the size of nickels. He dropped his pants as unceremoniously and the cocoon of his cock sprouted from a small trim patch of brown hair. He was very slim, and gorgeous.

Robert's heart raced. It was beating in his dick, pumping blood to it.

He kneeled onto the bed and then turned and lay back with an arm under his head, so that Robert, without hesitation, climbed on top of him fully dressed. They made out, intensely, rolling over each other for quite some time until they'd removed Robert's clothes too. The kid straddled him then, his thighs warm on either side of Robert's waist, and reached over sideways to beside the bed, so that their torsos were stretched along each other. Robert ran a hand across his back, feeling the skin there, which was amazing. It was wildly soft, like running a hand across warm cream.

When he righted himself, the kid held a small brown bottle, which he shook. He unscrewed the cap and held it under one of Robert's nostrils, deftly closing the other with his thumb. Though poppers were on his list of the many things that he had marked as triggers, Robert took a slow deep inhale, looking into the guy's eyes as he did, and felt a great, long-awaited wash of relief. It was as though he'd stepped out of a large cumbersome lead suit, and felt light again, in his own skin, unburdened. A great discomfort had left him, as his blood began to thump in his ears and a growing rush pulled him forward.

Done his own hit, the kid screwed the lid back on quickly and leaned back slightly so Robert could sit up. He met his face, and rubbed his nose across one side of Robert's, then the other, and then he slipped his tongue into his mouth and kissed him.

They made out this way, a rhythm of intensity, ramping up the heat with occasional hits from the bottle. The kid was tender at first and then increasingly rough, full of subtle changes, and trading back again, a complex mix that challenged Robert to try to keep up, building the energy between them, making him occasionally desperate for another taste of this corner of his body, or to have a hand placed here, then here. The salt of his skin pulled Robert's tongue, snail-slow, from behind the kid's ears on down to the indent at his ankle. Robert felt hunger for him, his body opening up to the sensation of their skins passing over each other.

They must have been wrapped up together an hour, the kid giving them a nice long draw on the bottle, then humping Robert slowly, running his shaft along the crack of Robert's ass, when he let it rest, finally, exactly in place.

I want it, he said in Robert's ear, his first words, his voice breathy but low in his throat, as smooth as his skin. With the rush in his limbs, and the boy pressing against him, he relaxed, and felt them slide, slowly, together. It was ecstasy. Home. The first home he'd found, after he'd run away, the warmest kind, his favourite, for there was nothing outside of that moment, nothing but their bodies, the uncomplicated generosity of skin responding to skin. The body knew what it liked. The body knew what to do. As easy, as mindless, as breathing.

He leaned between Robert's legs, stretching, again, sideways across his torso, humping. When he pulled himself upright, his hips were rhythmic, sweet, a melody. Robert groaned. Above him, the flick of a lighter sounded. His friend had a glass pipe between his teeth. He passed the flame under the bottom of the pipe, staring down at the bowl. Immediately, Robert smelled ammonia. Meth. He saw the smoke collect in the bowl, the kid inhale, and the grey strands dart through the pipe's neck. He held it a moment, not losing the rhythm in his hips, then bent over, his mouth a crooked line, looking him in the eye. And because he was already inside him, already barebacking, the harm done, Robert let himself be kissed, open-mouthed, to accept what was being offered.

WHILE HELEN WAS talking to Dave, Piché pulled out her rolling pin. She poured her usual glass of ginger ale and turned on the television in the front room so she wouldn't miss the start of her afternoon soap opera. She was timing it so that while the pie was in the oven she could sit down to her show, which was the only French one she could get without cable.

She turned on an element, added water and sugar to a pot to begin the filling, then took up mixing the dough. Her hands wanted to be busy. Making the pie was a means to not sit around arguing with her neighbours in her head, both the pair of dead ones — god rest their souls — and their daughter, but maybe she hadn't been concentrating when she'd added ingredients because she wasn't doing a very good job of that either. Were her hands too hot? She was having trouble keeping the dough dry enough. It was oily, which only made her work it too much until it was tough. Pitching that batch in the sink she sat down a second, her heart pounding. She was short of breath. Moments later, not feeling much better, she rose and took a sip of ginger ale. The bubbles tingled right up into her nose and made her want to sneeze. She stirred the peach slices into the pot and set the lid on it.

Taking up the measuring cup, she began again, more from

irascibility than enthusiasm. She didn't get any further than adding ingredients for the second batch before she felt short of breath, then light-headed and weak, and went into the living room to sit. Rather than her usual chair, she went to the couch to lie down.

When Helen pulled in the drive she saw a wispy grey coil of smoke twirling up the back of Piché's house. She ran to the back door, which was open, fortunately, with smoke rolling up the sides of the kitchen walls and across the ceiling. A stainless steel pot had boiled over, and the contents caught fire on the element, and must have burned there for some time. The top of the stove was blackened with a thick crust, the pot was blackened dry, and there was no fire but smoke everywhere. Helen turned the element off and left the pot where it was. She called for Piché, terrified that nobody would answer.

Annick?! she called again, hacking with cough. Annick!

Helen found her asleep on the couch, a rasp in her breath, with her hair flattened wet against her temples, her arms folded across her stomach, and her sandals still on, which made it look as though she'd only just laid down.

Helen rocked her awake and asked what was wrong.

She told Helen she was fine, just feeling a bit gassy. She didn't notice the smoke, but coughed.

Helen chatted with her a few minutes to help her wake up and to see how badly off she was.

How long has that filling been on the stove?

There was no answer. Alarmed, Piché turned her head, suddenly, to see into the kitchen.

Annick? How long have you been lying here?

Piché said she'd been there a half hour or so.

What time did you lie down, do you know?

Before my soap.

Your soap is over, Annick. You must have fallen asleep.

I'm good there me, she said. She tried to right herself, but only raised a few inches off the pillow, straining, too out of breath to sit up. I finish the pie in a minute, she croaked and lay back down.

The pie is a bit ruined, Hon.

Piché looked alarmed.

You left the stove on, Annick. I turned it off. It's fine. A bit smoky. Can you smell the smoke?

Piché sniffed, and nodded. Her brow was creased. She was clearly alarmed but trying to not let Helen know.

I clean that up.

I think we might want to visit the clinic instead, just in case?

No, she said, dismissive, drawing in her chin. She looked cartoonish, childlike. I just fall asleep. I'm fine.

You might have taken in some smoke, Helen said, rising to open the front door.

No no. Piché waved a hand. No, she said. I'm good. See?

Don't you smell that? You can probably see it. Look, it's smoky over there. Helen gestured to the band of light, thick with smoke, slanting in from the windows.

Bah, she said, and tried to roll herself off the couch, but coughed again, hacking, and rocked back on the cushion like a soft toy, holding her arms across her abdomen.

Annick! Just lie there. I'm calling an ambulance.

I'm good, I'm good, Piché protested, then barely paused and said, You drive me. I go.

Deal.

The clinic was only twenty minutes away, on this side of the city. Helen got Piché into the car, though that took nearly twenty minutes too, from getting her off the couch, into shoes, and down the stairs to the side of the car. Piché couldn't even manoeuvre herself into the seat. Helen took her hands and had her squat backwards onto the cushion. She wondered if this was a mistake, if an ambulance would have been quicker. As Helen helped her swing her legs in, Piché was silent. Sweat had flattened another finger of hair across her forehead. She was wetting her lips by drawing them into her mouth and chewing on them, quickly, so that her mouth was in a constant quick motion. Helen wondered if she knew what she was doing, if she noticed how nervous she was.

As they were about to leave, Helen felt smart for thinking of it and ran back into the house for Piché's purse, which was thankfully by the front door where she left it.

Climbing into the driver's seat and pulling the car door closed, Helen could hear Piché's breathing was heavy. It rattled, as though her chest were full of phlegm. She drove, working out the problem of time: if she'd have called the ambulance to come, how long would they have taken there and back? To strap her up, which would have been easier, but not faster. But then, if this was an emergency, they'd be monitoring her right now, they'd be helping. Helen's assent to drive her might be the very thing that kills her, though that wasn't a helpful line of thought. She prayed it wasn't serious, that she wouldn't regret this. Piché would be fine.

In the parking lot of the clinic, Helen told her, You stay here. I'm getting you a wheelchair.

Moments later when the nurse came out to get her, Piché, to Helen's surprise, hadn't moved a muscle. They took her information in the waiting room and wheeled her straight into a back room. Piché looked grim, an arm pressed to her chest, wheezing and sweaty.

At least a dozen people went in and out while Helen waited. She did what she'd usually done when she'd come here with her mother: studied the wood panelling on the walls, following the faux grain, counting the average number of lines in each section, looking for where the patterns repeated themselves. Many of the panels were upside down, which was a clever way to get variety. Little had changed in this place. Many of the magazines were the same, despite her two-year absence. The same murder mystery book, a little more dog-eared. By the front entrance, though, there was a new chair, second-hand, but yellow. Helen would have remembered such bright fabric.

A family came in, the parents each carrying a toddler. Twins, maybe. Both expelling a wet, deep cough into the shoulders of either parent. Watching the mother at the counter fill out forms, Helen rapped her fingers on the wooden armrest of the chair. The scene was all too familiar.

Waiting in the lobby, being called in for Piché's diagnosis — her heart was beating too slowly, affecting circulation and all manner of other things and causing disorientation, as if she needed more of that — taking her home, putting her to bed, preparing herself to spend the night in one of the spare rooms opposite, cleaning up as best she could in the kitchen, scrubbing the stove and cleaning what she could from the walls and floor, the blackened pot, throwing out the mess, Helen had to admit Piché was deteriorating.

A crescent of black under her fingernails, hands full of thin hardened chunks of burnt filling, Helen stopped over the garbage pail, struck with the notion that this house would soon be planted up the road, with Piché in it, only, no, she wouldn't be living on her own for long, not anymore.

Who then?

Asking the question told Helen that she couldn't live here, couldn't take care of another dying parent.

Before she would talk herself out of it, she was on the phone with Marcel — on Piché's line, so he'd know it was serious, someone else calling from their mother's number — and told him his mother needed help. In short order, he agreed to call his brothers. They'd work something out. He thanked her for phoning and hung up, without, Helen realized, much of a clue how involved she'd been in Piché's life. How invaluable she'd been. Without a sense what duty he was taking off of Helen's shoulders.

She set the phone in the cradle and sat down, exhausted. Seeing the dirty dish rag on the counter, darkened from cleaning the stove, Helen drew a hand across her forehead to block out the sight.

The boys would figure out what to do for their mother. This house would be moved and Helen would be somewhere else, no longer a neighbour.

It was undeniable that these were final days. Helen would lose the house.

The future, then, was inevitable.

She had been delaying signing the paperwork as a means to stop demolition, without recognizing that she wasn't preventing the loss of her house, only slowing down the process. Though, no, she hadn't even done that much. The Power Authority was ahead of schedule.

How is it that, with a thought, things could be made so much simpler? She'd been guarding the past, making or avoiding decisions based on a random set of feelings, and suddenly, here, before her, was the one question she hadn't been able to understand. Is this what I want? It was the I in that question which had been difficult. So many years looking out for others, feeling as though she'd been cheated from her true life, and now with that life revealed as a hoax, Helen had her self back. This was her life. How could she not have recognized that she was living today?

What do *I want*? she asked herself.

She couldn't find the answer. But sitting at Piché's kitchen table surrounded by the diminishing smell of smoke, she could feel her future, like a mare in the distance, coming for her.

WEDNESDAY

WHAT CAME NEXT was far too familiar. They were awake the entire night, stopping only to watch porn, to give themselves a break. Some time in the late morning, as the sound of cars became steady down on the street, the kid decided they should go online looking for someone else. His interest in Robert was waning, or the thrill was, because they'd done what they could do between them, so he'd find another to add to the mix, or a few, to give them some variety. He lay on his belly typing into the computer for a long while. The DVD ended, and Robert could feel the restlessness in his bones from too much crystal and too little sleep. He was tired, shaking with the drug, like an extreme case of caffeine jitters after pulling an all-night shift. He hated this — being hyper and exhausted in his skin — and couldn't get the boy, Toby, to kiss him. He thought if he could just make out through the worst of it, he might pass on through, or at least grow calm enough to stay still. How much had he smoked? They'd only used one bowl, and because it had been pre-treated, Robert couldn't say how much had been in there. He'd had three, or four, inhales. Second-hand. How much was that? He wanted out of his skin.

Reaching over, he ran a hand across the boy's slim back. Can we please just make out? ... Toby.

He was typing quickly, punching the keys.

Toby!

The boy turned his head to look at Robert, fingers on the keyboard. Man, you gotta chill. You want something to drink? There's pop in the fridge.

I don't want Coke in the morning.

There's juice. Get some juice. Get me some too. He went back to the screen, typing in a dialogue box.

Let's make out. I'm too buzzed to sit here. It's making me crazy.

I'm working on it.

I don't need someone else here. Let's just do something.

Take a shower.

Robert lay watching the ceiling, following the cracks in the stucco, one splintered line to the next. Maybe a shower would be a good idea, the water would be nice. He was thirsty. He climbed off the mattress and padded naked to the kitchen, which was a mess of dishes. The sink was piled full. Pasta stuck to a large number of plates and bowls, but there weren't any pots or pans.

Two white plastic folding chairs — IKEA, Robert thought — were on either side of a narrow wooden desk being used as a table. There were no curtains on the window, but a rod was suspended above it. Sunlight glared off cars passing in the street outside, but they were only three storeys up, next to another high-rise, which kept the light from coming into the suite.

In the cupboard, Robert found coffee mugs. He poured two glasses of orange juice from the fridge, drank one glass down, and refilled it, then returned to the bedroom.

He sat down beside Toby and set a mug next to the keyboard. Robert ran a hand along his back again. Toby's skin was damp, and cool, sweating the drugs out. Robert took another gulp of juice, which felt amazing going down his throat, cool right into his belly.

Do you have a towel? he asked. He kissed Toby's shoulder, and regretted it, for it too was slick with acrid sweat. Toby clicked back and forth between windows. The pictures were faceless.

He spoke again, in his ear. Toby.

There was a pause, then Toby rose up — forcing Robert to lift off of him — walked to a cluttered pile of clothes on the floor in the open closet, and pulled up a green towel from the centre of it. He tossed it on the carpet next to Robert and dropped down to the computer again.

Robert looked at the towel, which was clearly not fresh, then looked to the closet to confirm there weren't any clean ones. The closet shelves were a mess of boxes, mostly, and a couple of stacks of stiff-brimmed ball caps. Robert wondered if there were clean towels somewhere else. He couldn't decide if Toby was actually frustrated with him, or over it, or fixated on the next hook up, or simply irritable from the crystal. He disliked this kid's kind of high, because he couldn't read irritable correctly. He had poor instincts on when he should get out and when it was fine to stay. If some other guy did come, would Robert be welcome? Maybe. He couldn't tell.

Toby rolled left, onto his back, and propped an arm under his neck, as he had when they'd first started. He stared at Robert's torso, then lifted a leg, slid it between Robert's legs and tried to grab his dick with his toes.

We could go to your place, he said. You got anything at home? I don't.

Toby gave the smallest nod, taking that in. When their eyes met, he scrunched his brow, in a kind of concern, which read false. Why would you come without some?

Robert paused a moment, evaluating. Really, he'd no idea what the tempo was on that question. Toby's foot was massaging his dick.

I haven't used in six years, he said. And four before that.

Toby pulled himself up to sit more upright against the wall, crossing his legs as he did so. He put the tip of a finger in his mouth and chewed three times, fast, on a hangnail, looking at Robert, then away.

You can't just smoke other people's shit, he said, muffled from his finger. You gotta buy some of your own sometime.

I've been clean for most of ten years, buddy. I don't smoke other people's shit.

I just ... He looked at his fingernail, then sucked on it a second, releasing it with a smacking sound. I fucking hate that. People should buy their own shit.

Yeah, that's it for me, Robert said and took a final swig of his orange juice. He bent over and picked up his underwear from the carpet, setting his mug down. Toby scratched at his elbow, unconsciously picking at the loose skin. He wasn't looking at Robert, which seemed deliberate.

As Robert dressed, slowly, putting on each item — pants, T-shirt, button-up, then each sock — he knew it was time to go, that no good was to come from here on in, and still wished that Toby would say something, that he'd soften and remember a fresh pipe he'd forgotten about, and they'd be right again, for a couple of hours anyhow. He considered taking them in a cab to the other side of downtown, where he used to score. Get some cash from the bank machine first, though he knew it would be rotten out on the street with this kid. If he had him over, he might never get him out of his place. He could go home now and be done with it. Relapse done. But then it would be a long time till he used again, wouldn't it, another six years, it'd have to be, so it only made sense that if he'd already slipped he should take advantage while it was here. The best way to take care of himself was to find someone else, someone safer, who had a better, cleaner high.

THE NEXT MORNING when Helen returned to her own place after a night at Piché's, she was about to take a shower when she remembered the phone that she'd unplugged the night before. She picked up the receiver to check for messages and heard a man clear his voice on the other end.

She said Hello and Dave asked, first thing, Have you been out yet today?

She was on the hall phone. She hoped he couldn't hear in the background the toilet tank still filling up.

No, why?

Go check the tires on your car, would you? Someone slashed mine last night, all four. Could be coincidence, but I doubt it.

Helen put the phone down without a word. She felt rushed. Piché was still sleeping and Helen had only come home to shower quickly and to make them breakfast on her stove — to spare Piché the memory or embarrassment — and to bring it over super-quick.

She stepped outside, looked past the clematis, and saw that the car tires were intact. The car looked fine.

As she returned to the front door, she felt the air around her expand, as though the air held closed rooms whose doors were opening, one after the other, such that there was increasingly more space, the world expanding around her. She felt light on her feet, as though there were large bubbles of air underfoot which she couldn't avoid stepping on.

She picked up the cordless, exchanging phones, and told Dave all was fine on her end. He said, That's a good sign, I guess. I'd park it in the garage if I were you, Helen. And lock the door.

To the garage?

To the house too, sure.

Helen got goosebumps, and for good measure, went to the front door to shut and lock it before her shower. As she was closing the door, a dark blue sedan pulled up in front of the house. Helen watched the car stop and the two men in the front seats look at each other. The driver was talking, then they both sort of nodded.

Hey, you there? Dave said.

Yes, Helen answered, not really paying attention. If either

man noticed Helen in the doorway, they gave no indication as they stepped out of the car. They hadn't looked to the house, but came walking up her driveway. Yeah. I gotta go, she said.

Helen? What's going on?

She whispered, Company, I'm in my housecoat. I'll call you back. I gotta go, and hung up.

The taller man, the blond, finally looked to the doorway and smiled as he came across the walk, followed by his partner in a grey suit. His hair was a bit too short to be becoming.

Helen, feeling emboldened, stepped out onto the front steps, hands pressed into the pockets of her housecoat, clutching the cordless receiver.

Maybe we caught you at a bad time, the blond said, quizzical, but still smiling. I thought it might be a bit early but we haven't been able to reach you in the afternoons this week ...

When they arrived at the bottom step both men placed their briefcases beside them. The blond introduced them: he was Rodney and his partner was Brian. They were representing the Power Authority. They offered to wait if Helen wanted a moment to herself, but she was impatient to get back to Piché so she simply reached behind her and closed the door tight.

I was just heading over to a neighbour's, actually.

They started to chit-chat with Helen, mentioning the heat and the groundbreaking ceremonies at the museum site, but she was short. I don't have a lot of time, she said. What can I do for you?

We're making rounds in the community to make sure everyone is aware of the changes that were announced at the meeting on Monday. Were you at that meeting?

Yes.

So you know that this section, the blues, are being moved forward.

I heard that, yes.

You likely saw the house-mover this week. It's not back yet, is it? They moved one neighbour already, who was good to go.

Rodney looked up the road. I think the Alsagers are scheduled to be next. Things are picking up speed and we know we haven't finalized our details with you —

My house isn't being moved.

Yes, I understand that. We're making rounds to just ... check in. We have you booked for a consultation in a couple days ...

Sorry, which?

Randy looked to his partner. We wondered if you had missed that invitation. We have been trying to confirm you for that meeting. You should have received a registered letter. We have unconfirmed blues booked for the weekend in case folks didn't want to miss work. You were to phone us to confirm that appointment, or to change it if there was some inconvenience and you couldn't make it.

Uh huh, Helen said, trying to sound as though she had some idea what he was talking about.

So can we confirm you for Friday, if that's a good day for you?

Brian dragged his satchel across the ground to between his legs and pulled a leather folder from it. He flipped over the cover flap to a chart.

We have you down for eleven a.m., he said.

How does that sound? Rodney asked her.

Sure, Helen said, unthinking.

Brian wrote something on a small card, and handed it to Rodney, who looked at it briefly, then held it out to Helen, who took it. The handwriting was neat and tiny.

We are here today partly to let you know about some changes in your meeting. Same time and place as your registered letter, but we now have you meeting with Dan Cruikshank.

Helen paused, regarding him. Cruikshank? He does these?

Yes, of course. Sometimes. We're down to the wire, here, aren't we? Dan has a great sense of what can make this an easier process for you. Which is the other reason we're here, Rodney said, falling into his pitch. Sometimes the business side of the organization can be a bit much, *ergo* — and he smiled — this is a less formal way for us to get some feedback from you, to see if there's anything we can do to help make your relocation more comfortable. It's a good idea for us to collect some of your thoughts in advance of the meeting so we can do our best to accommodate you. Have you thought where you'd like to move? Maybe you have plans that don't involve the new town site. Or maybe you have questions about the site that you haven't had an opportunity to ask. We're here to help with whatever those concerns might be. We like to get any kind of feedback so we can help you make the best decision. Maybe we overlooked something, or you have some request that you forgot to mention in our initial consultation.

A request?

Rodney perked up a little, thinking he'd found a selling point with Helen. Some people have special requests, an item they need moved, that sort of thing. Most people are only delayed because they don't realize what we can do for them, what's in the cards.

Brian was nodding as Rodney spoke.

A little thing like having a second bathroom or moving a favourite water fountain — Helen thought of Ruby's sister — can slow down a decision, so we like to check in and find out what we can do to facilitate.

We bring that back to the table, Brian added, and see what we can come up with for you.

Rodney turned to look at him, with just a moment's hesitation before turning back to Helen and speaking again.

So if there is something you need, we want to have that conversation and see what options are available to us, he said, his tone altered, such that Helen thought Brian must have deviated from their usual script.

Helen paused. She was warm in her housecoat. It was hotter outside in the sun than it was inside. The breeze off the river was sheltered by the house. She was feeling a bit self-conscious in her robe, in case Ruby came out and saw her dressed like this with two men in suits. Though, she reasoned as well, Piché's situation was alarming, so who cared what Helen looked like. She could feel anxiety rising hot in her belly, bubbling up her insides, and tried to slow down, slow her breathing down. Step back a second.

Helen breathed deeply, slow and heavy, and just that intention made it seem as though everything untangled itself, that she was behind a screen watching every little thing happen.

Brian said again that they would bring her concerns to the table for her, and again Rodney seemed put out by him, nearly talking over him, nodding his head, and Helen recognized that it was damage control. Rodney was trying to talk them past that comment. To whom, Helen wondered, would they bring her concerns? If these two weren't the people to make the decision, who were they?

Who do you work for? she asked, her voice rising at the end.

You could say we're the people-people of the organization, Rodney said.

But do you work at the Power Authority?

Rodney hesitated, just a hair. Yes.

Yes-yes or yes-maybe?

We've been charged with helping to negotiate the settlement, Brian said, but he sounded more like a small child trying to impress than someone with any confidence.

Rodney raised a calming hand. We're not here to rush you, or get you to sign anything. We're here to listen, mostly. To see if there's anything we can do for you.

Helen spoke slowly as though they required her to be infinitely patient. You're not answering my question very well, though, Rodney. She turned to Brian. Do you work in the Power Authority?

Brian glanced quickly at his partner and then met Helen's eyes again. She saw the answer in his face.

Helen crossed her hands. How can we negotiate the settlement if you aren't the people doing the settling?

Rodney began to speak but Helen cut him off. I'm sorry, she said, that wasn't meant as a question. Who do you work for?

Neither man answered.

You don't know who you work for, is that it? Let me put it

this way, how can you give input into the private terms of my agreement if you aren't the people drawing up that agreement? Is that not a breach of confidentiality?

Rodney looked at Brian and answered. We do work for the Power Authority. I assure you this visit is perfectly legitimate.

I don't feel very assured. You still haven't answered me. What do you do for the Power Authority?

We're under contract.

To do what?

We facilitate the negotiation process, Rodney said, and counted on his fingers. We meet with clients. Answer questions. We help explain the terms of the settlements. We listen to clients like yourself who ... who aren't ready to sign for any host of legitimate reasons, and we determine what we can do to help them meet their needs.

I see, so the Power Authority hired you to look out for my best interests?

Yes, actually, you could say that.

She looked Brian in the eye and fixed him there. I would like to know who you work for. What company do I phone if I want to hire you as well?

Brian hesitated, with his mouth open.

Helen frowned. Do you have a business card?

Brian patted his pockets. I'm sorry, I don't. He looked to Rodney. Rodney?

We've obviously come at a bad time. Maybe we can reschedule? Rodney said, producing a card from his inside pocket. You can reach us here any time during business hours, including evenings until eight p.m.

Thank you, Helen said, holding the card in cupped palms as if it were precious.

Again, I'm sorry to have caught you at a bad time, Rodney apologized. We'll consider that meeting fixed then. Don't hesitate to be in touch. We enjoy finding ways to help people with what must be a difficult task ahead.

When Helen didn't answer, he nodded, and looked to Brian, and said, Well, you have yourself a nice day.

Helen was impressed at how steady he was, not a trace of irony, or resentment.

Thank you, Brian added, before turning to follow Rodney up the driveway. Rodney stopped just before the car to extend a hand to Brian, who gave him the keys. Neither of them looked back at the house — doing so might have gone against protocol.

As the car pulled out and headed farther up the highway, away from the direction they came, Dave drove into Helen's yard in his old high school Chevy. Helen was surprised to see him, and relieved. She still had the cordless phone in her pocket.

The car door squeaked as it opened, in bad need of some oil. Looks like I missed the fun, Dave called, adjusting his ball cap as he got out of the car. He wasn't hopping as he had the other day with his bad toenail, but he limped a little as he walked.

I don't know what that was, Helen said.

How do you mean?

She held their card out to him. I don't know. Power Authority people. Maybe.

When he reached her and took the card, she could smell stale booze on him from the night before, and sweat. He wasn't rank, but a bit off. Helen shot him a look, crinkling her nose.

Dave smiled and sniffed one of his pits quickly. I'm a little morning-breathed, sorry. I usually shower before I head out for the day, but you had me worried for you. I wanted to make sure you weren't being visited by the boys who came to see my truck tires last night.

I wished you'd have seen these two. I doubt they're the same, but they sure were interesting.

Dave read the company name on the card. Well, someone likes you.

How do you mean?

I know these guys. They came asking at the Loucks's too. Last week. You haven't signed your papers yet.

No.

Worked out good for Loucks. I think he got an in-ground swimming pool out of it. Well, Loucks paid for the parts, but they got the labour free. Why not, I guess, eh? It's nothing for them. They've got the equipment and men lined up. Quiet day, few extra hands, the pool's done.

I don't want a pool.

Well, did you tell them what you do want?

Helen rolled her eyes. I kinda brushed them off.

Dave chuckled and shrugged.

But I have their card. They said to call. They just pissed me off so much.

Yeah, well, Helen, Dave said, lifting his hat and scratching his scalp with a dirty fingernail, looks to me like somebody wants you to be happy. Maybe you should just take their advice.

Helen grimaced, and nodded. Thanks, Dave, she said, and drew the robe around her more tightly. You want to come in?

I'm not being ass-y. I'm just saying.

I know ... I just don't want to sign a paper that says, Sure, go ahead and tear down my house.

Especially when you don't know where you're going.

Dave was guessing, but Helen again wondered how well he could read her.

No, I don't. Helen looked across the street to Ruby's. You coming in?

Nah. Dave ran a hand through his hair, adjusting his ball cap again, and Helen spied a small hole in the underarm seam of his T-shirt. His skin made a light oval spot against the dark fabric.

She gestured to the Chevy. I'm surprised that still runs.

I had to drive something. You didn't answer the phone.

I was just going to turn it on when I talked to you. I get pranks at night.

Dave cocked his head. We might have the same friends.

It's been off and on for weeks. I don't even think of it. I just turn it off when I go to bed and on in the morning. Kids, right? You think it was just kids that did your tires?

Helen figured she knew the answer, but she wanted him to say *yes*, and have it be that easy.

I figure I asked one too many questions yesterday. Or one too many people.

She must have looked hopeful for some answers, because Dave raised a hand and said, I didn't find anything out. We aren't going to win any popularity contests, I can say that much.

Will insurance cover the tires? Will you phone the police?

Dave frowned and cocked his head. I doubt they'll care too much. It'll be a prank to them.

Helen's foot tingled from the small feet of an ant crawling across it. Two of them. Maybe I should, she said.

Dave chuckled. You going to charm them for me, Helen?

No, I mean maybe I should phone them about the accident. What if it wasn't an accident?

But there were other people there, right?

They can't pour concrete on a dead body though, can they? she asked, shaking her foot to throw the bugs off. She leaned over and scratched the spot where they'd been.

I don't know, Helen. I don't know what's smart and what is just making trouble for yourself.

Glinny said her boss killed the story before she'd even told him about it.

Maybe the police are already involved then.

How do you mean?

Well, where else would Dyson hear about it? Glinny phoned the police, didn't she? If there's an investigation, it would make sense that they wouldn't want it in the papers while they're collecting evidence.

I hadn't thought of that. But then why's no one come to talk to me?

Dave's lower lip extended, considering it, and then he shrugged. They got other witnesses.

I guess so, Helen said. She looked over at Ruby's picture window again and spied a flash of colour passing just beyond the frame. She rubbed a hand across her forehead. It was damp with a light sweat.

I should take a bath, Dave.

Good idea, he answered, then hesitated. Are you going to be okay here? If you want to call the cops I'll stick around. Or we can go down there together. It's been a while since I've seen the insides of that place.

I'm a big girl, Dave.

All right. I'm just saying. He took a step behind him, swivelling on one foot, sort of bent forward leaning on his heel, with a look that was making sure leaving was the right thing to do.

Thanks, Dave, she said. Maybe we split the cost of those tires?

He waved it off. I got two other sets, from the dump, been sitting there for a year. Just didn't have time to get them on.

At the door to the Chevy, he raised a hand, his elbow exaggeratedly cocked ninety degrees. Later, he said. He ducked into the seat, then swung himself up by the edge of the doorframe to peak over the top. You let me know if you need anything else. I'll let you know if I hear anything.

Will do, Helen said. She didn't wait for him to back out before returning inside. She closed the door behind her, and kept her hand on the knob a second, thinking. The engine of Dave's car revved alive, and reversed out her driveway.

She crossed into the kitchen, set the appointment card down on top of the fridge, and went to the bathroom to run the water for a bath. She wanted time to herself; Piché could wait half an hour. She wiped down the tub with a rag, tested the water with her hand, stoppered the plug and poured in some salts. She watched the water run in the tub for a second or so, listening to its hard rumble, then grunted a heavy sigh, returned to the kitchen, took the card down, read it over again, put it in her robe pocket, collected the manila envelopes and carried them into the living room. She set them on the coffee table and sat down on the couch, surveying them. Using her finger, she slit the remaining envelopes that still hadn't been opened and pulled out the papers from each.

By the end, the paperwork filled the table. Helen found there were multiple versions of the initial contract. They'd sent her the forms twice after the first set, which she still had in her purse. She flipped through the most recent contract, and spied some numbers in red, which, when she compared them to the first two contracts mailed out, she found to be increases in her proposed settlement. Had she signed the other day at the meeting, she'd have been taking a lesser offer.

A single letter confirmed what Rodney had said; she was scheduled for a consultation at the Power Authority office in the city.

Amongst the remaining papers was a document explaining the relocation of her mother's remains. Helen flipped to the last page with the diagram of the new cemetery and ran a finger over the options for plots where her parents could be buried. Nowhere near water. They were to be in any number of plots on the far side of the L-shaped grounds farther up the highway where it ran north, more than a mile from the river.

Did Robbie still care where they went? She recalled the gesture as he spread his coat on the ground at their gravesite. Eventually, he'd forgive his mother. Helen would, because what other choice did she have? She'd understood long ago that her parents had done the best they could — her father's drinking taught her that — and if that was too little, well, that was their weakness and not for lacking in love. Her mother had adored them both. She wished she could convince Robbie of that. She wished for some way of making amends, which was a means of putting their histories to rest. If she was going to keep this appointment, perhaps that was a chance to negotiate her parents' plots. They could be moved to her mother's home town, because it had a riverfront cemetery, although neither she nor Robbie ever went there. But that was better, wasn't it? Closer to something that would make them happy. An acknowledgment. A gesture, to make something right despite the deal they'd been given.

ARE YOU DONE? Colin asked.

Robert had found a payphone in the hallway of a seventies-style mall. It shared an entrance with a smaller library branch downtown, so he could see the checkout counter from the hall. Anyone exiting the building would see him on the phone.

I don't know, he answered.

Well that's up to you, right? Do you want to be done? Or do you want this to go on? You get to step off this train anytime. But I'm not coming to get you if you aren't done.

I'm sorry, Robert said.

You don't have to apologize to me, Rob. You haven't done anything to me. You're not being so good to yourself, though.

A woman with a red stroller outside pressed a button for the automatic door. She had a full knapsack on her back and her hair tied in a tight ponytail.

I know, he said, and added, his throat choking through the

words, I don't want to be here. He turned his face to the painted cinderblock wall.

But you are. And you get to choose where you go from here, right? You want to stay out on the street, or are you done?

. I want to be done.

Okay. Does that mean you are done? Colin asked, patient. There was no judgment in his voice. Robert was relieved to hear it.

I'm terrified I'm not done.

That's up to you, right?

Six years I've been sober. And I use again?

Rob, you are the one in control of this. You've just been through a nasty weekend, right? Colin waited a moment. Well, that is enough to set anyone off. You phoned me. But what do you learn from that? Right? You're not perfect. You get to make mistakes. Just let's not make them big ones, right? Let's not make this any bigger.

Robert leaned his head against the wall, which was cold against his forehead. He was hot all over. The coolness pressing against his scalp felt relaxing. Okay, he agreed.

There's no reason to be hopeless. It's a small slip, so far, yes?

I barebacked.

Fine. But what time is it? It's noon. It's been a half day and you're calling someone. You phoned me. You're done after a half-day slip. That's a good slip. You be happy about that. It's not three days, or three months. A half-day slip. You do not need to be hopeless. That's only adding to the problem, right? You know this, Colin said forcefully.

I do.

A small slip.

Robert didn't answer. He heard a woman at the checkout cackle, her voice piercing, and wondered if the staff would shush her. Oh, no, *you*, the voice said.

He tilted his head, to see what was happening. His cheek still pressed against the cool wall. A large woman in flip-flops pulled a big bag off the counter, wrapping her arms around it. She was grinning, and bellowed *Ciao* over her shoulder, but the woman at the desk was already dealing with the next client in line. The woman shuffled to the exit in her flip-flops and gave the door a kick to open it. She nearly beamed a guy standing outside finishing a cigarette.

Rob?

Robert could hear Colin breathing into the phone.

Yes, Robert said. Come get me.

Okay, good, he said. Where are you?

Robert hesitated, the wall felt comforting against his cheek. He was anxious. His belly was a mess of manic energy.

The smoker outside entered the building, throwing his cigarette butt out on the street behind him. He rolled up the cuffs on his loose-fitting shirt as he approached the washroom door.

Rob. Where are you?

The guy glanced at Robert as he entered the washroom, and held the door open for a couple of seconds, his arm stretched behind him, as though he was waiting for someone. The door swung closed slowly.

Robert heard Colin's mechanical voice on the phone say, Rob? Rob, where are you? as he set the receiver in the cradle.

THE CREW ARRIVED in the afternoon to begin the work of jacking up Ruby's house. Five men in hardhats and overalls and three in jeans and T-shirts, despite the heat. There must have been some rules passed down about dress code, because nobody in town ever wore that much to work outdoors in this weather. Helen was in Piché's front room when she saw them pull up. Piché had spent the morning in bed, barely touching her eggs at breakfast, but Helen had managed to get some soup into her. It was amazing how frail she could become in a day. Had it come on this suddenly, and was she old enough that she could just decline that easily? Her mother's death had been very slow. Her father's, too. Had Piché been on the verge of this, had she been slipping towards this slack-jawed weariness? Or was it a phase, and she'd eat, and get her strength back, and rebound? It was hard for Helen to see her in her worn flannel robe and imagine she was going to get out into her garden anytime soon.

Helen pulled back one of the white lace sheers to get a look at what it was they actually did to a house before a move. Three men on one of the trucks were using a hydraulic to unload a flat of lumber. Each of the ends was colour-coded. A pair of men was measuring a side of the house and chalking the concrete, without any rhyme or reason Helen could determine.

Folks on the road decelerated as they passed. A truck slowed right down, so that Helen thought it was pulling into Ruby's yard, but it was Bill, turning into Helen's driveway again.

Helen released a long, slow sigh. She turned her attention to listen up the hall, but there was no sound from Piché, so she stepped out onto the porch. Bill spotted her right away, and waved, shouting, Hey, Midget!

Helen held a finger up to her mouth, to shush him.

When he got to the bottom of the steps Bill lifted his hands in the air, showing her his palms. Now I was just driving by. I'm not here for anything, I was driving by and wanted to see how you were.

Oh, Bill, don't do that. I'm not mad at you.

Well, okay, then. Okay, he said and climbed the steps. I heard Piché was in the clinic yesterday, gave you a bit of a scare.

Well, I'm still scared. She nearly burned the house down.

You're a nursemaid again, are you?

It's only keeping me from my gardening.

Bill chuckled. Yeah, well, you could get help for that, you know. You could get them boys to do it, he said, and gestured across the road. Then he raised his hands again. I know, I know, you don't want to hear it and I'm getting my nose in where it isn't my business, but — he sighed — why not have some men paid to do this kinda work do it? Why do it all yourself? Just to be stubborn?

Bill, let's not do this.

No, he said, and blinked at her, like he was puzzled. You're right. I didn't come for that anyhow, did I?

I hope not.

When he paused, about to say something, and hesitated, Helen said, I thought you were just driving by?

I heard something, Helen. Heard you were on the Keegan's property the other day, were you? And you saw something, I guess, and ... and you've been asking after it.

Helen's heart doubled in her chest.

Maybe that was before I talked to you, I thought to myself, when I heard it, and rightly so it was. So I'm sorry I wasn't more sensitive to you the other day. You must have been in some shock, eh? An accident like that has got to be something rotten to see. I know, I've seen some pretty grisly things I wish I hadn't. But believe me, from an old fart that's lived it a few times, you're better forgetting it happened, Midget.

Helen cocked her head and put her hand on her hip. When she spoke, she was blunt, but quiet. I saw a man die there, Bill, and they buried him inside the dam.

I know that, Helen. I know that. Accidents happen, Helen.

And I also know that. They didn't bother to stop their work long enough to pull his body out of there for a proper burial. He's up there, in the cement. They just poured it over him.

Now there are way more things to consider here than the obvious, he said, sitting back gingerly on the black metal rail of the landing.

Helen opened the screen door and pulled closed the inside one so Piché wouldn't hear. Just in case. She faced him square, to say she was waiting for him to explain himself. She had all the time in the world to see him hang himself, if that's what he wanted to do.

The construction company has its own deadlines and these guys, you don't know these guys that work up there. Some of them are ex-cons, and some aren't so ex, probably, if you know what I mean.

So they deserve less care than the rest of us?

His hands raised in front of his chest again, palms forward, with almost an apologetic tone in his voice, he said, They don't ask a lot of questions when they're hiring men who are willing to do that work. There aren't a lot of men who will, despite the money. There are risks, Helen, he said firmly. They know it. They sign their agreements before they get up there. And so I'm saying that maybe he's signed something that lets them do what is necessary after an accident. Maybe he has no family. Maybe there's no one to attend a funeral.

But he did, Bill. That's the thing.

You don't know that.

He had me, Bill, she said and felt her arms prickle with heat.

Bill waited a long minute. Then he surprised Helen by nodding. Right, he said.

He let out a large sigh, stood up, and took her elbow, saying, Come here.

He moved them down onto the step. Helen could hear his joints crackle on the way down. Across the street, the men at the truck were unlatching the fasteners from the wooden beams. One guy was standing on top of the pile, undoing the winch.

Listen, Midget, can I give you some advice? he said. No one in town is going to like you any better for trying to slow any of this down.

In her mind, Helen saw the tires on Dave's truck, slashed. Did Bill know about that too?

Piché in here might be loyal to you, he continued, but are you doing her any favours by holding her up? She wants to get resettled. The sooner it happens, the sooner she'll get used to the new idea. We aren't getting any younger, she and I.

Are we talking about the house again? Or the accident?

Well, both, I think, yes?

Two men across the street shouted to each other. They were unhitching the stack of lumber from the crane.

Now what do you want to do about this accident? Make it public? Make a big stink? The newspapers aren't going to help you.

Unless I give them a better story.

They don't need a better story. They don't need to sell papers right now. Your version of better isn't the same as their better. Haven't you seen the ads? Full page ads. Who do you think is paying for them? So when it comes time to write the articles, they want access to the progress being made on the site. They report some death and make it sensational, some accident by a guy who wasn't doing his job carefully, and they report on it, and everything slows down, do you have any idea how much money one lost day would cost? An hour even? Let me put it to you carefully. I'm not trying to insult you, Helen. More than your home is worth. More than the cost of your silence.

Bill scratched at a small scab on his thumb, lifting a corner of dried skin.

I'm saying, your brother shows up and look — now you have two peoples' interests to look out for. You've twice as many worries and half the money, right? And, I'm not sure what arrangements you two have made about the house —

We've not talked about it yet.

But the question here is, what's that mean for you personally? That, they understand. If you think you're getting a raw deal, and I know, you've a lot of memories here. Look at your garden. He swept his arm towards her property. Now that's the kind of concern you can approach them with. They aren't unreasonable.

He tapped the side of Helen's leg with his knuckle. You get me? There was an accident. Who cares? he said gently, opening up his palms, his voice tight.

I do, Bill.

He ran his hands along his knees and continued. Pick the battles you can win. You've got to look at the bigger picture. Choose your battles, Helen. That's all I'm saying. They are within their rights. It's right there in the law. The Power Authority doesn't need your consent to expropriate your land. They can fuck you so good and well, he said. His voice was nearly hoarse with the effort to whisper. Helen smelled the sourness of coffee on his breath.

These negotiations are a courtesy, to keep up a good face. They don't need you to say yes. So get what you can, while you can. You don't want these guys as your enemy. You want them as your friend.

He patted her knee, then stood, grabbing the rail. Helen watched his broad back rounded some in the shoulders as he lumbered back to the truck without a goodbye. He didn't so much as wave at her before he hop-stepped into the truck.

He'd not made it out of the driveway before Helen heard the questions stacking up with some clarity. He'd left without giving her time to respond. How had Bill known the guy wasn't doing his job carefully? Was he simply assuming it? Did someone on the construction crew tell him that? Or who had? Was that the truth? Did Bill know? He might have found out the man's name.

Helen wondered, once Bill had heard about the accident, once he'd heard that Helen was asking questions, had he come on his own, or was he sent here? She wished she'd have had the wherewithal to have asked him at the time, because he might have answered, out of some guilt, or allegiance, perhaps, but now that he'd said his piece, the job was done, and something in how he'd left told her he'd be hardened, resigned. He'd done his bit and wouldn't have to say any more.

ROBERT LOST THAT day too. He spent most of it out on the street, like a fool, or trying not to be a fool. Trying to blend in. He wondered how normal he seemed. To have any success it was important for him to appear normal, to present well. There were two minds when he was in the addiction: there was the usual Robert, who was rational, who could see what was happening and reflect on it, who knew the other mind — the weird dark automaton taking over the driver's seat of his actions — was almost helplessly compelled to act. In a moment of great, desperate willpower, his better mind pulled his wallet from his back pocket and dropped it in a mailbox so he wouldn't have access to his cards. Then he spent an hour pacing the street trying to determine how to get it back. He couldn't figure out how to get in there without someone seeing. He didn't want to be arrested. How would he explain what he was doing if he was caught? His licence would prove who he was, but it was illegal anyhow, wasn't it? How would he explain how the wallet got in there?

Eventually he gave up, bent on a new idea. He went to a nearby branch of his bank, and tried to convince them he needed forty bucks, just forty, to get home, maybe they had a photo of him on file, which was a long shot, ha ha, but did they? He could tell them his account numbers, he had them memorized. And his password. The clerk at the counter thought he was charming, but creepy too. She didn't trust him one bit. She smiled very sweetly, almost giggling, each time he proposed a solution and she said no.

He sped back to the mailbox and thought maybe he'd run into the postal worker who came to collect the day's drops. He spent nearly another agonizing hour wondering if he'd missed the driver because it was just before the time they had listed as the daily pickup. Through the afternoon, he was also trying to cruise any men that passed. His mind swung quickly between thoughts, the same ones, back and forth, how to get into the mailbox, fearful that people would see him do so, finding a hookup on the street, finding the postal worker, getting caught by the postal worker. He imagined he might find a twenty in the road. He imagined he'd run into an old hookup who would take him home. Robert would let him fuck his brains out on condition that he could have a hit.

It was just past three in the afternoon when he remembered his passport at home. He had ID at home. He was stupid for having forgotten. Did he have change on him for the bus? No. He could be home in a half hour if he walked fast, and could be at the bank by four. During the walk home, he imagined the passport in his desk drawer, and knew it was a mistake. Maybe he'd stay in the apartment. Yes, he'd stay inside once he got home, this was a good strategy, to use the passport to get himself home, but once there, he'd stay. Robert could hear himself trading thoughts, and he knew the addict was devious, that the talk was more to do with convincing him to get home so he could have access to the passport and the bank, rather than any real desire to stay in. The addict could use the cautious mind to sidestep any fears, to nimbly overlook the damage. Sometimes, though, in the past, he'd been able to rein it in, sometimes he'd been lucky and had somehow turned the tricks against the addict, and had managed to step out of it long enough to find help, or to come down enough to make a solid decision. That felt like a long time ago. He wondered what those tricks were. Could he find one? A key to the door, to step out of the machinery. Which mind would win out was a coin toss. Going home was gambling.

The passport was exactly where he'd thought it would be. He took a terrible dump in the bathroom and then, washing his hands, looked in the mirror. His hair was matted to his forehead with sweat. His face was slick with it. He didn't look as tired as he thought he should, but his pupils were still large black circles. It was obvious. Too obvious. He'd wear sunglasses. But he stank, didn't he? A day and a half without showering, sex all night, he was filthy.

He stood under the shower until the water had collected in the tub to halfway up his calves. The tub drained slower than the water came out. The sensation on his back was amazing. He turned the taps off and, grabbing a towel, realized he hadn't bathed. He hadn't actually cleaned himself. He sat down, the level rising in the tub, and quickly lathered himself up. In the short time it took to be done, the water level was too low for him to even squish himself down and rinse off properly.

He turned the taps back on, the temperature too cold, and rinsed.

Both handsets of the telephone rang from either side of the apartment, like they were talking in unison. Robert turned the taps off and towelled dry. The phones stopped ringing. The silence was surprising; the apartment was still. Everything hushed. From a block over, the hum of street traffic sounded outside. Then a low boom, like a plastic bag popping behind a closed door. The six-o'clock gun? It couldn't be six.

He walked to the bedroom, and sure enough, his clock radio read 5:58. He'd lost an hour. The nearby banks had closed, some of them an hour earlier. He'd have to go downtown to find one open till seven.

The air on his skin, the smell of his sheets, drew him onto the bed. He lay on the warm cotton covers, the duvet sort of settling around him in a nest the shape of his body. The sun was still bright through the window. He closed his eyes against the glare and slept.

THERE WERE NIGHTS like this after her father died when Helen felt, just by stepping into the house, she'd travelled beyond any place she could be reached. She'd spent the day tending to Piché, cooking meals for both of them, she'd seen Dave, and Bill, and watched the house slowly get mounted on wood planks across the street. She'd cleaned Piché's bathroom, which was in a state, and had done a little more work, late in the afternoon, in both of their gardens. Around nine, she left a cordless phone on Piché's nightstand so she could sleep in her own bed, but the second she stepped out of the house, she felt profoundly alone, as though she wasn't even herself anymore, but less than that. Less than herself.

She wasn't in her own home more than an hour before she couldn't stand the indifference of the walls any longer. The dim light over the sink, the dishes in their rack from the previous day. Helen walked outside in the cool air, to the water's edge, and stared out at the river.

The air was thick with the smell of grass. She listened to the water licking between the stones and felt lonelier still. The river felt oddly removed. It was an object, a thing, out there, being manipulated. She owned nothing of what she once took for granted. Not the river, nor her home, not even the plants in the yard were hers in any true sense of the word. She had once had dominion, and with her home going, no, it was more than that, with her memories pulled out from under her, her memories corrupted, she hadn't the past that she'd imagined. She hadn't the alternate life in which she'd moved, a shadow self, imagining the home with Garrett, counting his birthdays, their anniversaries. She'd been living make-believe.

She pulled the back of her shirt stuck to her skin, to get a breeze in there, then had a better thought and removed her shoes, then her socks, slipping them inside the empty mouths of canvas. She folded her pants neatly, laying them on top of the shoes, making a pile of clothes. Her bobby pins she slid into the front pocket of her blouse before folding it, and her bra she tucked under the blouse. Her hair, loose on her shoulders, tickled her skin, and saddened her. The sensation so sweet, and empty. There was that blackness to her mood, like the sky inside her, voided. She inherited this feeling from her father;

it's why he drank. It's why she'd hated him and also why she'd pitied him enough to love him.

Leaning back on her heel, she slipped her toe into the water and felt drawn out of herself a little, with another sensation, below the water. With the change in temperature, her toe felt separated from the rest of her body, part of something else. She stepped forward, cautious on the slippery stones, feeling the cool water crawl up her body and tickle her skin with sensation, goosebumping her, until only her head was independent, absurdly floating in the air, hovering above the rest of her. She swam out slowly a few metres, looking to the black water before her, the peaks catching bits of moon and tossing the light around. When she took a breath and jackknifed downwards, pushing her body beneath the surface, the air warm in her lungs, she could feel her body being taken up by the river, the contact a sort of union, she was part of something greater than herself, vulnerable, and held, a great watery hand cupping her. Her skin prickled with the temperature, her heart beating steady and clear, a drum against the water.

She swam through the river, pushing, until she was a few dozen metres from land, a bit breathy, and stimulated, her skin alert to the river and air. She turned onto her back and looked up at the stars caught in the netting above her, but they didn't add to the feeling running through her blood. She closed her eyes and floated in the river, present but placeless, a location she could never quite find again, and felt the immediacy of the moment.

She felt she could crawl out of herself, slide out of her skin like she'd been trapped headfirst inside a sleeping bag and could emerge into the fresh air reborn. She'd step into town a new woman, ready to be held, long and deeply, by anyone, anyone kind enough to notice she was alone, anyone with half a care for what she could possibly do to keep herself busy in that house by herself.

The water was gorgeous, its cold hands over her everywhere at once. How many nights did she feel ridiculous to be sleeping on one side of the bed? Like she was in training. For what? A decade of waiting, denying herself the full use of a bed that was getting no other use. She infuriated herself. What's the point of hoping if there is no reward? And was it optimism? Garrett was dead; the one she knew and another she didn't, both dead.

She swam further out, kicking, on her back, the water cold against her as she moved, her breathing steady, measuring her pace, using her abdomen to really push the air, until she was a hundred yards out in the river, surrounded by water, the weeds too deep to brush her legs. Treading water. She felt exception-ally alert, looking around, huffing for breath, so much inside herself, so aware of her body in contact everywhere with the river, and her head above the waves, surrounded by the night sky, the sound of the water clicking against itself. The river felt alive between her legs. She moved it, kicking lightly, brushing her arms back and forth to stay afloat. Water itched as it dripped off her face.

There was an echo in her body to the hug Robbie had given her. She realized she hadn't held anyone since her parents passed. She'd spent her adult life not being held. The water around her felt more real. Her senses were coursing. Her body was a teenager, coming alive.

Garrett had made her feel this way.

Men had seen him dead and filled out paperwork to say as much. He'd been buried. His name was printed in the papers and added to a list. People knew him and had seen him dead. At some point, her hope needed to let him rest.

At some point.

She looked upstream to the dark outline of the riverbank, which would never, in a few months, look like this again. Nobody would be here, seeing this, again. It was not that the landscape wouldn't or couldn't change, naturally, but that she in her lifetime could not stop this other progress.

She didn't want to drag the dead behind her anymore; she didn't want to wrap herself in them. She wanted her life back, but that thought made her realize, with the water on her face, the stars above her, that she was alone. Nobody was going to come take care of her. No one was going to solve her problem.

None of the lights were on in her house. Like the other day, it looked abandoned. If the appointment was scheduled for two days from now, she'd be damned if she didn't get her head settled first. When she thought of the contracts, though, she came back to the same roadblock: she didn't want to move. Or, more precisely, she didn't want their massive backhoe pulling up onto her property and destroying it. She didn't want to give them the opportunity to take away her home, even though they legally had the right. So what did she have? What was available to her?

The falling man. The man who fell, for he'd fallen already, he was no longer falling. She had him, didn't she? There was leverage in what she knew, power in what she'd witnessed, or why else would they have arranged for her to meet with

Cruikshank? But how could she use that knowledge? To what purpose? It didn't seem fair to use him for her own gain. But she wasn't after gain. She was after an acknowledgment. A kind of respect, wasn't it? She wanted them to recognize what they were asking her to give up, what they were taking from her. *Witness*, she thought, and her blood zigged down her back, cold. *Witness*. Like the fallen man they refused to acknowledge.

Here she'd been resolved to get the business over with Robbie so she could negotiate with a clean conscience, sign the contracts, be done with it. She'd imagined they'd write changes in like Ruby had, in pen, on the three copies. Only that wasn't right, because it brought her back to the same place. She didn't want to negotiate. She didn't want to agree to terms. She didn't want to agree. She wanted to be seen.

The man who fell, then, was leverage. Cruikshank would acknowledge his death, print an obituary, hold a memorial, do him justice.

Her hands were cold. There was an ache in her lower back from the weeks of stress. Her face in the warm air above-water felt enormous. Everything she missed, everything she didn't want to live without, here, before her, had made her. It persisted. She suddenly felt her body become terrifically precious. She was full with the richness of herself. That richness, the events that led to who she was, the living memory in her, presented itself — a secret door she'd been staring at for years and could never see, opening — and she, Helen, having had no idea she'd missed the obvious, realized that she could be the constant, she could persist, she could live, she could love herself.

In the distance, through the screen door to her house, she

heard the distant ring of her phone and seized, briefly, for fear that it was Piché. But her light wasn't on. She was asleep, surely. Pranksters again, for it was after nine, and that was when the calls usually started. Or maybe, as Bill had said, she was naïve. Maybe the calls were more malicious. The slashed tires, the Power Authority sending some kind of spin doctors to her house, the fancy appointment, the multiple contracts, Glinny having her story cancelled. Bill, very likely — Helen could see she'd made the wrong assumption — had come with a warning, not on their behalf, but hers.

Helen looked upstream, to the two spots of light on Hooper's cottage on the other side of the river. *Cast downstream*, her father would direct them in the boat, *so the fish can't see what's coming at them*. That had been Helen, she'd not been able to see what was coming at her for watching what had already passed. Well, if someone was trying to intimidate her, they were granting her permission. If they were threatened it was because she had some kind of power to be threatening to them. And that power was not going to be wasted.

Her brother had remade himself. There was more to her life than what had happened to her and the fallout from that. The future could be determined, and influenced. Helen discovered the same sort of hope, simple as tomorrow, that she'd buried with Garrett. She was in the river; naked, and never moreso.

THURSDAY

BEFORE GETTING ON the phone in the morning, Helen ate breakfast with Piché. She'd sliced more peaches and made oats so Piché could stay in bed.

She perched beside Piché, noticing how she held her spoon in her fist, rather than her usual way. Piché's hand was unsteady.

Maybe, she said, and paused, without meeting Helen's eye. She took another bite of oats, chewing slowly, staring into the bowl. She seemed to swallow with difficulty.

Maybe my house, Piché shrugged.

Helen lowered her bowl to rest in her lap.

You like to live with me? In my house? What you do when they move this house?

Helen shook her head. I don't know, she said.

Piché leaned back against the pillow, closing her eyes. Maybe you live somewhere, she said. She waved a hand in the air, gesturing over there, then took Helen's hand. Not here.

Maybe, Helen said.

Maybe, Piché echoed. She was considering that answer, or asking Helen to consider it.

Marcel, he come, Piché said. Marcel come see me and we find what we do. What I do.

Helen recognized what she was telling her and was embarrassed she didn't feel she could offer more, though she was sure Piché wasn't asking it of her. Quite the opposite. But how to divorce herself from Piché's life and not feel responsible?

When the dishes were done, she made three phone calls. She was light, dialling the numbers, moving through the house on the cordless. She began with Marcel, who, in short order, said he had talked to the boys and he was coming. Either he was uncomfortable or upset, because he cleared his throat a number of times, loudly, into the phone.

The next call was to Markou, who ran the cemetery, to ask about a different gravesite for her mother. It was early, just before eight, but he answered the phone.

Helen asked him to confirm the graveyard in her mother's hometown was waterfront.

Yup, he said. You can move her there, sure, but you need permission from the district.

How hard is that?

Should be easy, if you get the Power Authority to ask. Nobody says no to them, he said bitterly.

Helen remembered his sign at the back of the school, *WITH WHOSE POWER*. She thanked him, and he said, sincerely, in his deep voice, It's good you honour your mother's wishes. They don't all do that. My pleasure. You take care now.

When she clicked the phone off, she held a finger to the button.

The last call was to her brother. When he didn't answer and the machine kicked in — a cheery message — she panicked and hung up the receiver.

Immediately, she regretted it. Could she phone back? Was he home and ignoring her call? Regardless, if she phoned again and he had call display, well, he'd know she was eager to talk to him. He didn't answer the second call and again she hung up. She sat by the phone for a half hour, doing little else than working out the puzzle of what to do, and phoned a third time, without an answer.

That decided it. She packed herself in the car and drove to the lodge. She told Norm at the front desk that she was getting a head start on the books, because things would be getting so busy at home by month-end. She went into the back room, took out the previous week's receipts, sat at the small counter there for no more than three minutes, rifling through them until she found the one she was looking for, and photocopied it. She waved bye to Norm who was busy checking in a client, drove back to the house, and dialled.

Colin picked up immediately.

I'd like to meet you, she said. She could hear him wondering who it was. Before he could ask, she added, I phoned Robbie, but he didn't answer.

Helen.

Can we meet? I mean all of us? Today. I'll drive down today. I can't get Robbie on the phone. I thought maybe he was there. With you.

She suspected she sounded harsh. She was clipped. Not so much out of anger, but because she didn't want to get into a conversation on the phone and be forced to say her piece there. She didn't want to hear the answers to her questions over the phone. She wanted to read his face. Being short was the easiest way to avoid any extra talk.

He's not here, no.

Can you make it today?

Any time. I'm not sure... I mean, I don't know if I can get a hold of Rob though. I can try... I'm not sure what his plans are for the day. When are you thinking?

I can be there by three, with good traffic.

We'll meet you at the coffee shop on the corner of Parker and Fourteenth. It's the only one there. Parker is the second exit off the highway. Just head north and you can't miss it; the cross streets are numbers. Drive to Fourteenth.

Okay.

And I'll get Rob, so you don't have to. He doesn't have a cell, so I'll have to try to find him. I don't know what he's doing today.

But you'll come, regardless? You won't leave me.

I can give you my cell, but I'll be there.

Thank you, she said, and paused. Well ... I look forward to meeting you.

I can say the same.

Okay then. Goodbye, she said, and set the receiver in the cradle before he could say any more.

ROBERT WOKE TO the sound of a clink from around the corner, in the kitchen. Dishes bumping together. His throat was prickly with dryness. Rolling over into a pillow, he realized he was on top of the covers and only for a second did he wonder why. The events from the day before flashed an answer. His knees pulled up to his chest and he pushed his face further into the pillow. He moved his tongue in his mouth, to get the saliva running, so he could swallow. The spit accumulated. Bit by bit his tongue spread the liquid around and his mouth smoothed itself out in swatches. He was in bed. It was daytime. He hadn't any sense what hour it was.

A door to a kitchen cupboard closed. Robert wondered how long he could lie in bed. Could he stay here long enough to outlast Colin? Would he come in to check on him? The bedroom door was open. Colin must know Robert was here. He wouldn't leave without coming to take a peek. What if Robert closed the door, then? What if he locked it and refused to open the door? He imagined dropping out the window, tumbling out. It was dramatic, to avoid facing Colin. To avoid the day, and the support group, and the therapy, and himself. He didn't want to go through the tedious motions. The shame and the obviousness of having fallen, and after so long being clean. Fucking shit, he thought. He was enraged to think that he'd gone home with such strength and had been undone, after so long, so easily.

Go home, he bellowed.

You're up, Colin said from the next room.

I said go away! he screamed.

Colin's footsteps paused a second, then continued to the doorway. He said, matter-of-fact and still warm, I thought you might want some company.

Robert didn't answer. He felt the bed sink next to him and a hand on his ankle.

He was terrifically ashamed of himself. He wanted to disappear, evaporate. Throw himself out the window.

I can't, he sobbed into the pillow. I can't.

Can't what, Rob?

I don't want you to see me, he blubbered.

Well, I do. And you're kinda naked.

He rubbed a hand along Robert's thigh and let it rest there. Robert sobbed for the relief of that hand, for being at home in bed, with someone there. Colin swung himself around and lay down next to him. He scooped his arm across his chest and pulled Robert into him.

I got you, he said, quietly. I got you, Rob. You're right here, ya? You're here. You're right here and I got you.

When Robert slowed, and his breathing softened, Colin squeezed him even harder and said into his hair, I made a sandwich.

Robert's stomach was acid at the thought of it. You have your shoes on my bed, he said.

Let's eat it. I'm hungry.

He stood up gingerly, taking Robert's hand and pulling him off the bed. Once Robert had slipped on pyjama bottoms, Colin walked them to the kitchen. There was a sandwich cut in half on a plate on the table, with a pickle beside it. A butter knife rested against the lip.

You eat half. I can make us another if we want more.

Robert sat down without saying a word. Colin picked up a side of the sandwich and handed it to him. Robert brought the bread to his mouth and took a bite, then dropped his hand in his lap. They ate in silence. Robert rested the sandwich hand on his leg each time while he chewed. His arm felt heavy, his whole body dead weight.

He cried again, halfway through eating, and then stopped, and stuffed the rest of the food into his mouth, chewing slowly, because it was more than he'd bargained for. Colin picked up the knife and cut the pickle in half and offered one to him.

No thanks, he said. I got enough sour pickle yesterday.

Colin belted out a laugh. I bet you did. He took a bite, rubbed his cheek. So ... what now? Do you have a plan?

I go to a meeting.

Colin gave a nod. You go to a meeting.

See my therapist once a week for a while. Double up.

Yes.

And ...? Robert asked, looking to Colin.

Weigh your behaviour with your values.

Measure. Measure my behaviour against my values. He's a good therapist. You think that's enough? I can't believe I'm in this place again.

You aren't, Rob. You aren't in it again. You've never been here. You've never gone six years clean and slipped.

I know.

This is a different place. It's important to recognize that. Your 'six years clean' is not undone because of this. That exists. You did that. And this, this is part of the history of that success. We make mistakes. They don't undo our successes.

What then?

What what?

What *do* they do then?

Colin looked at the bite of sandwich in his hand. They remind us where we don't want to be. That's part of the line of measure, isn't it? Here, not here.

Why aren't you a lawyer?

Colin laughed again, which made Robert feel lighter in his bones. He could be funny, so the world was not spoiled. Some things were right. Maybe that was the route back, that all was not spoiled.

You're a good best friend, Robert said.

So are you, Colin replied. Give or take.

Robert smiled.

Colin swallowed a bite of his sandwich, then regarded it in his hand again. I'm not sure if you're ready for this ...

What?

It should be sobering: Your sister phoned me. She's coming to visit.

Fuck, Robert said. Maybe I tripped out for nothing. Or is she coming with a gun?

Not with a gun. I don't think with a gun.

So, that's a good thing.

Yes, Colin said from the side of his mouth, chewing his last bite of sandwich.

When?

That's the weird thing, he said, picking up Rob's plate. He stacked it with his own. Today.

Today?

She's en route. Be here in a few hours. Do you want to go?

Yes, I guess.

You don't have to, he said. He carried the plates to the sink and turned on the hot water tap, to wash them.

Of course I do.

No, you don't, he said, soaping a rag. She invited us both.

How did she get your number?

So there's no reason I can't go alone. That can be enough for now.

I don't know. I should go.

That's another should.

I want to go.

Okay, if you do. But you don't have to. You don't have to do this now. Self-care, right? What do you need right now?

Sleep. A babysitter.

Colin put a plate in the dish rack. Let's phone Ingrid. She can come over and you can sleep through her movie choices.

I only fell asleep once.

The hotel. She got my number from the hotel, I imagine.

Okay, Robert said, and walked into the living room.

Are you going to phone Ingrid?

Robert paused, mid-step, then sat on his overstuffed chair. If Colin went, he could do the telling, and Robert could let someone else do the hard work. Maybe it was cheating, but why not have someone look out for him? If Colin didn't want him there, he'd not fuck this up for him again.

Yes, he said, and picked up the handset for the phone. I'm dialling Ingrid.

THE DRIVE WAS too long. She couldn't look at her hands on the steering wheel without being reminded of her drive home from the dam. Maybe it was the echo the nerves in her belly made, this time to that.

Despite her best efforts, she was hesitant on the roads once she got to the capital. She didn't like the speed of traffic on the four-lane highway, especially how people changed lanes so quickly, squeezing between cars without more than a couple of feet between their bumpers. Every time she tried to create a safe distance between herself and the vehicle ahead, someone pulled into that space and stayed. She was trying to calculate how little room she could leave that was reasonable, but unless she was less than a car's length away, someone inevitably squeezed in front of her. Her face in the rear-view mirror when she parked was pale and pulled tight. She looked as though she'd been crying, but she hadn't.

She'd put on a pink skirt and a slim white cotton top that was her attempt to appear big city, but she doubted the outfit now that she was here. When she reached Colin sitting in one of the two back booths of the coffee shop, she was self-conscious of the slightly frayed hem on her skirt. She'd clipped loose threads before she'd left but had the prickly feeling more were showing.

Colin was in a green polo shirt, good with his sandy hair. He was handsome; Garrett would have thought so too.

She stood at the edge of the table and offered to buy him a tea, trying to be the host, but he'd already ordered a pot. At the counter, she ordered her own, and found herself looking to the door each time it opened, hoping Robbie would be stepping through it. Clearly it was obvious, for when she'd returned with both their teapots — the girl at the counter had given her Colin's pot too — Colin told her that Robbie wouldn't be coming.

It's not that he didn't want to, he said. He just couldn't get away. I didn't know his plans for the day.

Helen wrinkled her brow. She could tell by his tone that he was trying to hide a thin excuse.

Colin added, I know you wanted to talk to both of us, but I think for all our sake it's better you and I do this on our own.

She could feel herself hesitating. She had thought she'd present Robbie the contracts, and the settlement for their father's estate, before the appointment tomorrow, to have it be done with. She would then tell Robbie of the plans to move their mother, and all would be well. But without Robbie here, what then?

I don't know how much you know, she said, hoping, in a kind of panic, that she could get out of the meeting. She wasn't sure she could face this man without her brother.

Colin looked at her blankly, unclear what she meant. She added, About Garrett, I mean.

He gave the faintest smile, which might have seemed cruel except for the paleness of him, too. He said in a low tone, Everything, yes.

And then, the moment, somehow, fit, because if she was here with Garrett's lover, what was there to do but listen?

I'd like to hear it, she said.

He picked up one of the white china teapots and poured tea into his cup, set the small pot down and looked up, steady. We were lovers. At camp. Nobody there knew it. Well, maybe.

For eight months. And after he was killed, and I came home, I found your brother. So I know everything.

Helen felt the air around her go heavy, for one black second the world stopped moving, the dust still in the air — and then her heart whumped lower in her chest and the blood ran hot in her limbs, up her neck, humming through her ears.

She was about to speak, the words about to pour out of her gut, when Colin raised his finger to her, and spoke slowly. You take a breath. And sit on that a minute. On what has happened to me. What I lost. I'm not done.

A young woman opened the door to the café and a white-blond toddler waddled in ahead of her, a boy, in red runners and a polka-dot one-piece unbuttoned down the front. Colin turned his head to the door and Helen saw a few hairs above his jawline that he'd missed shaving. As he turned to address her again, she stared at those hairs.

I saw them pick up the pieces of my lover blown apart by a landmine, all five of them worth picking up, with a shovel, so he could be buried for the family who never returned my calls. I have earned this.

He swallowed.

I have earned the right to his memory. And if you give me one bad word, you — he paused, and lowered his finger.

Helen looked him in the eye again.

One bad word and I'll tell you things you'll wish you'd never heard — he coughed — I'm sorry if that's harsh. I'm sorry. I'm angry. I've been angry. I think I came here to forgive you.

Me? Helen cried, incredulous.

If it weren't for you — he paused again, swallowing hard, to contain himself — he'd never have left. If he'd not been so shamed by what he'd been doing ... Colin stopped dead, and his face softened, briefly, a split second. There's more than you in this room with mixed feelings. More than you who lost someone precious.

His hands smoothed the cloth along the edge of the table-top. I want to like you, Helen. I may even find I love you for reasons you would rather not know. He looked to his cup for a second, and as his eyes came back onto her, there were pools threatening to spill over.

We will be fine through this, he said hoarsened, over time ... but no harsh words. No looks. No eye-rolling, side-stepping, uncomfortable, judgmental looks. Please. He meant too much to me to tolerate contempt. We will not talk of him, his voice softened, with contempt.

Helen hadn't the means to answer. Images of Garrett, the stacked-up memories she had of him — pressed into him on the bottom of the filthy fishing boat, driving his car up her driveway, on the living room couch, his warm hand on her leg, the hair on his knuckles, leaning on his knees into the car looking under the seat for a quarter for the parking metre — each said the same thing. *Not Garrett.*

That Garrett could be two people. That he could be this other person too. There was Garrett and this other Garrett, same person.

I'm a little more than you bargained for, I bet. But I'll tell you everything, if you're asking. I'll tell you more than Rob would. I have nothing to hide.

Helen nodded. Colin poured her tea for her, and pushed her

cup towards her. She looked at it, and picked it up, aware that the cup was hot in her hands. She sipped, lightly, and noticed her hands trembling. She barely managed to set the cup down without upsetting it.

Rob would hold back for fear of hurting you. More. He'd be willing to have you hate him a little more than he deserves, than to soil too much Garrett's memory. I'd rather not speak ill of the dead, because Garrett didn't have the opportunity to make it right, but Rob ... Rob didn't do anything wrong.

No?

He just feels like he did. You can thank your parents for that.

They were lovers, Helen said, and could barely get the word out.

Rob got there first, Colin said flatly. Although that isn't quite the way to put it, either, because Garrett refused to speak about what they were doing. When Rob came home from a night at the gas station — I think this was only about two months or so after their first shag — he found you and Garrett wrapped up on the dock.

A cold stone pounded on Helen's chest. That was our first kiss.

Rob threw up in the bathroom for an hour, Colin said, then paused to let it sink in with Helen that she should note Robbie's reaction, because it meant something.

Helen nodded, to say it was clear.

So he stopped their trips to the hay fields, and the months passed, and the two of you were an item. Rob got his licence so he could drive the three hours to the gay bars on weekends.

A few weeks before he ran away, he was in a club, and there was Garrett, at the bar, with another man.

Another man?

When he confronted him, Garrett said, *It's not what you think*. Which didn't mean he wasn't cheating on you, but only that he didn't think there was anything wrong with it. In some confused logic, he explained to Rob it wasn't cheating because he wasn't in a relationship with another woman. Somehow, by some mental trick, Garrett thought he could have both, a male lover and a girlfriend, because one of each meant he wasn't unfaithful with either. And because it wasn't cheating, he didn't have to tell you.

At the door, the blond toddler was pressing his face against the glass, leaving slobber marks. His mother flipped pages in a magazine. He smushed his face, then rolled his head along the glass to see if she was looking, then again pressed his face, making open-mouthed *ah* sounds into the glass.

Rob told Garrett to break it off with you, or he'd have to tell you what he'd seen.

Fuck, Helen said. She picked up her teacup and had to bend over to drink, holding it in both hands. I just don't understand this to be the same Garrett. How is this the same Garrett?

Colin considered an answer. To give him some credit, or some peace, he said, I don't believe he was malicious, or selfish, exactly. His reasoning ... wasn't convenience; it was blind. He'd told me he'd tried his best to be everything he wanted and everything everyone else wanted him to be, too. It was the only way he knew to get everything he wanted. He was the politician's son: he couldn't accomplish all those things at once without the contradictions, so, being blind to them, they remained possible.

Which is pretty ugly, he said, with a shrug. Rob talked until he was blue in the face and reason didn't do any good, so Rob threatened him. He gave him two weeks — to muster the courage, and some sense — to do it. He'd agreed to just two weeks. And then Garrett tried to renegotiate. When Rob refused, Garrett was firm: Rob could tell you if he wanted to, but Garrett wouldn't. Rob could betray him, but he wouldn't betray you, he said.

He was desperate, I think, for a solution that meant he wouldn't have to choose. The night Rob was kicked out came because Garrett still hadn't told you, so Rob told your mother most of the story. He was hoping for advice. An ally. I understand that she was a wreck and told your dad.

Helen released a groan. That her brother had done this to not have her waiting for a man who wasn't coming back to her, or not coming back as the man she'd imagined him to be, and her parents had said nothing, and she'd waited regardless.

This is the great part: your dad suggested he take the job overseas. The politician's son. Good PR for the rebuild. It's ironic I have your father to thank for meeting him.

Colin cleared his throat.

I flew home, he said, on the flight with his body, and then never saw him again. His parents refused my phone calls. I didn't know anyone else to contact. I didn't dare go to the funeral, which I regret. I still don't know where he's buried.

Colin coughed, and took a sip of his tea. Helen thought maybe she should speak, speak now, but she didn't. She felt dissociated, clicked off. She wanted Colin to be done first, she wanted him to say his bit and have it be done before she turned herself back on.

A few months passed, and driving to work one morning, I remembered Rob's name, out of the blue. He was in the capital. He lived twenty blocks away.

Your brother might be shy with you, timid, or resistant, because he'd rather be a fake than angry. Angry being the fastest way to lonely. I think I've been such an important friend to Rob these years because I'm the closest thing to his past and also not his past. I've seen him do just about everything to avoid being that lonely. And he's come through the parties and the drugs and the rest of it and still ... I've never seen him so vulnerable as I did last week.

The toddler, like a jack-in-the-box, bounced up at their table, gripping the edges. His whisps of hair arced upwards into little points.

Jody, get over here, his mother said. Come here, baby.

Jody turned to her, then turned back, bit the table with his small teeth, and ran away, to his mother, grabbing onto her leg. Neither Colin nor Helen had addressed him, though Colin had grinned when he'd bit the table, and Helen had felt a pang of hatred for him, and for the boy and his mother.

I liked him less, he said, making Helen think he'd read her. Then he continued, and she understood him. Seeing him last weekend, but maybe it was a relief, too, to see him there, making so many mistakes. It made him make more sense. I'll tell you this: I would have come much sooner, a decade ago, but he wouldn't allow it. He was too ashamed, too fearful, I think, of losing what he had, which really are only memories of family, and memories based on deceit. I think he realizes that. I think he came to reclaim his family, so now that he's found you, he's loathe to see himself rejected. I'm not sure it was the better choice, though. I might regret having finally convinced him to let me meet you.

Colin picked up his teacup, and sipped, and set it down. He looked at Helen and shrugged, uncertain of himself after having said so much. He was waiting, she thought, for her to say something comforting. To reassure him.

I'm glad you did, she said. You haven't done anything wrong.

She knew immediately, as the words were coming out, that she wasn't saying it correctly. She sounded patronizing, but couldn't think how better to say what she was feeling. She was trying to forgive, to show she wasn't cold to him, that she wasn't resentful, and suspected, in her gut, that she was, or she wouldn't have thought it.

Colin bristled just slightly, a calm wave of intense patience spread over his face. No, I haven't, he said. He bent down to reach an arm into his bag, and continued, I'd come to see you to put something to rest, Helen. I'd come to give you this.

He produced a letter, worn and dirty on the edges, sealed, addressed to *Helen* in a familiar script she recognized but couldn't immediately identify. There was no postage, nor a last name. Just *Helen*, which made her doubt it was for her.

What is this?

It's an apology, I suspect. Or an explanation.

For who?

For you, of course. It is addressed to you. Fifteen years late, but my conscience is clean. I'd read it somewhere else, I think.

Puzzled, Helen looked him in the face for an answer. What do you have to be sorry for? she asked.

His face softened. It's not from me, Helen. It's from Garrett.

She was unstoppered, every bit of energy flushed out of her system. The letter dropped onto the table and she leaned forward in her seat, hands and arms shaking. She was ghost-cold.

Woah, honey. Colin was beside her, his warm hand on her back. Let's get you some water. Lean against the wall there.

At the sideboard, Colin poured her some water. He returned with a cup and made her drink it. She was shivering. The water was room temperature. She wanted to be outside, in the sunshine, in the fresh air, but was worried she hadn't the legs for it.

Colin sat back down, and started to talk, but Helen wanted him to shut up. She'd heard enough. Wouldn't he just shut up for now.

I was the terrified one. It was a crazy place to work. I wrote letters out of some superstition. I would fold them up and tuck them into his old envelopes from home. It was a great system. We could say the things we wanted, we could keep them in our pockets, here — and he touched his breast — and no one would be the wiser. Except I didn't die. And he did. So I stole them from his locker. You would think that might have been the hardest day of my life. But it wasn't. You move forward or you die. It was reading them. It was coming home after the bloody business was over and being stupid enough to open a letter and read it. I had six months on some very nice drugs to come to grips with myself.

Helen glanced at the letter on the table and Colin added, That gem was amongst the others. It's not dated. I don't know when he wrote it, or if he'd even intended to mail it to you. But by my mind, it's yours.

She picked up the envelope, turned it over, and was tempted to smell it. Its paper felt gritty on her fingers. She wanted to read it immediately, her chest sore with a dull stab, but Colin was watching her. She imagined tearing it up in front of him. Or ripping it in halves quietly, in the bathroom, and leaving it there. Though she'd come back for it and what would that look like, especially if he saw her. She could throw it at him, and storm out the door, but thought then maybe he'd read it. What to do with it? A letter. She felt ridiculous holding it. She would take it with her. She could put it in her purse and take it with her and decide later what to do.

Helen folded it in half, unzipped her purse, and slid it in next to the contracts. She turned to Colin and thanked him. He nodded. She could tell by the look around his eyes that he was tired by this, and it loosened her, comforted her, to think this wasn't easy for him either.

He asked her what she was going to do next and she told him she didn't know.

This can be a clean slate, can't it?

Although she knew he was talking about Robbie, or she assumed so, the idea struck Helen that he was right. Half right. She could start over, though that didn't mean wiping the past away. She couldn't erase what had happened, but if it was what had brought her here — and it was — then it was a tool. And if it was a tool, she wanted to use it.

FRIDAY

THE POWER AUTHORITY temporary branch office was in the city, in the stone post office that had sat empty for a decade. There had been much celebration when the office opened, a clapping of hands that they had revitalized a downtown building with such great historic significance. Situated at the corner of what was once the heart of downtown, the building's clock tower had always been a centrepiece, so with the clock face restored and the graffiti removed, the block looked remade. When Helen arrived at reception, she was asked to wait in the long narrow lobby for someone to collect her. The first floor entrance was a large open space divided behind the counter with cubicles made of red maple and glass. One could see straight to the back wall if you centred yourself to look through the glass-top of the first cubicle.

Not five minutes passed before a woman clicked around the corner in black leather pumps. She was patting the upper button on the collar of her blouse. Her skin was pale, with freckles on her hand.

I thought I'd lost a button for a second, she said, laughing. I'm sorry. Helen Massey? She held out her hand. I'm Sylvie. I'll take you upstairs.

As they returned to the entrance and ascended the grey marble stairs — the lower steps had a dip in their centres from wear — Helen tried to steady herself by asking how her day was.

Oh, it's a tight push, Sylvie said, waving a hand, if we're to open on schedule. Too much overtime. But there's no delay allowed if we're trying to get royalty to come, right?

At the second floor, the staircase led directly onto a hallway with three corridors off to the left. The ceiling was much lower. The walls were white, lined with photographs blown up from archives, detailing various stages of settlement in the area. Homes having been built, a new water tower from the turn of the last century that Helen had never seen, fishermen in knee-high boots holding their catches, and what must have been the opening of the lodge, for it was decorated in flowers across its entrance and a full staff of twenty posed together in uniforms. They turned down the first hallway and Helen was surprised to see that each corridor was cut in half, smartly, by another hall, so that the offices were in blocks of four, easier to get to than walking the whole way to the front.

They passed the nameplate for Sandy Peterson, whose door was closed, and entered the last, wider corridor at the back of the building. There were four doors there, not maple like the others, but frosted glass. A long leather bench sat in the middle of the hall, on the right. Sylvie gestured to the bench and invited Helen to sit. She asked if Helen wanted coffee or water.

When Helen declined, Sophie excused herself, saying, Good luck, then walked further up the hall and turned the corner. Within seconds, her shoes stopped clicking and Helen knew she was in a nearby cubicle, which she found comforting.

Moments later, the first of the doors opened and Cruikshank stepped out, with his hand extended before he'd even passed through the door. He was a large man — taller than he'd seemed behind the table at the town meeting — in a handsome grey suit. Helen wasn't sure she could go through with it. How could she convince this man of anything?

Dan Cruikshank, he said, shaking her hand. He invited her into his office, thanking her for coming.

The first room beyond the doors was a reception area. Dan introduced her to Mary-Lynn and then brought her through into the adjoining room. It was large, spare, and tidy, with a few more of the same type of photos on the wall, black-and-whites of houses and landscapes Helen couldn't quite recognize but found familiar. Two chairs faced the desk. Dan stood next to the farthest one, and gestured for Helen to sit with him there. His back was to a good-sized window, looking out onto the top of the Chinese food restaurant next door. The office had nice light, but a horrible view.

Once seated, he introduced himself as the manager of financial operations for the Power Authority. There was a nameplate on his desk, in front of them, saying so.

There were nerves in her belly, but behind that, riding them, was a rush, because Cruikshank was the man who would know something. He could do things.

He asked if he could get her anything and when she declined, he said, Then let's begin with the obvious place. Let's look at our proposal because I really want to address some issues there, he said. He reached behind him to collect his own copy, but Helen was already pulling out the agreement from her purse.

As she flipped to the last page of the most recent contract, searching for the red-inked numbers, she noted Cruikshank's name at the bottom, which she hadn't seen before.

That's you there, she remarked, surprised.

It is my name, correct, he said matter-of-factly. Mine is one of the names stamped on the cheques too. One of three. The last of three, he chuckled. Not the first.

He flipped open his copy of the contract and pulled a pen from atop the desk, clicking it. Good to get that out, yes. Just so you know who you're talking to, he said. Some context. Let's say there are a lot of mountains I can move to help you be satisfied with your relocation.

Helen hadn't time to think before he'd launched into much of the same line of thought as Rodney and Brian regarding proposed suggestions for her, things she might like, such as having them hire a professional to move her garden for her, to save her the work. Unlike Rodney, he sounded genuine, and earnest, which made Helen think he must be good at his job. His offers, though, sounded researched, which unnerved her. He knew she had a garden, and that it mattered to her. Had the two men consulted back with him? Or could he have been talking to Bill? Or someone who knew Bill? The Power Authority had assessed the property — they knew things — but how much did he guess what her big concerns were, and how much did he have investigated?

She was unsettled. And encouraged. She chose not to discuss her mother's grave until she had the big thing settled, in case he would feel he'd done enough. Helen smoothed a hand along her skirt and sat up straighter, subtly, her jaw raised.

Helen began haltingly. I noticed your offer. For the house.

Cruikshank flipped the contract closed. Now that's exactly why we've asked you to come in because — and I'm embarrassed to admit this — we have our property assessments reviewed by a nonpartisan third party, and you can imagine how much work that is. Anyhow, long and short, they found we'd made an error and your property is worth more than we'd assessed.

You offered me more on the last contract, she said carefully.

We did. And that was part of our review. But it's come to my desk, which is why you're here, he said, gesturing with his pen to where she was sitting. I want to apologize for the mix-up and clear the slate. Here is the new assessment — he picked up a folded piece of copier paper and handed it to her. I have contracts for this figure drawn up ready to go.

As Helen opened it, he rose and stepped around his desk to sit down at the chair, giving her time to review the number.

You don't have to sign anything you don't want to today. Think about it. I can send you home with the paperwork and you can let it sit for a few days.

The total was sixty thousand more than the previous offer. Helen hadn't expected more money, and, given the circumstances, resented the gesture. She didn't want the man's death to mean more money for her, but how exactly do you negotiate less? Was it her place to accept less, if she was also splitting the settlement with her brother? If she'd given Robbie the papers the day before, he might have been here to help her. He might have given her permission to take less.

She folded the paper in half again and tucked it into her purse, next to Garrett's letter, unopened.

Why offer this now? she asked calmly, then swallowed. Is it the accident?

She waited a moment for that question to sink in, but not long enough to let him speak. She felt her heartbeat in her temples and fingertips.

You want me to shut up about the man who fell from the dam.

Cruikshank adjusted himself in his seat, leaning back a little. He appeared calm. He was surprisingly steady in his answer.

You were witness to an accident?

Isn't that why you've offered me more money?

You're here, he said, giving his pen a slow twirl, because you haven't negotiated your contracts, and I'd like to help you do that so we can both move forward.

I thought I was here — she had to swallow again — because Glinny Ouderkirk asked questions about the man I saw fall to his death on the job site.

And why were you on-site at the time?

I wasn't on-site. I had binoculars. You can't tell me I didn't see what I saw.

Cruikshank set his pen across the contract.

When men die on a construction site, everyone feels it. It is a tragedy. There is nothing worse.

Then why wasn't there some mention in the paper? A memorial. Did he get a memorial? You should give him one, she blurted out.

Forgive me for being blunt, Miss Massey, he said, leaning his elbows on the desk, but if there's an accident — in the case of an accident — what good would that do? Say someone does fall. Say we report it in the papers. Then what? What do you think they would have us do? Stop construction? Tell our accountants we'll be another few hundred thousand over budget?

Yes, she said.

And where do you think that money is coming from? It's your money. And my money. It's the money of those men too.

Some things are worth more than money, she said, though the phrase felt too slight to bear the importance of what she meant.

Nobody wants a safe site more than me — he leaned back in his chair — because in the end my colleagues and I are the ones who have to answer the hard questions and I don't like the hard questions, because I'm lazy. We run a tight ship because we don't want the hard stuff.

When Helen didn't respond, didn't pick up on whatever cue that was, he continued. I don't want to make more work for myself. A newspaper article isn't going to make it any better for anyone: not for you, not for me, and not for the poor guy up there either.

Up there. Helen recognized the detail, an indirect admission.

Publishing a news report is only going to slow the work down, waste money, which will not be helping the greater good. And not serving anyone's memory. Those men are workers, they're proud men — coming in over budget isn't something anyone working on that dam wants, because we have pride in what we do. And that means doing the job right.

Helen looked him in the eye. She wanted to say that what they did on that job site wasn't part of doing the job right. Money wasn't a good enough answer. Neither was pride, but what else was there? What else mattered to him? She could have known that coming in here. Her plan now seemed ridiculous because there was no convincing someone the importance of a man falling to his death, let alone the insult of being buried where he fell. If Cruikshank could see it, he would have already.

Helen nodded her head.

Misinterpreting the gesture, Cruikshank nodded back at her, once, to acknowledge they had an understanding.

Now, he said, picking up his pen, we have an offer here to negotiate. It's a generous offer. Far more than what your house is insured for, at any rate, if there were an accident. More than its assessment. So I'm asking, is there something more we can do for you?

He held his pen above the paper, waiting to write. Helen sat a moment. Swallowed.

Could I have some water?

Certainly, he said, standing. He stepped a foot out of the office, briefly, and Helen heard him say, Do we have a bottle of water in the fridge for Miss Massey?

As he sat, Helen wished she had more at her disposal. She had failed, because what had she given him? A weak argument. Not even an argument. Words meant little to his numbers or none of this would be happening.

What else do I have, she thought. And in her head she saw the letter in her purse. And her mother's grave. And her brain made a sort of click, like double doors opening. She couldn't prove she'd seen what she'd seen, the men on the dam weren't talking to Dave, and there was no way to exhume the corpse from the dam. Not now. But she had her own body, didn't she? She had something of value in that. Something to work with.

Mary-Lynn entered with a bottle of water. Helen thanked her, taking the plastic container, already slick with condensation, in her hands. She twisted the neck and took a sip. The water was ice cold down her throat. Slick. She was a million times better. Her mind was clear. If numbers beat words, maybe actions, she thought, could beat numbers. Something had to be more important than numbers.

I would like, she said calmly, twisting the lid on the bottle, for you to move my mother.

Where is she now? he asked. You want your homes placed beside each other?

She's in the cemetery. Two years now, Helen said. He hadn't done as much research as she'd thought. It pleased Helen that he'd been caught in a delicate mistake.

I'm sorry. My condolences, he said. He held the pen between his hands. That whole cemetery is being moved to Gardenview. You should have received papers to that effect. I'm sorry if you didn't. I can look into that for you. That's easily done.

I have those papers. I haven't signed them either. I want her moved to her hometown.

That might be tricky, but I'm sure we can make this work, he said, and jotted notes on a pad of paper.

I'm not sure you can, Helen said flatly.

Cruikshank looked up from writing, quizzical.

I'm not going to sign these today, she said.

You don't have to.

I know that. You write that in, you sign it, and give it to me, and I'll think about it.

You do realize we're offering far more than your insurance?

You realize that it is my house. My land.

Well, yes ... though that's just a matter of time, isn't it, he said. He'd sounded calm, kind even, though Helen was sure the point was meant to be sharp.

Shall we continue? he asked.

Helen gave him the necessary details. At the same time, her mind was racing with a new plan. She was lining up how to approach Markou to get him onside. And Dave. Dave would help. She would invite Robbie, and he'd come, and together they would bury their parents.

ROBERT DIDN'T WAKE till eleven, with the sun hot on his face. He was covered in sweat, and although he'd slept a long time, his body still felt tired. Drained, like when he hadn't eaten well the first few months he'd been couch-surfing, or bed-surfing, and had ended up anaemic. Despite being tired, or perhaps because of it, he felt calm. Amazingly, surprisingly still. He felt such clarity; hot with conviction.

He took the receiver to the washroom while he peed so he could phone Colin immediately. They'd agreed he was to check in regularly for the next few days, while Robert got himself together. He'd booked an emergency appointment with his therapist and intended to buy a cellphone, which seemed to satisfy Colin that he was taking recovery seriously — a cellphone was serious. They'd spent the better part of the night reviewing what Colin had said, or didn't say, and mostly how he'd said it. *I was a bit fierce*, Colin had told him, *but we settled down, both of us. I was kind.*

Robert had said *Good*, emphatically, but knew he was disappointed, for his sister had been cruel and there seemed some unfairness in that. Colin had told her everything, far more, Robert realized, than he'd have said. So maybe Colin had saved him, but from the perspective of the next day, Robert felt like, again, he'd chickened out. Helen had invited him, thinking she'd apologize, and they'd eventually speak, soon, and be well and good. Regardless, it was fifteen years later, and he'd be damned if he'd be guilty anymore. She knew now. He was innocent. And there was no shame in what had happened. It was unfortunate, but he had no cause for shame. Shame was on his parents. Shame was on Garrett, if it came to that. Shame was on her, because he had acted in good faith, as a teenager, and he wouldn't let that cycle of self-loathing run its course again.

The phone in his hand rang before he could dial and the call display said it was Peter Massey. It gave him a jolt to see his father's name. He raced to sit himself on the couch. He took a big breath on the third ring, and let it out, then answered, trying to sound natural.

Hello, Robbie, Helen said, her voice warm.

He felt his legs tremble against the lip of the couch as he cleared the blanket so he could sit on the cushion.

I missed you yesterday. And I have a crazy suggestion. I'd like to invite you back, she said, without hesitation. *Take two? Tonight, actually. I think you're still off work, right?*

I go back to work Saturday afternoon. I work dinner shift.

She didn't apologize, or offer any acknowledgment that she'd spoken with Colin. Knew the truth. But she was asking him back. He could return, invited.

I want you to meet me at the Tourangeau's intersection tonight, ten o'clock? Could you do that?

She wouldn't say why; she only said she had something to give him. Her voice was serious, laced with a sort of restrained urgency.

Robert was sure she sounded apologetic, but he wanted her to say it too. He tucked his feet below the wool blanket. Was he fooling himself to think he could do this? He'd only just got back.

I don't know, he said, and then thought he would trust her. Or test her. I've kind of been fucked up since I came back.

I wasn't much help, she said, pausing. But I'd like to be. I think you should come. We need this.

He was convinced, simply, by that *we*. By what it meant.

Okay, he said, leaning his head against the arm of the couch. Tourangeau's.

Wear something comfortable that you can throw out, she said, shoes and all. Something dark. Bring extra clothes.

Then, with a quick goodbye, and without ceremony, she hung up.

He laughed from the absurdity and, with relief for it, stared at the phone. He would need to talk to the post office to find his wallet. First he called Colin, and told him — tried to convince him — not to worry, but he was driving back.

DAVE DID HIS usual trick before Helen could knock and yelled from inside his place, Come in.

Helen had hung up the phone from talking to her brother and had driven straight to Dave's place. She found him on the couch, in cut-offs and a singlet, with reading glasses slid low on his nose, looking over bills and receipts spread out on the couch around him. He was surrounded by paperwork.

I need your help again, she said.

Something more dangerous? he asked, chuckling. He set his reading glasses on the coffee table.

Helen replied, Sort of. More illegal.

Perfect, Dave said. Nothing better to leave home for.

Helen couldn't tell if he was kidding or not. Can you come with me? she asked, and Dave, surprising her, agreed.

Gingerly, he rose from the couch, leaving the slips of paper where they were.

Can I ask where we're going, he said at the door, putting on his shoes. He was enthused with the adventure.

We'll need a few friends. I've asked Robbie. He's coming. She hesitated. And I need help from Markou.

Old Tony? Or Vince?

Vince, yes. I want him to know you're onside. You know him. I mean, it's illegal, but fair. You trust me?

Sure, Helen, he said.

Once outside, he didn't lock the door behind him. Helen shot him a look and he said, Nothing worth stealing. They can have it.

When they were on the old highway, nearly there, she could tell he was twitching to say something.

What, she said.

I'll do this, but, just out of curiosity, you know, you going to tell me what this is?

Eventually, she said, coyly, which made him laugh.

Markou's house, when they pulled into his lot next to the cemetery, was jacked up on stilts. It wasn't long before he would be moved. They found him in the office. Dave knocked and walked in and Helen followed.

Markou had made the living room into an office by closing off the archway into the rest of the house with another dead-bolted door. Being the caretaker, and before that the caretaker's son, he'd grown up in the bungalow. His father had retired and moved south, to Florida, for most of the year — he only came back a month or two in the summer — so Markou had the house, and the job, mostly to himself.

Hey Vinnie, Dave said, slapping his hand in Markou's palm. They did a complicated handshake and Dave slapped Markou on the shoulder.

Helen has something for us. Eh, Helen? She's going to make us gangsters.

Not quite, she said. Dave's enthusiasm both made her nervous and was a comfort, because he was relaxed. The men were friends.

Can we sit? she asked.

Oh yeah, sure, Markou said, clearly curious. Here.

He pulled out an extra folding chair in rather bad shape and rolled over a chair from in front of the computer. I don't get a lot of folks in here. I don't entertain, he said, laughing self-consciously. He was a large man sitting in his chair.

Helen began by telling them about the accident, then her meeting with Cruikshank, and, in fits and starts, explained her plan.

I'm not sure I get you, Dave said. He was scratching at the stains on his hands, which were black with grease, a streak of it right up to his elbow, likely from the lawn mower.

I know, I might be crazy, Helen said, but I think we should do this. She leaned forward in the folding chair and scratched at her ankle.

Sure, Dave said. But are you sure this is what you want, Helen?

Robbie is coming, and I figure we'd need four sets of hands. That's you and Markou and the two of us. I'd like you to do this, because I don't know anyone else who's crazy enough to say yes. Or at least shut up about it.

No no, I can do it. I will do it. If Markou is onside —

Markou shrugged. The meaning wasn't clear to Helen.

Can I ask why? Dave continued.

Markou piped in. You can go to the media. You can make a pretty stink, right? There's more available to you than the local paper.

I could, she said, unsure how to answer.

Dave cleaned dirt from under his nail, what he'd scratched off his arm, and let it drop to the floor. She'd be very public then. A lot of reporters, he said, nodding at her. Maybe not your thing.

Maybe not, she said, thankful that he was looking out for her. Mostly I want to do this for Robbie. And for me, I think.

Sure, Dave said. But I don't have to enjoy it.

I don't think that's in the cards, no.

And then what? Markou asked.

Then what? Helen repeated.

Then what? What do you do after that?

She shrugged. Markou looked her in the eye. His were deep green, picking up some colour, either from his shirt or from the grass outside, through the window. He waited for her to answer, and she didn't. She wouldn't offer more, so he set his hands on his knees, giving a sort of nod, acknowledging that she was entitled to her privacy.

Any last words? Dave asked.

She looked out the window, to the highway and the farmland across the road, full of stalks of corn.

It's personal, she said. I'm doing this for personal reasons. A personal message, if that makes sense.

I'm onside, Dave said, shrugging. I like illegal.

Okay, Markou said, but if we're going to do this, we have to do it soon. Let me look. Picking up a binder from his desk, he flipped pages till he found the one he wanted. Woah, he said. Before Monday.

Wow, Dave said.

Actually, I was thinking tonight. Robbie works tomorrow afternoon. And I don't want to chicken out.

Tonight, Dave chuckled. Well, I've got a date tomorrow, so why waste time, eh?

Helen looked to Markou. I invited Robbie; he comes tonight, she said firmly.

Good, Markou said and paused, for a moment. He gave a small nod to himself, saying, Good, I'm in.

LATE THAT AFTERNOON, packing another sweater and pants, slipping on his old runners and painting clothes, Robert was nervous. There was something ridiculous about going through the motions, and something unsettling in his gut that turned itself over and again every half hour during the long drive back to a place he didn't want to be. He was visiting under volatile circumstances because he was that desperate, he knew, for an apology. For some recognition. He wasn't entirely safe within himself. It felt like there was no guarantee — no reason other than his own dumb will — that he'd return with any conviction to stay clean. He was taking himself back to the place that had driven him to drugs, he now realized, more or less, twice.

He remembered his therapist's advice, and Colin's too: Robert got to choose if he used again. It was Robert who made the decision. Robert who was in charge. So often, for years, he'd wished for someone to tell him what to do, where to live, what job to take, what to eat for supper, who to date or who to dump. He wanted advice. He wanted someone else to be responsible. It was parenting, wasn't it, that he was wishing for? But, his parents were dead, and that was irreversible. Robert had to decide, then, what his future would be. The world isn't a just place. *The world is unjust* is how Gary had phrased it. Which meant terrible things happened whether Robert deserved them or not. His parents had made terrible decisions, but Robert had to decide what he did with those injustices. He could ride them, or he could climb off and walk a different path. He wasn't ready to see Helen again. But he didn't want to turn his back either. He didn't want to go home and feel sorry for himself. Regardless what she said to him, he'd be himself.

Although he was a good twenty minutes early, Helen was at the Tourangeau intersection when he arrived, standing beside her car in jogging pants and a light sweater zipped up to the neck. When he pulled in, she walked up beside the car door so that he had to roll down his window to talk to her. She didn't want him to step out.

Hi. Leave it running, she said calmly, leaning in and putting her hand on the doorframe. I want you to follow me. Her voice was soft, again apology in her tone, but also a directness. She put her hand on his shoulder.

Okay, he said, nodding.

She didn't pause, but stepped back and got into her car. She drove them up the highway, past Graffiti Rock, past the Johnsons' farm, and signalled, then braked too, at the turnoff for the cemetery. The lights from Helen's car lit someone at the gate, whom he didn't recognize at first, his stomach tight. The guy was opening the gate and then stepped back quickly behind the bushes inside the entrance as Helen drove in and turned right. Robert followed.

Dave Handy was holding the ironwork, motioning with his hand for Robert to drive forward, and then gesturing to park it to the right, beside Helen, whose car had stopped. He turned the ignition off, and the engine ticked. Helen was out of her car and saying something to Dave too low for him to hear. Robert stared out at the machinery before him, parked in a row at the end of the lot. Then he opened his door and stepped out into the night air.

The grounds were dark. He could smell the damp earth, a heavy smell. The moon was half-cycle, its light playing on the river. The air felt cold on his face and hands, though he doubted it was even cool. The sound of the car door slamming shut seemed a loud interruption in the air.

Helen was at her trunk, unlocking it.

To the left of them, the backhoes and trucks looked to be mechanical beasts, slumbering. They were giants, quieted in the night, heavy and waiting.

Helen lifted the trunk of the car. She pulled out a long rod and handed it to him. It was a shovel. A spade. The metal handle, when he gripped it, was much colder than the wood shaft.

Robert looked to her, but she had turned back to the trunk. She pulled out a second spade for herself, then handed him a set of gloves. He waited for her to say something, but she only put her hand on his shoulder again and then turned for the grounds.

They walked across the graves in the dark, without a flash-light, as Dave locked the gates behind him and ran to a truck across the road in the makeshift crew lot. Dave's engine rumbled and faded down the highway. Robert felt sweat in his armpits. They were passing the gravestones, in a dream. There was only the shushing of the river against the bank, the leaves of the trees across the road brushing against each other in the wind, and their shoes in the grass.

They reached her gravesite. Robert recognized the location. There was a shallow line dug into the grass, a rectangle, around his mother's grave. Helen put the spade to its nearest corner and dug in, lifting a pile of dirt and dropping it three feet away. She repeated the gesture, and then again. And again.

Robert opened his mouth but nothing came out. Through the glove, the spade was warming in his hand.

When he stepped towards her, she stopped. In the dark, her voice was clear. We're moving her to waterfront, she said. Ourselves. We'll bury them both. I want us to do this. Together.

He could recognize it was crazy, but he didn't speak. There was no way to do this thing and speak. He took Helen's hand, quickly, so she would know. She squeezed his. And they set to work.

Three hours. Four — he couldn't tell. They took breaks. They traded off as they got deeper and the space more cramped. Twice Helen stepped away and wretched into the grass. Occasionally a car passed on the highway. Towards the end, Helen would look up, then go back to work, until one slowed, they could hear the engine soften, and he turned to see it pull up in the crew parking lot across the street. His heart sank, but Helen put her hand on his arm; she was expecting someone.

They were three-quarters done, or had to be, by the depth of where they were standing. He was soaking wet, and he could see, as Helen stepped away to meet the men approaching them, his sister's sweater was glued to her back with sweat. He took up digging again, only stopping when she returned with the two men. It was Dave and a man Robert couldn't recognize in the dark. Dave extended a hand and helped pull Robert up. Both men were silent. The big guy took the shovel from Robert and lowered himself into the hole. Dave took Helen's shovel. She removed her gloves, gave them to him, and her hands dropped to her sides like dead weights. He took off his own gloves, and

in the cool air noticed then his hands were burning. His forearms ached. He leaned over the edge to offer his gloves to the
other guy, but he only raised his. He'd brought his own.

They made quick work of it. Helen offered him some water,
which must have come with the men. Her hair was matted with
sweat and dirt.

It seemed like no time before there was the thump of metal
on wood. His heart jumped. Everyone's did. They stopped. Helen
let out a strange guttural grunt, which sounded as much like a
belch as a groan. Less than half an hour after that the men had
shimmied straps beneath the box. The bigger man jumped
out, and headed off to the far end of the grounds. When he
returned with machinery, Robert realized this was Markou,
the caretaker's son. His nose and jaw were suddenly clear in
the moonlight.

He hadn't even wondered how they would get the coffin out
of its plot, he was so bent on the job at hand. They never would
have been able to do it alone. Helen and he watched as Markou
and Dave put the lift in place, the straps and pulley, until
Markou swung his arm wide, to have them step back. He bent
down and flipped out a handle at the back of the device and
began to crank it. Robert could hear the dirt falling from the
coffin. The wood lifting from the earth. He was panicked. Helen
gripped his hand as the casket rose. The crank's squeak was
fierce in the night air. It seemed to carry for miles, up and down
the river, until Dave threw a heavy blanket over it, which helped.

When the coffin was above ground, Markou secured the
device's latch, and Dave headed to the gates of the cemetery
again at a quick jog.

Markou wet his palms with some water and wiped his hands. He then produced a small bottle out of his shirt pocket and twisted the lid as he approached Robert. He slipped a finger in the jar and then swiped it under Robert's nose — the smell of Vicks filled his head — then Markou did the same to Helen.

Breathe from your nose, he said. We're going to do this quick-like, but you breathe from your nose, and you breathe away from the box when you can. Like this, and he turned his head to the side and inhaled quickly, letting the air out in a hushed whistle so they could hear him do it.

Helen took his hand again; his blisters burned where they met her palm. Their mother's casket was a large solid mass suspended two feet above her plot. It felt, somehow, quiet. The casket had a stillness about it. This must have been something of what Helen saw the first time. To see this again.

He began to sweat anew, in the extreme. Helen must have felt his palm slippery against hers, and she turned to face the truck as it pulled into the cemetery. Dave drove the periphery with his lights off so that he came right around and pulled past the grave, and backed it up flush with the casket. He jumped out quickly, and Markou nodded, motioning for them to follow. He slipped his fingers under Dave's nose, then his own, and slid the bottle back in his pocket.

Markou pulled two wide straps out of the cab of the truck and handed one to Dave, then walked Helen and Robert round to the other side of the casket. He placed Robert at the front, and Helen at the rear. Dave dropped the back of the truck. One side of the bed was packed full of dirt, but they'd saved a spot wide enough for the casket in the other half. Dave crossed in front and took up the position on the other side of Robert. They were to lift the thing up into the bed of the truck.

Like this, Markou said. He turned to his right shoulder and took a fast deep breath and held it. Then he slipped his arm under the casket, Helen meeting him, and they pulled the strap up on the sides. There were handles on either end.

We're going to bend at the knee and lift from the shoulder. We need one second up and one step forward and she's on the cab. We'll push from there.

Robert took a breath, mirrored the same gesture, meeting Dave's hand underneath.

One second, Helen cried out. She took a step away, holding the strap's handle with an extended arm, and wretched again into the grass. A moment later, she stepped back.

Dave nodded at Robert, who nodded back. Markou counted to three and they bent down. His face next to the dirty wood of the casket, Robert forgot to breathe from his right side, forgot to breathe again before he bent down. He inhaled without thinking and through the camphor and menthol was the rank smell of what he was lifting. For a moment his head was full of it and he nearly missed standing up, lifting a second too slow, they wobbled upright, the wood slamming his shoulder.

One step forward in an instant and the box was on the back of the truck. Markou pushing it the whole way up in a matter of seconds, and immediately Robert dropped away, his head on the ground, the cold wet dew of the grass pressed against his forehead, his arms limp beside him, his head throbbing, and the smell, the smell of menthol and the other smell both, and he realized he must have fainted. His blood was pumping in his head with one thought. He coughed.

A door of the truck closed. Helen put her hand on his back. She was kneeling beside him, stroking his hair. He was slick with sweat. The air along the ground cooled him.

I found these, Markou said, and handed Helen something. A set of binoculars. Are they yours?

Kind of, she answered, standing. Without hesitation, she walked to the empty grave and tossed them in. We'll just leave them here.

The truck's engine rumbled to life and the metal slowly rolled away from Robert. Helen leaned beside him, her hand stroking his hair again, their hips touching. Her body was warm next to him, the grass cold and damp on his cheek.

He pushed himself upward, and hugged Helen, whose face was steady and contained.

He whispered in her ear, Won't somebody wonder about the vomit?

He felt her cheek as she smiled. I doubt it'll be the first time they find vomit on this site.

The truck had left without Markou, who was at the front, waiting for them at the gate on this side of a bush. Markou was going to lock up behind them and meet up when he was done. Helen rode with Robert so Markou would have her car.

She had blankets to cover the seats. Once they were in his rental, he felt a touch more normal. The factory-clean smell of the car soothed him. His hands on the steering wheel were filthy, especially his nails. On both palms, the pads of his hands burned like hot coins were pressed into them.

Can you drive? Helen asked.

I'm fine, he said, calmer than he thought he should be. He turned the key in the ignition and started the engine. The sound of the motor turning over felt like a relief. They'd done this thing and were leaving.

You want to turn left out of the gates, Helen instructed.

Robert clicked his signal light on, though it was the middle of the night. They had seen no other cars for an hour.

I just don't know how we're getting away with this.

Helen answered, No witnesses.

Are we allowed to do this?

She shrugged, opening up her purse. We're not taking anything that isn't ours. And they can't say the same.

Jesus, Robert thought.

It's fine. Markou maintains the records on the grounds.

But why would he do this?

I'm giving him a treat, she said, sheepishly.

You're paying him?

No no, she said, then gestured. Turn here, left. The guy signing the contracts is going to ask about moving Mom because I made other arrangements this morning. Markou will tell him the body is missing. Cruikshank, if he's smart, will know what's happened. He'll know we did this. A missing body. It's a slap in his face.

Robert looked at Helen. Markou loves the idea, she said, pleased with herself.

Her smile made Robert marvel at her, that she'd thought this through, at least enough to have gathered what tools they needed, and to have phoned him, and convinced the men, and brought them here.

Left again, she said. Just up here. You can pull over anywhere.

As he parked, Helen took from her purse a large envelope and a pen. She held the envelope out to Robbie.

This is yours, she said.

He took it, puzzled. Who's it from?

They're for the house. I only signed the papers this afternoon. You're entitled to half.

So what is this?

Contracts. You sign them, you own half the house. While he paused, Helen added, It's your inheritance, Robbie. You sign those, and it's a done deal.

You don't have to do this, he said.

I didn't, she said, and waited a moment, to see if he'd catch on. Dad did. The first one is Dad's will, here, on top.

She pulled the papers from out of the envelope and showed him their father's name heading the document.

Dad left you half the house. It's an old will, from before you left. But he never changed it, so you have that. You can have that.

Even with just the light from the moon, she could see that information sinking in, his eyes darting back and forth across the width of the envelope.

He held it out to her. I don't want it.

She looked from the papers to him and leaned back against the car door. It's yours. As much as mine. I don't want what isn't mine.

He lifted the papers and gripped them as if he'd tear them in half, but she put a hand on his and took the papers back. She flipped a few pages, then handed him a pen, which he didn't take.

You only have to sign three places. There's the papers for the will — date them for yesterday, like I did, just to be safe — and the Power Authority contracts. Date those for today.

Robert shook his head.

This is yours, she said gently and put the pen in his hand. I want you to sign now. Like it or not, you own it. It's yours. Half yours. Half mine. You sign here, here, and — she flipped a page — here. Do it now.

I don't want his money.

It's not his money anymore. It's ours. And we can do with it what we want. We get to decide what we do with it, Robbie. We get to decide.

He waited a long moment, blinking, and took the pen from her. He signed the first line. Quickly, she flipped through the pages with Post-its stuck to them, for all three copies, until they were done. Then she did the same for the will. They both giggled when she pulled out the final document, for the ridiculousness of it. That done, Helen felt her back relax. She opened the car door to a chill on the air and took a deep inhale, smelling the wildflowers in the field.

They crossed the road and walked along a fenceline, marking an orchard on their right, the rows of trees rustling beside them as they stepped through the long grass. They followed tire tracks until they came to a clearing, with a large, waist-high boulder. Dave was there with the truck.

Robert wondered if Helen had planted that stone already too, and how she'd gotten it there. She walked to the far side of it and was at the mouth of an open grave, dirt piled beside it.

Yours is cleaner, she said.

This should be quick, Dave answered.

Markou arrived within minutes and it wasn't long before the casket was in the ground. The lowering device was silent as the casket descended. Markou said a small prayer, beginning with a lovely line — We are here to witness — which Robert appreciated for its simplicity. He was grateful to be there, to witness. Markou pulled out a baggie of dirt he'd taken from the pile they'd dug at the cemetery and passed it around for each of them to draw some.

When the first handful landed on the coffin, from Dave, Helen slapped her leg. Oh, shit, she said, and everyone laughed nervously. Take this, she said and put her dirt into Markou's free hand.

Robert held his cool clump of dirt as best as he could without losing any while Helen ran to the cab of the truck.

Oh, thank god, Markou said.

Helen came back carrying something in a plastic bag about the size of a breadbox. She set it at her feet and pulled the bag down, revealing a silver urn.

I almost forgot Dad.

She hesitated what to do with it, until Robert came alive and seized the other handle with his free hand. Helen nodded at him and released the urn. She held out her cupped hands to take Robert's dirt, which he dropped into her palms.

It was unreal — small, for all the fact of it — that he held in his hands what remained of his father. He wanted to say aloud, *I forgive you*, but couldn't trust himself to get the words out without blubbering. His back prickled, his shoulders released, and then, like a warm wave against him, the rage came back, travelling up inside his guts, and he said aloud, *I forgive you*, and noticed he was addressing himself.

His breath rattled up his throat. Helen touched his arm with her cupped hands, to say they hadn't a lot of time, they were here together so they could revisit this moment later, but right now there was work to do. He carried the urn to the edge of the fresh grave, held his breath and kneeled down with one hand on the ground, lowering himself to place the ashes on the coffin.

He barely had time to stand before Helen released Robert's dirt back into his hands. Markou returned Helen's portion to her. They each tossed their handful of earth into the grave — Robert kissed his first — and they were still for a brief moment, with crickets sounding in the field and the trees rubbing together.

When Dave picked up a shovel, Robert reached out to take it, but he handed it to Markou. We got this.

Helen took him by the hand and pulled a flashlight out of her pocket, drawing him to the far side of the rock, on the side of the river. Across the water, he noticed, was the new dam, lit up bright as day. He marvelled that he hadn't noticed it.

Helen shone the flashlight on the stone. He's here, Robbie, she said.

He looked to the rock, and there, embedded in its face, was Garrett's name, and his dates.

Oh fuck, he said in a small voice.

Now you know where to come. You can bring Colin, she said.

Robert couldn't answer. Helen turned off the light and Robert squatted down, to feel the letters in the stone. She stepped around the other side again, to give him a moment.

Do people come here? he asked. His palm rested over the inscription for *GARRETT*.

How do you mean?

He removed his hand and stood, to see her. Does family come here? Won't they wonder about Mom?

We have this, she said, and shone the light again into the back of the pickup. The whole one side wasn't full of dirt, but plants.

From my gardens. They had to go somewhere. I doubt anybody does come here. If they do, they'll just think we planted flowers for him. Which we did.

Fuck, he said, and tears came burbling out of him.

Helen walked over to him and took his hand again. The boys ignored them, bent on shovelling.

The day you came, she said, I witnessed an accident here.

Robbie was drying his eyes on the sleeve of his other arm. Whether he heard her or not, he didn't ask her for more.

Here, let's get warm, she said. We're freezing.

She picked up the blanket from the lowering device and wrapped it around their shoulders. That's better, she said, and the men both took a second from shovelling to wave at her.

Five minutes, Markou said. Then the garden.

Yes.

Helen walked them back across the flattened grass with the sound of shovels getting quieter in the night.

Does this have anything to do with Garrett's letter? Robbie asked.

I haven't read it, she said. It's at home. On the kitchen table.

Okay, he said.

This isn't about Garrett, she added, trying to be clear. It's you and me. Can you handle this?

Yeah, he said, we've been through much worse.

Helen cupped a hand on the side of Robert's head, for a moment, then tousled his hair. She stood on her toes a little and scowled with concentration above his ear, untangling something. She held out a small, rough stone.

You don't want to sleep on that.

No.

She took his hand again, to squeeze it, he thought, but she set the stone in his palm, closed his fingers around it, and nodded.

Robert looked around them, then up to the sky, wishing for something to prove what they had done was right, but everything was the same. The sky was the same. That had to be good enough.

ACKNOWLEDGEMENTS

I BELIEVE IT'S true that the stories we tell help shape our futures, so I would like to thank the generous support of the Canada Council for the Arts in my small attempt to make for the world a better tomorrow.

I would like to thank the many friends who lent an ear, an eye, a shoulder, a home, or a spot of time over the many years, especially: Treena Chambers, Jeffrey Rotin, Billeh Nickerson, Marie Gillan, Don Falk, Max Rada Dada, Adela Krupich, Shauna Lancit Baitz, Dana Baitz, Sylvain Bombardier, Yani Mitchell, Leah Bailey, Caitlin Alsager, Karma Lacoff, Adrian Nieoczym, Elizabeth Bachinsky, Amber Dawn, Kim Kinakin, and Trish Kelly. I thank my family, especially my mother, Liz Smith, and my sister, Leica Prevost. Thanks to George K. Ilsley, Brett Josef Grubisic, and David Chariandy, who saw this book in its first days. Wonderful thanks to Matt Rader and Colin Thomas, who offered great insight and clarity at key times.

Also thanks to UBC, Okanagan Campus, especially my colleagues in the Faculty of Creative and Critical Studies, and most especially: Sharon Thesen, Nancy Holmes, Anne Fleming, Neil Cadger, Denise Kenney, Alwyn Spies, and Claude Desmarais, who are nothing less than wonderful.

Thanks to Frank Stonner at Kelowna Memorial Park Cemetery for invaluable information about the grisly act of exhumation. And the UBC Library at Robson Square, the UBC Bookstore, and the lovely folks who work there, for being so supportive so many years.

Thanks to my agent, Carolyn Swayze, for her confidence and kind words and hard work. Many thanks to the wonderful people at Cormorant Books who do so much hard work to make a book appear seamless.

Nobody has championed me more than my wonderful publisher, Marc Côté. I dearly thank him for his decade of insight, patience, friendship, enthusiasm, and support.